REDSHIRTS

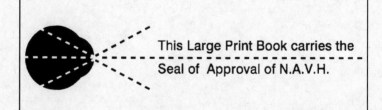

This Large Print Book carries the
Seal of Approval of N.A.V.H.

REDSHIRTS

JOHN SCALZI

THORNDIKE PRESS

A part of Gale, Cengage Learning

Farmington Hills, Mich • San Francisco • New York • Waterville, Maine
Meriden, Conn • Mason, Ohio • Chicago

GALE
CENGAGE Learning·

LIBRARY OF CONGRESS CATALOGING-IN-PUBLICATION DATA

Scalzi, John, 1969–
  Redshirts / by John Scalzi. — Large print edition.
    pages ; cm. — (Thorndike Press large print mini-collections)
    ISBN 978-1-4104-7607-4 (hardcover) — ISBN 1-4104-7607-3 (hardcover)
    1. Space warfare—Fiction. 2. Human-alien encounters—Fiction. 3. Large type books. I. Title.
  PS3619.C256R43 2014
  813'.6—dc23
                                                                    2014036881

Published in 2015 by arrangement with Tom Doherty Associates, LLC

Printed in Mexico
1 2 3 4 5 6 7 19 18 17 16 15

Redshirts *is dedicated to the following:*
To Wil Wheaton, whom I heart with all
the hearty heartness a heart can heart;
To Mykal Burns, my friend since the
TRS-80 days at the Glendora Public
Library;
And to Joe Mallozzi and Brad Wright,
who took me to space with them.

PROLOGUE

From the top of the large boulder he sat on, Ensign Tom Davis looked across the expanse of the cave toward Captain Lucius Abernathy, Science Officer Q'eeng and Chief Engineer Paul West perched on a second, larger boulder, and thought, *Well, this sucks.*

"Borgovian Land Worms!" Captain Abernathy said, and smacked his boulder with an open palm. "I should have known."

You should *have known? How the hell could you* not *have known?* thought Ensign Davis, and looked at the vast dirt floor of the cave, its powdery surface moving here and there with the shadowy humps that marked the movement of the massive, carnivorous worms.

"I don't think we should just be waltzing in there," Davis had said to Chen, the other crew member on the away team, upon encountering the cave. Abernathy, Q'eeng and West had already entered, despite the fact that Davis and Chen were technically their security detail.

Chen, who was new, snorted. "Oh, come on," he said. "It's just a cave. What could possibly be in there?"

"Bears?" Davis had suggested. "Wolves? Any number of large predators who see a cave as shelter from the elements? Have you never been camping?"

"There are no bears on this planet," Chen had said, willfully missing Davis' point. "And anyway we have pulse guns. Now come on. This is my first away mission. I don't want the captain wondering where I am." He ran in after the officers.

From his boulder, Davis looked down at the dusty smear on the cave floor that was all that remained of Chen. The land worms, called by the sound of the humans walking in the cave, had tunneled up under him and dragged him down, leaving nothing but echoing screams and the smear.

Well, that's not quite true, Davis thought, peering farther into the cave and seeing the hand that lay there, still clutching the pulse gun Chen had carried, and which as it turned out had done him absolutely no good whatsoever.

The ground stirred and the hand suddenly disappeared.

O*kay,* now *it's true,* Davis thought.

"Davis!" Captain Abernathy called. "Stay where you are! Any movement across that ground will call to the worms! You'll be eaten instantly!"

Thanks for the useless and obvious update, you jackass, Davis thought, but did not say, because he was an ensign, and Abernathy was the captain. Instead, what he said was, "Aye, Captain."

"Good," Abernathy said. "I don't want you trying to make a break for it and getting caught by those worms. Your father would never forgive me."

What? Davis thought, and suddenly he remembered that Captain Abernathy had served under his father on the *Benjamin Franklin.* The ill-fated *Benjamin Franklin.* And in fact, Davis' father had saved the then-Ensign Abernathy by tossing his unconscious body into the escape pod before diving in himself and launching the pod just as the *Franklin* blew up spectacularly around them. They had drifted in space for three days and had almost run out of breathable air in that pod before they were rescued.

Davis shook his head. It was very odd that all that detail about Abernathy popped into his head, especially considering the circumstances.

9

As if on cue, Abernathy said, "Your father once saved my life, you know."

"I know —" Davis began, and then nearly toppled off the top of his boulder as the land worms suddenly launched themselves into it, making it wobble.

"Davis!" Abernathy said.

Davis hunched down, flattening himself toward the boulder to keep his center of gravity low. He glanced over to Abernathy, who was now conferring with Q'eeng and West. Without being able to hear them, Davis knew that they were reviewing what they knew about Borgovian Land Worms and trying to devise a plan to neutralize the creatures, so they could cross the cave in safety and reach the chamber that housed the ancient Central Computer of the Borgovians, which could give them a clue about the disappearance of that wise and mysterious race.

You really need to start focusing on your current situation, some part of Davis' brain said to him, and he shook his head again. Davis couldn't disagree with this assessment; his brain had picked a funny time to start spouting a whole bunch of extraneous information that served him no purpose at this time.

The worms rocked his boulder again. Davis gripped it as hard as he could and saw Abernathy, Q'eeng and West become more animated in their attempted problem solving.

A thought suddenly came to Davis. *You're part of the security detail*, it said. *You have a pulse gun. You could just vaporize these things.*

Davis would have smacked his head if the worms weren't already doing that by driving it into the boulder. Of course! The pulse gun! He reached down to his belt to unclasp the gun from its holster. As he did so another part of his brain wondered why, if in fact the solution was as simple as just vaporizing the worms, Captain Abernathy or one of the other officers hadn't just ordered him to do it already.

I seem to have a lot of voices in my brain today, said a third part of Davis' brain. He ignored that particular voice in his brain and aimed at a moving hump of dirt coming toward his boulder.

Abernathy's cry of "Davis! No!" arrived at the exact instant Davis fired, sending a pulsed beam of coherent, disruptive particles into the dirt mound. A screech emanated from the mound, followed by violent thrashing, followed by a sinister rumbling, followed by the ground of the cave erupting

11

as dozens of worms suddenly burst from the dirt.

"The pulse gun is ineffective against Borgovian Land Worms!" Davis heard Science Officer Q'eeng say over the unspeakable noise of the thrashing worms. "The frequency of the pulse sends them into a frenzy. Ensign Davis has just called every worm in the area!"

You couldn't have told me this before I fired? Davis wanted to scream. *You couldn't have said, Oh, by the way, don't fire a pulse gun at a Borgovian Land Worm at our mission briefing? On the ship? At which we discussed landing on Borgovia? Which has fucking land worms?*

Davis didn't scream this at Q'eeng because he knew there was no way Q'eeng would hear him, and besides it was already too late. He'd fired. The worms were in a frenzy. Somebody now was likely to die.

It was likely to be Ensign Davis.

Through the rumble and dust, Davis looked over at Abernathy, who was gazing back at him, concern furrowed into his brow. And then Davis was wondering when, if ever, Abernathy had ever spoken to him before this mission.

Oh, Abernathy must have — he and Davis' father had been tight ever since the destruction of the *Franklin.* They were friends. *Good* friends. It was even likely that Abernathy had known Davis himself as a boy, and may have even pulled a few strings to get his friend's son a choice berth on the *Intrepid,* the flagship of the Universal Union. The captain wouldn't have been able to spend any real time with Davis — it wouldn't have done for the captain to show favoritism in the ranks — but surely they would have spoken. A few words here and there. Abernathy asking after Davis' father, perhaps. Or on other away missions.

Davis was coming up with a blank.

Suddenly, the rumbling stopped. The worms, as quickly as they had gone into a frenzy, appeared to sidle back under the dirt. The dust settled.

"They're gone!" Davis heard himself say.

"No," Abernathy said. "They're smarter than that."

"I can make it to the mouth of the cave!" Davis heard himself say.

"Stay where you are, Ensign!" Abernathy said. "That's an order!"

But Davis was already off his boulder and running toward the mouth of the cave. Some part of Davis' brain howled at the irrationality of the action, but the rest of Davis didn't care. He knew he *had* to move. It

13

was almost a compulsion. As if he had no choice.

Abernathy screamed "No!" very nearly in slow motion, and Davis covered half of the distance he needed to go. Then the ground erupted as land worms, arrayed in a semicircle, launched themselves up and toward Davis.

And it was then, as he skidded backward, and while his face showed surprise, in fact, that Ensign Davis had an epiphany.

This was the defining moment of his life. The reason he existed. Everything he'd ever done before, everything he'd ever been, said or wanted, had led him to this exact moment, to be skidding backward while Borgovian Land Worms bored through dirt and air to get him. This was his fate. His destiny.

In a flash, and as he gazed upon the needle-sharp teeth spasming in the rather evolutionarily suspect rotating jaw of the land worm, Ensign Tom Davis saw the future. None of this was really about the mysterious disappearance of the Borgovians. After this moment, no one would ever speak of the Borgovians again.

It was about him — or rather, what his impending death would do to his father, now an admiral. Or even more to the point, what his death would do to the relationship between Admiral Davis and Captain Abernathy. Davis saw the scene in which Abernathy told Admiral Davis of his son's death. Saw the shock turn to anger, saw the friendship between the two men dissolve. He saw the scene where the Universal Union MPs placed the captain under arrest for trumped-up charges of murder by negligence, planted by the admiral.

He saw the court-martial and Science Officer Q'eeng, acting as Abernathy's counsel, dramatically breaking down the admiral on the witness stand, getting him to admit this was all about him losing his son. Davis saw his father dramatically reach out and ask forgiveness from the man he had falsely accused and had arrested, and saw Captain Abernathy give it in a heartrending reconciliation right there in the courtroom.

It was a great story. It was great drama.

And it all rested upon him. And this moment. And this fate. This destiny of Ensign Davis.

Ensign Davis thought, *Screw this, I want to live,* and swerved to avoid the land worms.

But then he tripped and one of the land worms ate his face and he died anyway.

From his vantage point next to Q'eeng and West, Captain Lucius Abernathy watched helplessly as Tom Davis fell prey to

15

the land worms. He felt a hand on his shoulder. It was Chief Engineer West.

"I'm sorry, Lucius," he said. "I know he was a friend of yours."

"More than a friend," Abernathy said, choking back grief. "The son of a friend as well. I saw him grow up, Paul. Pulled strings to get him on the *Intrepid.* I promised his father that I would look after him. And I did. Checked in on him from time to time. Never showed favoritism, of course. But kept an eye out."

"The admiral will be heartbroken," Science Officer Q'eeng said. "Ensign Davis was the only child of the admiral and his late wife."

"Yes," Abernathy said. "It will be hard."

"It's not your fault, Lucius," West said. "You didn't tell him to fire his pulse gun. You didn't tell him to run."

"Not my fault," Abernathy agreed. "But my responsibility." He moved to the most distant point on the boulder to be alone.

"Jesus Christ," West muttered to Q'eeng, after the captain had removed himself and they were alone and finally free to speak. "What sort of moron shoots a pulse gun into a cave floor crawling with land worms? And then tries to run across it? He may have been an admiral's son, but he wasn't very smart."

"It's unfortunate indeed," Q'eeng said. "The dangers of the Borgovian Land Worms are well-known. Chen and Davis both should have known better."

"Standards are slipping," West said.

"That may be," Q'eeng said. "Be that as it may, this and other recent missions have seen a sad and remarkable loss of life. Whether they are up to our standards or not, the fact remains: We need more crew."

CHAPTER ONE

Ensign Andrew Dahl looked out the window of Earth Dock, the Universal Union's space station above the planet Earth, and gazed at his next ship.

He gazed at the *Intrepid*.

"Beautiful, isn't she?" said a voice.

Dahl turned to see a young woman, dressed in a starship ensign's uniform, also looking out toward the ship.

"She is," Dahl agreed.

"The Universal Union Capital Ship *Intrepid*," the young woman said. "Built in 2453 at the Mars Dock. Flagship of the Universal Union since 2456. First captain, Genevieve Shan. Lucius Abernathy, captain since 2462."

"Are you the *Intrepid*'s tour guide?" Dahl asked, smiling.

"Are you a tourist?" the young woman asked, smiling back.

"No," Dahl said, and held out his hand.

"Andrew Dahl. I've been assigned to the *Intrepid*. I'm just waiting on the 1500 shuttle."

The young woman took his hand. "Maia Duvall," she said. "Also assigned to the *Intrepid*. Also waiting on the 1500 shuttle."

"What a coincidence," Dahl said.

"If you want to call two Dub U Space Fleet members waiting in a Dub U space station for a shuttle to the Dub U spaceship parked right outside the shuttle berth window a coincidence, sure," Duvall said.

"Well, when you put it that way," Dahl said.

"Why are you here so early?" Duvall asked. "It's only now noon. I thought I would be the first one waiting for the shuttle."

"I'm excited," Dahl said. "This will be my first posting." Duvall looked him over, a question in her eyes. "I went to the Academy a few years late," he said.

"Why was that?" Duvall asked.

"It's a long story," Dahl said.

"We have time," Duvall said. "How about we get some lunch and you tell me."

"Uh," Dahl said. "I'm kind of waiting for someone. A friend of mine. Who's also been assigned to the *Intrepid*."

"The food court is right over there,"

Duvall said, motioning to the bank of stalls across the walkway. "Just send him or her a text. And if he misses it, we can see him from there. Come on. I'll spring for the drinks."

"Oh, well, in *that* case," Dahl said. "If I turned down a free drink, they'd kick me out of Space Fleet."

"I was promised a long story," Duvall said, after they had gotten their food and drinks.

"I made no such promise," Dahl said.

"The promise was implied," Duvall protested. "And besides, I bought you a drink. I *own* you. Entertain me, Ensign Dahl."

"All right, fine," Dahl said. "I entered the Academy late because for three years I was a seminary student."

"Okay, that's moderately interesting," Duvall said.

"On Forshan," Dahl said

"Okay, that's *intensely* interesting," Duvall said. "So you're a priest of the Forshan religion? Which schism?"

"The leftward schism, and no, not a priest."

"Couldn't handle the celibacy?"

"Leftward priests aren't required to be celibate," Dahl said, "but considering I was the only human at the seminary, I had celibacy thrust upon me, if you will."

"Some people wouldn't have let that stop them," Duvall said.

"You haven't seen a Forshan seminary student up close," Dahl said. "Also, I don't swing xeno."

"Maybe you just haven't found the right xeno," Duvall said.

"I prefer humans," Dahl said. "Call me boring."

"Boring," Duvall said, teasingly.

"And you've just pried into my personal preferences in land speed record time," Dahl said. "If you're this forward with someone you just met, I can only imagine what you're like with people you've known for a long time."

"Oh, I'm not like this with everyone," Duvall said. "But I can tell I like you already. Anyway. Not a priest."

"No. My technical status is 'Foreign Penitent,'" Dahl said. "I was allowed to do the full course of study and perform some rites, but there were some physical requirements I would not have been able to perform for full ordination."

"Like what?" Duvall asked.

"Self-impregnation, for one," Dahl said.

"A small but highly relevant detail," Duvall said.

"And here you were all concerned about celibacy," Dahl said, and swigged from his drink.

"If you were never going to become a priest, why did you go to the seminary?" Duvall asked.

"I found the Forshan religion very restful," Dahl said. "When I was younger that appealed to me. My parents died when I was young and I had a small inheritance, so I took it, paid tutors to learn the language and then traveled to Forshan and found a seminary that would take me. I planned to stay forever."

"But you didn't," Duvall said. "I mean, obviously."

Dahl smiled. "Well. I found the Forshan religion restful. I found the Forshan religious war less so."

"Ah," Duvall said. "But how does one get from Forshan seminary student to Academy graduate?"

"When the Dub U came to mediate between the religious factions on Forshan, they needed an interpreter, and I was on planet," Dahl said. "There aren't a lot of humans who speak more than one dialect of Forshan. I know all four of the major ones."

"Impressive," Duvall said.

"I'm good with my tongue," Dahl said.

"Now who's being forward?" Duvall asked.

"After the Dub U mission failed, it advised that all non-natives leave the planet," Dahl said. "The head Dub U negotiator said that the Space Fleet had need of linguists and scientists and recommended me for a slot at the Academy. By that time my seminary had been burned to the ground and I had nowhere to go, or any money to get there even if I had. The Academy seemed like the best exit strategy. Spent four years there studying xenobiology and linguistics. And here I am."

"That's a good story," Duvall said, and tipped her bottle toward Dahl.

He clinked it with his own. "Thanks," he said. "What about yours?"

"Far less interesting," Duvall said.

"I doubt that," Dahl said.

"No Academy for me," Duvall said. "I enlisted as a grunt for the Dub U peace-keepers. Did that for a couple of years and then transferred over to Space Fleet three years ago. Was on the *Nantes* up until this transfer."

"Promotion?" Dahl said.

Duvall smirked. "Not exactly," she said. "It's best to call it a transfer due to personnel conflicts."

Before Dahl could dig further his phone buzzed. He took it out and read the text on it. "Goof," he said, smiling.

"What is it?" Duvall asked.

"Hold on a second," Dahl said, and turned in his seat to wave at a young man standing in the middle of the station walkway. "We're over here, Jimmy," Dahl said. The young man grinned, waved back and headed over.

"The friend you're waiting on, I presume," Duvall said.

"That would be him," Dahl said. "Jimmy Hanson."

"Jimmy Hanson?" Duvall said. "Not related to James Hanson, CEO and chairman of Hanson Industries, surely."

"James Albert Hanson the Fourth," Dahl said. "His son."

"Must be nice," Duvall said.

"He could buy this space station with his allowance," Dahl said. "But he's not like that."

"What do you mean?" Duvall said.

"Hey, guys," Hanson said, finally making his way to the table. He looked at Duvall, and held out his hand. "Hi, I'm Jimmy."

"Maia," Duvall said, extending her hand. They shook.

"So, you're a friend of Andy's, right?"

25

Hanson said.

"I am," Duvall said. "He and I go way back. All of a half hour."

"Great," Hanson said, and smiled. "He and I go back slightly farther."

"I would hope so," Duvall said.

"I'm going to get myself something to drink," Hanson said. "You guys want anything? Want me to get you another round?"

"I'm fine," Dahl said.

"I could go for another," Duvall said, waggling her nearly empty bottle.

"One of the same?" Hanson asked.

"Sure," Duvall said.

"Great," Hanson said, and clapped his hands together. "So, I'll be right back. Keep this chair for me?"

"You got it," Dahl said. Hanson wandered off in search of food and drink.

"He seems nice," Duvall said.

"He is," Dahl said.

"Not hugely full of personality," Duvall said.

"He has other qualities," Dahl said.

"Like paying for drinks," Duvall said.

"Well, yes, but that's not what I was thinking of," Dahl said.

"You mind if I ask you a personal question?" Duvall said.

"Seeing as we've already covered my

26

sexual preferences in this conversation, no," Dahl said.

"Were you friends with Jimmy before you knew his dad could buy an entire planet or two?" Duvall asked.

Dahl paused a moment before answering. "Do you know how the rich are different than you or me?" he asked Duvall.

"You mean, besides having more money," Duvall said.

"Yeah," Dahl said.

"No," Duvall said.

"What makes them different — the smart ones, anyway — is that they have a very good sense of why people want to be near them. Whether it's because they want to be friends, which is not about proximity to money and access and power, or if they want to be part of an entourage, which is. Make sense?"

"Sure," Duvall said.

"Okay," Dahl said. "So, here's the thing. When Jimmy was young, he figured out that his father was one of the richest men in the Dub U. Then he figured out that one day, he would be too. Then he figured out that there were a lot of other people who would try to use the first two things to their own advantage. Then he figured out how to avoid those people."

"Got it," Duvall said. "Jimmy would know if you were just being nice to him because of who his daddy was."

"It was really interesting watching him our first few weeks at the Academy," Dahl said. "Some of the cadets — and some of our instructors — tried to make themselves his friend. I think they were surprised how quickly this rich kid had their number. He's had enough time to be extraordinarily good at reading people. He has to be."

"So how did you approach him?" Duvall said.

"I didn't," Dahl said. "He came over and started talking to me. I think he realized I didn't care who his dad was."

"Everybody loves you," Duvall said.

"Well, that, and I was getting an A in the biology course he was having trouble with," Dahl said. "Just because Jimmy's picky about his companions doesn't mean he's not self-interested."

"He seemed to be willing to consider me a friend," Duvall said.

"That's because he thinks we're friends, and he trusts my judgment," Dahl said.

"And are we?" Duvall said. "Friends, I mean."

"You're a little more hyper than I normally like," Dahl said.

"Yeah, I get that 'I like things restful' vibe from you," Duvall said.

"I take it you don't do restful," Dahl said.

"I sleep from time to time," Duvall said. "Otherwise, no."

"I suppose I'll have to adjust," Dahl said.

"I suppose you will," Duvall said.

"I have drinks," Hanson said, coming up behind Duvall.

"Why, Jimmy," Duvall said. "That makes you my new favorite person."

"Excellent," Hanson said, offered Duvall her drink, and sat down at the table. "So, what are we talking about?"

Just before the shuttle arrived, two more people arrived at the waiting area. More accurately, five people arrived: two crewmen, accompanied by three members of the military police. Duvall nudged Dahl and Hanson, who looked over. One of the crewmen noticed and cocked an eyebrow. "Yes, I have an entourage," he said.

Duvall ignored him and addressed one of the MPs. "What's his story?"

The MP motioned to the one with a cocked eyebrow. "Various charges for this one, including smuggling, selling contraband and assaulting a superior officer." She then motioned to the other crewman, who

29

was standing there sullenly, avoiding eye contact with everyone else. "That poor bastard is this one's friend. He's tainted by association."

"The assault charge is trumped up," said the first ensign. "The XO was high as a kite."

"On drugs *you* gave him," said the second crewman, still not looking at anyone else.

"No one can prove I gave them to him, and anyway they weren't drugs," said the first. "They were an offworld fungus. And it couldn't have been that. The fungus relaxes people, not makes them attack anyone in the room, requiring them to defend themselves."

"You gave him Xeno-pseudoagaricus, didn't you," Dahl said.

The first crewman looked at Dahl. "As I already said, no one can prove I gave the XO anything," he said. "And maybe."

"Xeno-pseudoagaricus naturally produces a chemical that in most humans provides a relaxing effect," Dahl said. "But in about one-tenth of one percent of people, it does the opposite. The receptors in their brains are slightly different from everyone else's. And of those people, about one-tenth of one percent will go berserk under its influence. Sounds like your XO is one of those people."

"Who are you, who is so wise in the way of alien fungus?" said the crewman.

"Someone who knows that no matter what, you don't deal upward on the chain of command," Dahl said. The crewman grinned.

"So why aren't you in the brig?" Duvall asked.

The crewman motioned to Dahl. "Ask your friend, he's so smart," he said. Duvall looked to Dahl, who shrugged.

"Xeno-pseudoagaricus isn't illegal," Dahl said. "It's just not very smart to use it. You'd have to either study xenobiology or have an interest in off-brand not-technically-illegal alien mood enhancers, possibly for entrepreneurial purposes."

"Ah," Duvall said.

"If I had to guess," Dahl said, "I'm guessing our friend here —"

"Finn," said the crewman, and nodded to the other one. "And that's Hester."

"— our friend Finn had a reputation at his last posting for being the guy to go to for substances that would let you pass a urine test."

Hester snorted at this.

"I'm also guessing that his XO probably doesn't want it known that he was taking

31

drugs —"

"Fungus," said Finn.

"— of any sort, and that in any event when the Xeno-pseudoagaricus made him go nuts, he attacked and Finn here was technically defending himself when he fought back. So rather than put Finn in the brig and open up an ugly can of worms, better to transfer him quietly."

"I can neither confirm nor deny this interpretation of events," Finn said.

"Then what's with the MPs?" Hanson asked.

"They're here to make sure we get on the *Intrepid* without any detours," said Hester. "They don't want him renewing his stash." Finn rolled his eyes at this.

Duvall looked at Hester. "I'm sensing bitterness here."

Hester finally made eye contact. "The bastard hid his stash in my foot locker," he said, to Duvall.

"And you didn't know?" Duvall asked.

"He told me they were candies, and that if the other crew knew he had them, they'd sneak into his foot locker to take them."

"They would have," Finn said. "And in my defense, everything *was* candied."

"You also said they were for your mother," Hester said.

32

"Yes, well," Finn said. "I *did* lie about that part."

"I tried to tell that to the captain and the XO, but they didn't care," Hester said. "As far as they were concerned I was an accomplice. I don't even *like* him."

"Then why did you agree to hold his . . . candies?" Duvall said. Hester mumbled something inaudible and broke eye contact.

"He did it because I was being nice to him, and he doesn't have friends," Finn said.

"So you took advantage of him," Hanson said.

"I don't *dislike* him," Finn said. "And it's not like I meant for him to get in trouble. He *shouldn't* have gotten in trouble. Nothing in the stash was illegal. But then our XO went nuts and tried to rearrange my bone structure."

"You probably should have known your product line better," Dahl said.

"The next time I get something, I'll run it by you first," Finn said sarcastically, and then motioned toward the window, where the shuttle could be seen approaching the berth. "But it's going to have to wait. Looks like our ride is here."

CHAPTER TWO

The *Intrepid*'s four other new crew members were met on the ship by a petty officer named Del Sol, who quickly marched them off to their stations. Dahl was met by the *Intrepid*'s chief science officer, Q'eeng.

"Sir," Dahl said, saluting.

Q'eeng returned the salute. "Ensign Junior Rank Dahl," he said. "A pleasure to meet you. I do not always greet my department's new arrivals in this manner, but I have just come off duty and I thought I would show you your station. Do you have any personal items you need to stow?"

"No, sir," Dahl said. His and the others' foot lockers were going through ship's security for inspection and would be delivered to their quarters, the locations of which would be uploaded to their phones.

"I understand you spent several years on Forshan, and that you speak the language," Q'eeng said. "All four dialects."

"Yes, sir," Dahl said.

"I studied it briefly at the Academy," Q'eeng said, and then cleared his throat. *"Aaachka faaachklalhach ghalall chkalalal."*

Dahl kept his face very still. Q'eeng had just attempted in the third dialect the traditional rightward schism greeting of "I offer you the bread of life," but his phrasing and accent had transmuted the statement into "Let us violate cakes together." Leaving aside the fact it would be highly unusual for a member of the rightward schism to voluntarily speak the third dialect, it being the native dialect of the founder of the leftward schism and therefore traditionally eschewed, mutual cake violating was not an accepted practice anywhere on Forshan.

"Aaachkla faaachklalhalu faadalalu chkalalal," Dahl sad, returning the correct traditional response of "I break the bread of life with you" in the third dialect.

"Did I say that correctly?" Q'eeng asked.

"Your accent is very unusual, sir," Dahl said.

"Indeed," Q'eeng said. "Then perhaps I will leave any necessary Forshan speaking to you."

"Yes, sir," Dahl said.

"Follow me, Ensign," Q'eeng said, and strode forward. Dahl raced to keep up.

35

Around Q'eeng the *Intrepid* was a hive of activity; crew members and officers moved purposefully through the halls, each appearing to have someplace very important to get to. Q'eeng strode through them as if he had his own bow wave; they would magically part for him as he came close and close behind him as he walked past.

"It's like rush hour in here," Dahl said, looking around.

"You'll find this crew to be quite efficient and effective," Q'eeng said. "As the flagship of the Universal Union, the *Intrepid* has its pick of crew."

"I don't doubt that, sir," Dahl said, and looked briefly behind him. The crew members behind him had slowed down considerably and were staring at him and Q'eeng. Dahl couldn't read their expressions.

"I understand you requested at the Academy to be stationed on the *Intrepid,*" Q'eeng said.

"Yes, sir," Dahl said, returning his attention to his superior officer. "Your department is doing some real cutting-edge work. Some of the stuff you do on board is so out there we had a hard time re-creating it back at the Academy."

"I hope that's not a suggestion that we're doing sloppy work," Q'eeng said, with a slight, tense edge to his voice.

"Not at all, sir," Dahl said. "Your reputation as a scientist is unimpeachable. And we know that in the kind of work your department does, initial conditions are both significant and difficult to re-create."

Q'eeng seemed to relax at this. "Space is vast," he said. "The *Intrepid*'s mission is to explore. Much of the science we do is front line — identify, describe, posit initial hypotheses. Then we move on, leaving it to others to follow our work."

"Yes, sir," Dahl said. "It's that front line science that appeals to me. The exploration."

"So," Q'eeng said. "Do you see yourself participating in away team missions?"

Directly in front of them, a crew member seemed to stumble over his own feet. Dahl caught him. "Whoa," Dahl said, propping him back up. "Careful with those feet, now." The crew member pulled away, his mumbled "Thanks" very nearly dopplered as he hastened off.

"Agile *and* polite," Dahl said, grinning, then stopped grinning when he noticed Q'eeng, also stopped, staring at him very intently. "Sir," he said.

"Away teams," Q'eeng said again. "Do you see yourself participating in them?"

"At the Academy I was known more as a lab rat," Dahl said. Q'eeng seemed to frown at this. "But I realize that the *Intrepid* is a vessel of exploration. I'm looking forward to doing some of that exploration myself."

"Very good," Q'eeng said, and started moving forward again. "Being a 'lab rat' is fine at the Academy and may be fine on other ships. But the reason that the *Intrepid* has made so many of the discoveries that interested you in the first place is because of its crew's willingness to get into the field and get its hands dirty. I'd ask you to keep that in mind."

"Yes, sir," Dahl said.

"Good," Q'eeng said, and stopped at a door marked "Xenobiology." He opened it, showing the laboratory beyond, and stepped through. Dahl followed.

It was empty.

"Where is everybody, sir?" Dahl asked.

"The *Intrepid* crew does a lot of cross-consultation with crew members in other departments, and often have secondary or supernumerary postings," Q'eeng said. "You are supernumerary with the Linguistics Department for your facility in Forshan, for example. So people don't always stay chained to their workstations."

"Got it, sir," Dahl said.

"Nevertheless," Q'eeng said, pulled out his phone, and made a connection. "Lieutenant Collins. The newest member of your department is at your laboratory to present himself to you." A pause. "Good. That is all." Q'eeng put away his phone. "Lieutenant Collins will be along presently to welcome you."

"Thank you, sir," Dahl said, and saluted. Q'eeng nodded, saluted in return and walked off into the hallway. Dahl went to the door and watched him go. Q'eeng's bow wave preceded him until he turned a corner and went out of sight.

"Hey," someone said behind Dahl. He turned. There was a crew member standing in the middle of the lab.

Dahl looked back out the door, to where Q'eeng had turned, and then back to the new crew member. "Hi," Dahl said. "You weren't here two seconds ago."

"Yeah, we do that," the crew member said, and walked over to Dahl and stretched out his hand. "Jake Cassaway."

"Andy Dahl." Dahl took his hand and shook it. "And how exactly *do* you do that?"

"Trade secret," Cassaway said.

A door opened from the other side of the lab and another crew member entered the

39

room from it.

"There goes the trade secret," Cassaway said.

"What's in there?" Dahl asked, motioning to the door.

"It's a storage room," Cassaway said.

"You were hiding in the storage room?" Dahl said.

"We weren't hiding," said the other crew member. "We were doing inventory."

"Andy Dahl, this is Fiona Mbeke," Cassaway said.

"Hello," Dahl said.

"You should be glad that we were doing inventory," Mbeke said. "Because now that means that it won't be assigned to you as the new guy."

"Well, then, thanks," Dahl said.

"We'll still make you get coffee," Mbeke said.

"I would expect nothing less," Dahl said.

"And look, here is the rest of us," Cassaway said, and nodded as two new people came through the hallway door.

One of them immediately approached Dahl. He saw the lieutenant's pip on her shoulder and saluted.

"Relax," Collins said, and nevertheless returned the salute. "The only time we salute around here is when His Majesty

40

comes through the door."

"You mean Commander Q'eeng," Dahl said.

"You see the pun there," Collins said. "With 'king,' which is what his name sounds like."

"Yes, ma'am," Dahl said.

"That's a little nerd humor for you," Collins said.

"I got it, ma'am," Dahl said, smiling.

"Good," Collins said. "Because the last thing we need is another humorless prick around here. You met Cassaway and Mbeke, I see."

"Yes, ma'am," Dahl said.

"You've figured out that I'm your boss," she said, then motioned to the other crew member. "And this is Ben Trin, who is second in command of the lab." Trin came forward to shake Dahl's hand. Dahl shook it. "And that's all of us."

"Except for Jenkins," Mbeke said.

"Well, he won't see Jenkins," Collins said.

"He might," Mbeke said.

"When was the last time you saw Jenkins?" Trin said to Mbeke.

"I thought I saw him once, but it turned out to be a yeti," Cassaway said.

"Enough about Jenkins," Collins said.

"Who's Jenkins?" Dahl asked.

41

"He's doing an independent project," Collins said. "Very intensive. Forget it, you'll never see him. Now . . ." She reached over to one of the tables in the lab, grabbed a tablet and fired it up. "You come to us with some very nice scores from the Academy, Mr. Dahl."

"Thank you, ma'am," Dahl said.

"Is Flaviu Antonescu still heading up the Xenobiology Department?" Collins asked.

"Yes, ma'am," Dahl said.

"Please stop appending 'ma'am' to every sentence, Dahl, it sounds like you have a vocal tic."

Dahl smiled again. "All right," he said.

Collins nodded and looked back at the tablet. "I'm surprised Flaviu recommended you for the *Intrepid.*"

"He refused at first," Dahl said, remembering the discussion with his Academy department head. "He wanted me to take a post at a research facility on Europa."

"Why didn't you take it?" Collins asked.

"I wanted to see the universe, not be down a sixty-kilometer ice tunnel, looking at Europan microbes."

"You have something against Europan microbes?" Collins asked.

"I'm sure they're very nice as microbes go," Dahl said. "They deserve someone who really wants to study them."

"You must have been pretty insistent to get Flaviu to change his mind," Collins said.

"My scores were high enough to get Commander Q'eeng's attention," Dahl said. "And as luck would have it, a position opened up here."

"It wasn't luck," Mbeke said.

"It was a Longranian Ice Shark," Cassaway said.

"Which is the opposite of luck," Mbeke said.

"A what?" Dahl asked.

"The crew member you're replacing was Sid Black," Trin said. "He was part of an away team to Longran Seven, which is an ice planet. While exploring an abandoned ice city, the away team was attacked by ice sharks. They carried Sid off. He wasn't seen again."

"His leg was," Mbeke said. "The lower half, anyway."

"Quiet, Fiona," Collins said, irritated. She set down the tablet and looked back at Dahl. "You met Commander Q'eeng," she said.

"I did," Dahl said.

"Did he talk to you about away missions?" Collins asked.

"Yes," Dahl said. "He asked me if I was

43

interested in them."

"What did you say?" Collins asked.

"I said I usually did lab work but I assumed I would participate on away missions as well," Dahl said. "Why?"

"He's on Q'eeng's radar now," Trin said to Collins.

Dahl looked at Trin and back at Collins. "Is there something I'm missing here, ma'am?" he asked.

"No," Collins said, and glanced over at Trin. "I just prefer to have the option to indoctrinate my crew before Q'eeng gets his hands on them. That's all."

"Is there some philosophical disagreement there?" Dahl asked.

"It's not important," Collins said. "Don't worry yourself about it. Now," she said. "First things first." She pointed over to the corner. "You get that workstation. Ben will issue you a work tablet and give you your orientation, and Jake and Fiona will catch you up on anything else you want to know. All you have to do is ask. Also, as the new guy you're on coffee duty."

"I was already told about that," Dahl said.

"Good," Collins said. "Because I could use a cup right about now. Ben, get him set up."

■ ■ ■ ■

"So, did you guys get asked about away teams?" Duvall asked, as she brought her mess tray to the table where Dahl and Hanson were already sitting.

"I did," Hanson said.

"So did I," Dahl said.

"Is it just me, or does everyone on this ship seem a little weird about them?" Duvall asked.

"Give me an example," Dahl said.

"I mean that within five minutes of getting to my new post I heard three different stories of crew buying the farm on an away mission. Death by falling rock. Death by toxic atmosphere. Death by pulse gun vaporization."

"Death by shuttle door malfunction," Hanson said.

"Death by ice shark," Dahl said.

"Death by *what*?" Duvall said, blinking. "What the hell is an ice shark?"

"You got me," Dahl said. "I had no idea there was such a thing."

"Is it a shark *made* of ice?" Hanson asked. "Or a shark that *lives* in ice?"

"It wasn't specified at the time," Dahl said, spearing a meat bit on his tray.

"I'm thinking you should have called bullshit on the ice shark story," Duvall said.

"Even if the details are sketchy, it fits your larger point," Dahl said. "People here have away missions on the brain."

"It's because someone always dies on them," Hanson said.

Duvall arched an eyebrow at this. "What makes you say that, Jimmy?"

"Well, we're all replacing former crew members," Hanson said, and then pointed at Duvall. "What happened to the one you replaced. Transferred out?"

"No," Duvall said. "He was the death by vaporization one."

"And mine got sucked out of the shuttle," Hanson said. "And Andy's got eaten by a shark. Maybe. You have to admit there's something going on there. I bet if we tracked down Finn and Hester, they'd tell us the same thing."

"Speaking of which," Dahl said, and motioned with his fork. Hanson and Duvall looked to where he pointed to see Hester standing by the end of the mess line, tray in hand, staring glumly around the mess hall.

"He's not the world's most cheerful person, is he," Duvall said.

"Oh, he's all right," Hanson said, and then called to Hester. Hester jumped slightly at

46

his name, seemed to consider whether he should join the three of them, and then appeared to resign himself to it, walked over and sat down. He began to pick at his food.

"So," Duvall finally said, to Hester. "How's your day?"

Hester shrugged and picked at his food some more, then finally grimaced and set down his fork. He looked around the table.

"What is it?" Duvall asked.

"Is it just me," Hester said, "or is everyone on this ship *monumentally fucked up* about away missions?"

CHAPTER THREE

Dahl was at his workstation, classifying Theta Orionis XII spores, when Ben Trin's work tablet pinged. Trin glanced at it, said "I'm going to get some coffee," and headed out the door.

What's wrong with my *coffee?* Dahl wondered, as he went back to his work. In the week since his arrival on the *Intrepid,* Dahl had, as promised, been tasked with the role of coffee boy. This consisted of keeping the coffee pot in the storage room topped off and getting coffee for his lab mates whenever they rattled their mugs. They weren't obnoxious about it — they got their own coffee more often than not — but they enjoyed exercising their coffee boy privileges from time to time.

This reminded Dahl that he needed to check on the status of the coffee pot. Cassaway had been the last one to get a cup; Dahl looked up to ask him if it was time for him to start another pot.

He was alone in the lab.

"What the hell?" Dahl said, to himself.

The outside door to the lab slid open and Q'eeng and Captain Abernathy stepped through.

Dahl stood and saluted. "Captain, Commander," he said.

Q'eeng looked around the laboratory. "Where are your crewmates, Ensign Dahl?" he said.

"Errands," Dahl said, after a second.

"He'll do," Abernathy said, and strode forward purposefully toward Dahl. He held a small vial. "Do you know what this is?" he said.

A small vial, Dahl thought, but did not say. "A xenobiological sample," he said instead.

"Very good," Abernathy said, and handed it to him. "As you know, Ensign, we are currently above the planet Merovia, a planet rich with artistic wonders but whose people are superstitiously opposed to medical practices of any sort." He paused, as if waiting for acknowledgment.

"Of course, sir," Dahl said, giving what he hoped was the expected prompt.

"Unfortunately, they are also in the throes of a global plague, which is decimating their population," Q'eeng said. "The Universal

49

Union is concerned that the damage caused by the plague will collapse their entire civilization, throwing the planet into a new dark age from which it will never recover."

"The government of Merovia has refused all Universal Union medical help," Abernathy said. "So the *Intrepid* was secretly assigned to collect samples of the plague and engineer a counter-bacterial which we could release into the wild, burning out the plague."

Counter-bacterial? Dahl thought. *Don't they mean a vaccine?* But before he could ask for clarification, Q'eeng was speaking again.

"We sent a covert two-man away team to collect samples, but in doing so they became infected themselves," Q'eeng said. "The Merovian Plague has already claimed the life of Ensign Lee."

"Damn plague liquefied the flesh right off her bones," Abernathy said, grimly.

"The other *Intrepid* crew member infected is Lieutenant Kerensky," Q'eeng said. At this, both Abernathy and Q'eeng looked at Dahl intensely, as if to stress the sheer, abject horror of this Lieutenant Kerensky being infected.

"Oh, no," Dahl ventured. "Not Kerensky."

Abernathy nodded. "So you understand

the importance of that little vial you have in your hands," he said. "Use it to find the counter-bacterial. If you can do it, you'll save Kerensky."

"And the Merovians," Dahl said.

"Yes, them too," Abernathy said. "You have six hours."

Dahl blinked. "Six hours?"

Abernathy angered at this. "Is there a problem, mister?" he asked.

"It's not a lot of time," Dahl said.

"Damn it, man!" Abernathy said. "This is *Kerensky* we're talking about! If God could make the universe in six days, surely you can make a counter-bacterial in six hours."

"I'll try, sir," Dahl said.

"Try's not good enough," Abernathy said, and clapped Dahl hard on the shoulder. "I need to hear you say that you'll *do* it." He shook Dahl's shoulder vigorously.

"I'll do it," Dahl said.

"Thank you, Ensign Dill," Abernathy said.

"Dahl, sir," Dahl said.

"Dahl," Abernathy said, and then turned to Q'eeng, turning his attention away from Dahl so completely it was as if a switch had been thrown. "Come on, Q'eeng. We need to make a hyperwave call to Admiral Drezner. We're cutting things close here." Abernathy strode out into the hallway,

51

purposefully. Q'eeng followed, nodding to Dahl absentmindedly as he followed the captain.

Dahl stood there for a moment, vial in his hand.

"I'm going to say it again," he said, again to himself. "What the hell?"

The storage room door opened; Cassaway and Mbeke came out of it. "What did they want?" Cassaway asked.

"Checking inventory again?" Dahl asked, mockingly.

"We don't tell you how to do your job," Mbeke said.

"So what did they want?" Collins asked, as she briskly walked through the outside door, Trin following, cup of coffee in hand.

Dahl thought hard about yelling at all of them, then stopped and refocused. He held up the vial. "I'm supposed to find a counter-bacterial for this."

"Counter-bacterial?" Trin asked. "Don't you mean a vaccine?"

"I'm telling you what they told me," Dahl said. "And they gave me six hours."

"Six hours," Trin said, looking at Collins.

"Right," Dahl said. "Which, even if I knew what a 'counter-bacterial' was, is no time at all. It takes weeks to make a vaccine."

"Dahl, tell me," Collins said. "When Q'eeng and Abernathy were here, how were they talking to you?"

"What do you mean?" Dahl asked.

"Did they come in and quickly tell you what you needed?" Collins said. "Or did they go on and on about a bunch of crap you didn't need to know?"

"They went on a bit, yes," Dahl said.

"Was the captain particularly dramatic?" Cassaway asked.

"What is 'particularly dramatic' in this context?" Dahl asked.

"Like this," Mbeke said, and then grabbed both of Dahl's shoulders and shook them. " 'Damn it, man! There is no *try*! Only *do*!' "

Dahl set down the vial so it was not accidentally shaken out of his grip. "He said pretty much exactly those words," he said to Mbeke.

"Well, they're some of his favorite words," Mbeke said, letting go.

"I'm not understanding what any of this means," Dahl said, looking at his lab mates.

"One more question," Collins said, ignoring Dahl's complaint. "When they told you that you had to find this counter-bacterial in six hours, did they give you a reason why?"

"Yes," Dahl said. "They said that was the amount of time they had to save a lieutenant."

"Which lieutenant?" Collins said.

"Why does it matter?" Dahl asked.

"Answer the question, Ensign," Collins said, uttering Dahl's rank for the first time in a week.

"A lieutenant named Kerensky," Dahl said.

There was a pause at the name.

"*That* poor bastard," Mbeke said. "He always gets screwed, doesn't he."

Cassaway snorted. "He gets *better,*" he said, and then looked over to Dahl. "Somebody else died, right?"

"An ensign named Lee was liquefied," Dahl said.

"See," Cassaway said, to Mbeke.

"Someone really needs to tell me what's going on," Dahl said.

"Time to break out the Box," Trin said, sipping his coffee again.

"Right," Collins said, and nodded to Cassaway. "Go get it, Jake." Cassaway rolled his eyes and went to the storage room.

"At least someone tell me who Lieutenant Kerensky is," Dahl said.

"He's part of the bridge crew," Trin said. "Technically, he's an astrogator."

54

"The captain and Q'eeng said he was part of an away team, collecting biological samples," Dahl said.

"I'm sure he was," Trin said.

"Why would they send an astrogator for that?" Dahl said.

"Now you know why I said 'technically,' " Trin said, and took another sip.

The storage room door slid open and Cassaway emerged with a small, boxy appliance in his hands. He walked it over to the closest free induction pad. The thing powered on.

"What is that?" Dahl asked.

"It's the Box," Cassaway said.

"Does it have a formal name?" Dahl asked.

"Probably," Cassaway said.

Dahl walked over and examined it, opening it and looking inside. "It looks like a microwave oven," he said.

"It's not," Collins said, taking the vial and bringing it to Dahl.

"What is it, then?" Dahl asked, looking at Collins.

"It's the Box," Collins said.

"That's it? 'The Box'?" Dahl said.

"If it makes you feel better to think it's an experimental quantum-based computer with advanced inductive artificial intelligence capacity, whose design comes to us from an advanced but extinct race of warrior-engineers, then you can think about it that way," Collins said.

"Is that actually what it is?" Dahl asked.

"Sure," Collins said, and handed the vial to Dahl. "Put this in the Box."

Dahl looked at the vial and took it. "Don't you want me to prepare the sample?" he asked.

"Normally, yes," Collins said. "But this is the Box, so you can just put it in there."

Dahl inserted the vial into the Box, placing it in the center of the ceramic disk at the bottom of the inside space. He closed the Box door and looked at the outside instrument panel, which featured three buttons, one green, one red, one white.

"The green button starts it," Collins said. "The red button stops it. The white button opens the door."

"It should be a little more complicated than that," Dahl said.

"Normally it is," Collins agreed. "But this is —"

"This is the Box," Dahl said. "I get that part."

"Then start it," Collins said.

Dahl pressed the green button. The Box sprang to life, making a humming sound.

On the inside a light came on. Dahl peered inside to see the vial turning as the disk he placed it on was rotated by a carousel.

"You have got to be kidding me," Dahl said, to himself. He looked up at Collins again. "Now what?"

"You said Abernathy and Q'eeng said you had six hours," Collins said.

"Right," Dahl said.

"So in about five and a half hours the Box will let you know it has a solution," Collins said.

"How will it tell me that?" Dahl asked.

"It'll go *ding,*" Collins said, and walked off.

Roughly five and a half hours later there was a small, quiet *ding,* the humming sound emanating from the Box's carousel engine stopped and the light went off.

"Now what?" Dahl said, staring at the Box, to no one in particular.

"Check your work tablet," Trin said, not looking up from his own work. He was the only one besides Dahl still in the lab.

Dahl grabbed his work tablet and powered up the screen. On it was a rotating picture of a complex organic molecule and beside that, a long scrolling column of data. Dahl tried to read it.

"It's giving me gibberish," he said, after a minute. "Long streaming columns of it."

"You're fine," Trin said. He set down his own work and walked over to Dahl. "Now, listen closely. Here's what you do next. First, you're going to take your work tablet to the bridge, where Q'eeng is."

"Why?" Dahl said. "I could just mail the data to him."

Trin shook his head. "It's not how this works."

"Wh—" Dahl began, but Trin held up his hand.

"Shut up for a minute and just listen, okay?" Trin said. "I know it doesn't make sense, and it's stupid, but this is the way it's got to be done. Take your tablet to Q'eeng. Show him the data on it. And then once he's looking at it, you say, 'We got most of it, but the protein coat is giving us a problem.' Then point to whatever data is scrolling by at the time."

" 'Protein coat'?" Dahl said.

"It doesn't have to be the protein coat," Trin said. "You can say whatever you like. Enzyme transcription errors. RNA replication is buggy. I personally go with protein coat because it's easy to say. The point is, you need to say everything is almost perfect but one thing still needs to be done. And

58

that's when you gesture toward the data."

"What'll that do?" Dahl asked.

"It will give Q'eeng an excuse to furrow his brow, stare at the data for a minute and then tell you that you've overlooked some basic thing, which he will solve," Trin said. "At which point you have the option of saying something like 'Of course!' or 'Amazing!' or, if you really want to kiss his ass, 'We never would have solved that in a million years, Commander Q'eeng.' He likes that. He won't acknowledge that he likes it. But he likes it."

Dahl opened his mouth, but Trin held up his hand again. "Or you can do what the rest of us do, which is to get the hell off the bridge as soon as you possibly can," Trin said. "Give him the data, point out the one error, let him solve it, get your tablet back and get out of there. Don't call attention to yourself. Don't say or do anything clever. Show up, do your job, *get out of there.* It's the smartest thing you can do." Trin walked back over to his work.

"None of this makes the slightest bit of sense," Dahl said.

"No, it doesn't," Trin agreed. "I already told you it didn't."

"Are any of you going to bother to explain any of this to me?" Dahl asked.

59

"Maybe someday," Trin said, sitting down at his workstation. "But not right now. Right now, you have to race to get that data to the bridge and to Q'eeng. Your six hours is just about up. Hurry."

Dahl burst out of the Xenobiology Laboratory door and immediately collided with someone else, falling to the ground and dropping his tablet. He picked himself up and looked around for his tablet. It was being held by the person with whom he collided, Finn.

"No one should ever be in that much of a rush," Finn said.

Dahl snatched back the tablet. "You don't have someone about to liquefy if you don't get to the bridge in ten minutes," Dahl said, heading in the direction of the bridge.

"That's very dramatic," Finn said, matching Dahl's pace.

"Don't you have somewhere to be?" Dahl asked him.

"I do," Finn said. "The bridge. I'm delivering a manifest for my boss to Captain Abernathy."

"Doesn't anyone just send messages on this ship?" Dahl asked.

"Here on the *Intrepid,* they like the personal touch," Finn said.

"Do you think that's really it?" Dahl asked. He weaved past a clot of crewmen.

"Why do you ask?" Finn said.

Dahl shrugged. "It's not important," he said.

"I like this ship," Finn said. "This is my sixth posting. Every other ship I've been on the officers had a stick up their ass about procedure and protocol. This one is so relaxed it's like being on a cruise ship. Hell, my boss ducks the captain at every possible opportunity."

Dahl stopped suddenly, forcing Finn to sway to avoid colliding with him a second time. "He ducks the captain," he said.

"It's like he's psychic about it," Finn said. "One second, he's there telling a story about a night with a Gordusian ambisexual, and the next he's off getting coffee. As soon as he steps out of the room, there's the captain."

"You're serious about this," Dahl said.

"Why do you think I'm the one delivering messages?" Finn said.

Dahl shook his head and started off again. Finn followed.

The bridge was sleek and well-appointed and reminded Dahl of the lobby of some of the nicer skyscrapers he had been to.

"Ensign Dahl," Chief Science Officer

Q'eeng said, spotting him from his workstation. "I see you like cutting it close with your assignments."

"We worked as fast as we could," Dahl said. He walked over to Q'eeng and presented the tablet with the scrolling data and the rotating molecule. Q'eeng took it and studied it silently. After a minute, he looked up at Dahl and cleared his throat.

"Sorry, sir," Dahl said, remembering his line. "We got ninety-nine percent there, but then we had a problem. With, uh, the protein coat." After a second he pointed to the screen, at the gibberish flying by.

"It's always the protein coat with your lab, isn't it," Q'eeng murmured, perusing the screen again.

"Yes, sir," Dahl said.

"Next time, remember to more closely examine the relationship between the peptide bonds," Q'eeng said, and punched his fingers at the tablet. "You'll find the solution to your problem is staring you right in the face." He turned the tablet toward Dahl. The rotating molecule had stopped rotating and several of its bonds were now highlighted in blinking red. Nothing had otherwise changed with the molecule.

"That's amazing, sir," Dahl said. "I don't know how we missed it."

"Yes, well," Q'eeng said, and then tapped at the screen again. The data flew off Dahl's tablet and onto Q'eeng's workstation. "Fortunately we may have just enough time to get this improved solution to the matter synthesizer to save Kerensky." Q'eeng jabbed the tablet back at Dahl. "Thank you, Ensign, that will be all."

Dahl opened his mouth, intending to say something more. Q'eeng looked up at him, quizzically. Then the image of Trin popped into Dahl's brain.

Show up, do your job, get out of there. It's the smartest thing you can do.

So Dahl nodded and got out of there.

Finn caught up with him outside the bridge a moment later. "Well, that was a complete waste of my time," Finn said. "I like that."

"There's something seriously wrong with this ship," Dahl said.

"Trust me, there isn't a damn thing wrong with this ship," Finn said. "This is your first posting. You lack perspective. Take it from an old pro. This is as good as it gets."

"I'm not sure you're a reliable —" Dahl said, and then stopped as a hairy wraith appeared before him and Finn. The wraith glared at them both and then jabbed a finger into Dahl's chest.

"You," the wraith said, jabbing the finger deeper. "You just got lucky in there. You don't know how lucky you were. Listen to me, Dahl. *Stay off the bridge.* Avoid the Narrative. The next time you're going to get sucked in for sure. And then it's all over for you." The wraith glanced over to Finn. "You too, goldbrick. You're fodder for sure."

"Who are you and what medications aren't you taking?" Finn said.

The wraith sneered at Finn. "Don't think I'm going to warn either of you again," he said. "Listen to me or don't. But if you don't, you'll be dead. And then where will you be? *Dead,* that's where. It's up to you now." The wraith stomped off and took an abrupt turn into a cargo tunnel.

"What the hell was that?" Finn asked. "A yeti?"

Dahl looked back at Finn but didn't answer. He ran down the corridor and slapped open the access panel to the cargo tunnel.

The corridor was empty.

Finn came up behind Dahl. "Remind me what you were saying about this place," he said.

"There's something seriously wrong with this ship," Dahl repeated.

"Yeah," Finn said. "I think you might be right."

Chapter Four

"Come on! We're almost to the shuttles!"
yelled Lieutenant Kerensky, and Dahl had
one giggling, mad second to reflect on how
good Kerensky looked for having been such
a recent plague victim. Then he, like Hester
and everyone else on the away team,
sprinted crazily down the space station corridor, trying to outrun the mechanized
death behind them.

The space station was not a Universal
Union station; it was an independent commercial station that may or may not have
been strictly legally licensed but that none-
theless sent out on the hyperwave an open,
repeating distress signal, with a second,
encoded signal hidden within it. The *Intrepid*
responded to the first, sending two shuttles
with away teams to the station. It had
decoded the hidden signal while the away
teams were there.

It said, *Stay away — the machines are out*

of control.

Dahl's away team had figured out that one before the message was decoded, when one of the machines sliced Crewman Lopez into mulch. The distant screams in the halls suggested that the second away team was in the painful process of figuring it out, too.

The second away team, with Finn, Hanson and Duvall on it.

"What sort of assholes encode a message about *killer machines*?" Hester screamed. He had brought up the rear of his away team's running column. The distant vibrating *thuds* suggested one of the machines — a big one — was not too far behind them at the moment.

"Quiet," Dahl said. They knew the machines could see them; it was a good bet the machines could hear them too. Dahl, Hester and the other two remaining crew members on the team hunkered down and waited for Kerensky to tell them where to go next.

Kerensky consulted his phone. "Dahl," he said, motioning him forward. Dahl sneaked up to his lieutenant, who showed him the phone with a map on it. "We're here," he said, pointing to one corridor. "The shuttle bay is here. I see two routes to it, one through the station's engineering core and the other through its mess hall area."

67

Less talk, more decision making, please, Dahl thought, and nodded.

"I think we stand a better chance if we split up," Kerensky said. "That way if the machines get one group, the other group might still get to the shuttles. Are you rated to fly one?"

"Hester is," Dahl heard himself say, and then wondered how he knew that. He didn't remember knowing that bit of information before.

Kerensky nodded. "Then you take him and Crewman McGregor and cut through the mess hall. I'll take Williams and go through Engineering. We'll meet at the shuttle, wait for Lieutenant Fischer's away team if we can, and then get the hell out of here."

"Yes, sir," Dahl said.

"Good luck," Kerensky said, and motioned to Williams to follow him.

He hardly looks liquefied at all, Dahl thought again, and then went back to Hester and McGregor. "He wants to split up and have the three of us go through the mess hall to the shuttle bay," he said to the two of them, as Kerensky and Williams skulked off down the corridor toward Engineering.

"What?" McGregor said, visibly upset.

"Bullshit. I don't want to go with you. I want to go with Kerensky."

"We have our orders," Dahl said.

"Screw them," McGregor said. "You don't get it, do you? Kerensky's untouchable. You're not. You're just some ensign. We're in a space station filled with fucking killer robots. Do you really think *you're* going to make it out of here alive?"

"Calm down, McGregor," Dahl said, holding out his hands. Beneath his feet, the corridor floor vibrated. "We're wasting time here."

"No!" McGregor said. "You *don't get it*! Lopez already died in front of Kerensky! She was the sacrifice! Now anyone with Kerensky is safe!" He leaped up to chase after Kerensky, stepping into the corridor just as the killing machine that had been following them turned the corner. McGregor saw the machine and had time to make a surprised "O" with his mouth before the harpoon the machine launched pushed into him, spearing him through the liver.

There was an infinitesimal pause, in which everything was set in a tableau: Dahl and Hester crouched on the side of the corridor, killing machine at the corner, the harpooned McGregor in the middle, dripping.

McGregor turned his head toward the

horrified Dahl. "See?" he said, through a mouthful of blood. Then there was a yank, and McGregor flew toward the killer machine, which had already spun up its slicing blades.

Dahl screamed McGregor's name, stood and unholstered his pulse gun, and fired into the center of the pulpy red haze where he knew the killer machine to be. The pulse beam glanced harmlessly off the machine's surface. Hester yelled and pushed Dahl down the corridor, away from the machine, which was already resetting its harpoon. They turned a corner and raced away into another corridor, which led to the mess hall. They burst through the doors and closed them behind them.

"These doors aren't going to keep that thing out," Hester said breathlessly.

Dahl examined the doorway. "There's another set of doors here," he said. "Fire doors or an airlock door, maybe. Look for a panel."

"Found it," Hester said. "Step back." He pressed a large red button. There was a squeak and a hiss. A pair of heavy doors slowly began to shut, and then stalled, halfway closed. "Oh, come on!" Hester said.

Through the glass on the already closed

set of doors, the killer machine stepped into view.

"I have an idea," Dahl said.

"Does it involve running?" Hester asked.

"Move back from the panel," Dahl said. Hester stepped back, frowning. Dahl raised his pulse gun and fired into the door panel at the same time the machine's harpoon punctured the closed outer door and yanked it out of the doorway. The panel blew in a shower of sparks and the heavy fire doors moved, shutting with a vibrating *clang.*

"Shooting the panel?" Hester said, incredulous. "That was your big idea?"

"I had a hunch," Dahl said, putting his pulse gun away.

"That the space station was wired haphazardly?" Hester said. "That this whole place is one big fucking code violation?"

"The killer machines kind of gave that part away," Dahl said.

There was a violent *bang* as a harpoon struck against the fire door.

"If that door is built like the rest of this place, it won't be long before that thing's through it," Hester said.

"We're not staying anyway," Dahl said, and pulled out his phone for a station map. "Come on. There's a door in the kitchen that will get us closer to the shuttle bay. If

71

we're lucky we won't run into anything else before we get there."

Two corridors before the shuttle bay, Dahl and Hester ran into what was left of Lieutenant Fischer's party: Fischer, Duvall, Hanson and Finn.

"Well, aren't we the lucky bunch," Finn said, seeing Dahl and Hester. The words were sarcastic, but Finn's tone suggested he was close to losing it. Hanson put a hand on his shoulder.

"Where's Kerensky and the rest of your team?" Fischer asked Dahl.

"We split up," Dahl said. "Kerensky and Williams are alive as far as I know. We lost Lopez and McGregor."

Fischer nodded. "Payton and Webb from our team," he said.

"Harpoons and blades?" Dahl asked.

"Swarming bots," Duvall said.

"We missed those," Dahl said.

Fischer shook his head. "It's unbelievable," he said. "I just transferred to the *Intrepid*. This is my first away team. And I lose two of my people."

"I don't think it's you, sir," Dahl said.

"That's more than I know," Fischer said. He motioned them forward and they made their way cautiously to the shuttle bay.

72

"Anyone else here rated to fly one of these things?" Fischer asked, as they entered the bay.

"I am," Hester said.

"Good," Fischer said, and pointed to the shuttle Kerensky had piloted. "Warm her up. I'll get started on mine. I want all of you to get into that shuttle with him." He pointed at Hester. "If you see any of those machines coming, don't wait, take off. I'll have enough space for Kerensky and Williams. Got it?"

"Yes, sir," Hester said.

"Get to it, then," Fischer said, and ducked into his own shuttle.

"Everything about this mission sucks," Hester said in their own shuttle, as he banged through the shuttle's pre-flight sequence. Finn, Duvall and Hanson were strapping themselves in; Dahl kept watch by the hatch, looking for Kerensky and Williams.

"Hester, did you ever tell me that you knew how to fly a shuttle?" Dahl asked, turning to look at Hester.

"Kind of busy now," Hester said.

"I didn't know he was rated to fly a shuttle, either," Finn said, from his seat. His anxiousness was needing a release, and talking seemed like a better idea to him than

73

wetting himself. "And I've known him for more than a year."

"Not something you'd think you'd miss," Dahl said.

"We weren't close," Finn said. "I was mostly just using him for his foot locker."

Dahl said nothing to this and turned back to the hatch.

"There," Hester said, and punched a button. The engines thrummed into life. He strapped himself in. "Close that hatch. We're getting out of here."

"Not yet," Dahl said.

"The hell with that," Hester said. He pressed a button on his control panel to seal the hatch.

Dahl slapped the override at the side of the hatch. "Not yet!" he yelled at Hester.

"What is wrong with you?" Hester yelled back. "Fischer's got more than enough space for Kerensky and Williams. My vote is for leaving, and since I'm the goddamn pilot, my vote's the only one that counts!"

"We're waiting!" Dahl said.

"For fuck's sake, *why?*" Hester said.

From his seat, Hanson pointed. "Here they come," he said.

Dahl looked out the hatch. Kerensky and Williams were hobbling slowly into the shuttle bay, propping each other up. Immediately behind them were the pounding of the machines.

Fischer popped his head out his shuttle hatch and saw Dahl. "Come on!" he said, and ran toward Kerensky and Williams. Dahl leaped out of his shuttle and followed.

"There's six of them behind us," Kerensky said, and they came up to the two of them. "We came as fast as we could. Swarming bots —" He collapsed. Dahl grabbed him before he could hit the floor.

"You got him?" Fischer said to Dahl. He nodded. "Get him on your shuttle. Tell your pilot to go. I've got Williams. Hurry." Fischer slung his arm around Williams and dragged him toward his shuttle. Williams turned back to look at Kerensky and Dahl, utterly terrified.

The first of the machines stomped into the shuttle bay.

"Come on, Andy!" Duvall yelled, from the shuttle hatch. Dahl put on a burst of speed and crossed the distance to the shuttle, fairly hurling Kerensky at Duvall and Hanson, who had unlatched himself from his seat as well. They grabbed the lieutenant and dragged him in, Dahl collapsing in afterward.

"*Now* can we go?" Hester said, rhetorically, because he slapped the hatch button

75

without waiting for a response. The shuttle leaped up from the shuttle bay deck as something slammed into the side and clattered off.

"Harpoon," Finn said. He had unstrapped himself and was hovering over Hester, looking at a rearview monitor. "It didn't take."

The shuttle cleared the bay. "Good riddance," muttered Hester.

"How's Kerensky?" Dahl asked Duvall, who was examining Kerensky.

"He's nonresponsive, but he doesn't look too bad," she said, and then turned to Hanson. "Jimmy, get me the medkit, please. It's on the back of the pilot's seat." Hanson went to get it.

"Do you know what you're doing?" Dahl asked.

Duvall looked up briefly. "Told you I'd been ground forces, right? Got medic training then. Spent lots of time patching people up." She smiled. "Hester's not the only one with hidden skills." Hanson came back with the medkit; Duvall cracked it open and got to work.

"Oh, shit," Finn said, still looking at the monitor.

"What is it?" Dahl said, coming over to Finn.

"The other shuttle," Finn said. "I've got a

feed from their cameras. Look."

Dahl looked. The cameras showed dozens of machines pouring into the shuttle bay, targeting their fire at the shuttle. Above them a dark, shifting cloud hovered.

"The swarm bots," Finn murmured.

The camera view wobbled and shook and then went blank.

Finn slipped into the co-pilot seat and punched the screen they had just been looking at. "Their shuttle's been compromised," he said. "The engines aren't firing, and it looks like the hull integrity has been breached."

"We need to go back for them," Dahl said.

"No," Hester said. Dahl flared, but Hester turned and looked at him. "Andy, no. If the shuttle's been breached even a little, those swarming bots are already inside of it. If they're already inside of it, then Fischer and Williams are already dead."

"He's right," Finn said. "There's no one to go back for. Even if we did, we couldn't do anything. The bay is swarming with those things. This shuttle doesn't have weapons. All we'd be doing is letting the machines get a second shot at us."

"We were lucky to get out at all," Hester said, returning to his controls.

Dahl looked back at Kerensky, who was

now moaning softly while Duvall and Hanson tended to him.

"I don't think luck had much to do with it," he said.

CHAPTER FIVE

"I think I'd like to dispense with the bullshit now," Dahl said to his lab mates.

The four of them were quiet and looked at each other. "All right, you don't have to fetch us all coffee anymore," said Mbeke, finally.

"It's not about the *coffee*, Fiona," Dahl said.

"I know," Mbeke said. "But I thought it was worth a shot."

"It's about your away team experience," Collins said.

"No," Dahl said. "It's about my away team experience, and it's about the fact all of you disappear whenever Q'eeng shows up, and it's about the way people move away from him whenever he walks down the corridors, and it's about that fucking *box,* and it's about the fact there's something very wrong with this ship."

"All right," Collins said. "Here's the deal.

Some time ago, it was noticed that there was an extremely high correlation between away teams led by or including certain officers, and crewmen dying. The captain. Commander Q'eeng. Chief Engineer West. Medical Chief Hartnell. Lieutenant Kerensky."

"And not only about crewmen dying," Trin said.

"Right," Collins said. "And other things, too."

"Like if someone died with Kerensky around, everyone else would be safe if they stuck with him," Dahl said, remembering McGregor.

"Kerensky's actually only weakly associated with that effect," Cassaway said.

Dahl turned to Cassaway. "It's an *effect*? You have a *name* for it?"

"It's the Sacrificial Effect," Cassaway said. "It's strongest with Hartnell and Q'eeng. The captain and Kerensky, not so much. And it doesn't work at all with West. He's a goddamn death trap."

"Things are always exploding around him," Mbeke said. "Not a good sign for a chief engineer."

"The fact that people die around these officers is so clear and obvious that everyone naturally avoids them," Collins said. "If they're walking through the ship, crew members know to look like they're in the middle of some very important errand for the crew chief or section head. That's why everyone's rushing through the halls whenever they're around."

"It doesn't explain how you all know to get coffee or inspect that storage room whenever Q'eeng is on his way."

"There's a tracking system," Trin said.

"A tracking system?" Dahl said, incredulously.

"It's not that shocking," Collins said. "We all have phones that give away our locations to the *Intrepid*'s computer system. I could, as your superior officer, have the computer locate you anywhere on the ship."

"Q'eeng isn't your underling," Dahl said. "Neither is Captain Abernathy."

"The alert system isn't strictly legal," Collins allowed.

"But you all have access to it," Dahl said.

"*They* have access to it," Cassaway said, pointing to Collins and Trin.

"We give you warning when they're on their way," Trin said.

" 'I'm going to get some coffee,' " Dahl said. Trin nodded.

"Yes, which only works as long as you two are actually here," Cassaway said. "If you're not around, we're screwed."

"We can't have the entire ship on the alert system," Trin said. "It would be too obvious."

Cassaway snorted. "As if *they'd* notice," he said.

"What does that mean?" Dahl asked.

"It means that the captain, Q'eeng and the others seem oblivious to the fact that most of the ship's crew go out of their way to avoid them," Mbeke said. "They're also oblivious to the fact that they kill off a lot of the crew."

"How can they be oblivious to that?" Dahl said. "Hasn't someone told them? Don't they know the stats?"

Dahl's four lab mates shared quick glances at each other. "It was pointed out to the captain once," Collins said. "It didn't take."

"What does that mean?" Dahl asked.

"It means that talking to them about the amount of crew they run through is like talking to a brick wall," Cassaway said.

"Then tell someone else," Dahl said. "Tell Admiral Comstock."

"You don't think that's been tried?" Cassaway said. "We've contacted Fleet. We've contacted the Dub U's Military Bureau of Investigation. We've even had people try to go to journalists. Nothing works."

"There's no actual evidence of malfeasance or command incompetence, is what we're told," Trin said. "Not us, specifically. But whoever complains about it."

"How many people do you have to lose before it becomes command incompetence?" Dahl asked.

"What we've been told," Collins said, "is that as the flagship of the Dub U, the *Intrepid* takes on a larger share of sensitive diplomatic, military and research missions than any other ship in the fleet. Because of that, there is commensurate increase of risk, and thus a statistically larger chance crew lives will be lost. It's part of the risk of such a high-profile posting."

"In other words, crew deaths are a feature, not a bug," Cassaway said, dryly.

"And now you know why we just try to avoid them," Mbeke said.

Dahl thought about this for a moment. "It still doesn't explain the Box."

"We don't have any good explanation for the Box," Collins said. "No one does. Officially speaking, the Box doesn't exist."

"It looks like a microwave, it *dings* when it's done and it outputs complete nonsense," Dahl said. "You have to present its results in person, and it doesn't matter what you say when you give the data to Q'eeng, just so long as you give him something to fix. I don't really have to point out all the ways that's so very fucked up, do I?"

"It's how it's been done since before we got here," Trin said. "It's what we were told to do by the people who had our jobs before us. We do it because it works."

Dahl threw up his hands. "Then why not use it for everything?" he asked. "It'd save us all a lot of time."

"It doesn't work with everything," Trin said. "It only works for things that are extraordinarily difficult."

"Like finding a so-called counter-bacterial in six hours," Dahl said.

"That's right," Trin said.

Dahl looked around the room. "It doesn't bother you that a science lab has a *magic box* in it?" he asked.

"Of course it bothers us!" Collins said sharply. "I hate the damn thing. But I have to believe it's not actually magic. We just somehow got hold of a piece of technology so incredibly advanced it looks that way to us. It's like showing a caveman your phone. He wouldn't have the first idea how it worked, but he could still use it to make a call."

"If the phone were like the Box, the only time it would let the caveman make a call would be if he were *on fire,*" Dahl said.

"It is what it is," Collins said. "And for some reason we have to do the Kabuki dance of showing off gibberish to make it work. We do it because it *does* work. We don't know what to do with the data, but the *Intrepid*'s computer does. And at the time, in an emergency, that's enough. We hate it. But we don't have any choice but to use it."

"When I came to the *Intrepid,* I told Q'eeng that at the Academy we had trouble replicating some of the work you guys were doing on the ship," Dahl said. "Now I know why. It's because you weren't actually *doing* the work."

"Are you done, Ensign?" Collins said. She was clearly getting tired of the inquisition.

"Why didn't you just tell me all of this when I came on board?" Dahl said.

"What are we going to say, Andy?" Collins said. " 'Hi, welcome to the *Intrepid,* avoid the officers because it's likely you'll get killed if you're on an away team with them, and oh, by the way, here's a magic box we use for *impossible things*'? That would be a lovely first impression, wouldn't it?"

"You wouldn't have believed us," Cassaway said. "Not until you were here long enough to see some of this shit for yourself."

"This is nuts," Dahl said.

"That it is," Collins said.

"And you have no rational explanation for it?" Dahl asked. "No hypothesis?"

"The rational explanation is what the Dub U told us," Trin said. "The *Intrepid* takes on high-risk missions. More people die because of it. The crew has developed superstitions and avoidance strategies to compensate. And we use advanced technologies that we don't understand but which allow us to complete missions."

"But you don't believe it," Dahl said.

"I don't *like* it," Trin said. "I don't have any reason not to believe it."

"It's saner than what Jenkins thinks," Mbeke said.

Dahl turned to face Mbeke. "You've talked about him before," he said.

"He's doing an independent research project," Collins said.

"On this?" Dahl asked.

"Not exactly," Collins said. "He's the one who built the tracking system we use for the captain and the others. The computer system AI sees it as a hack and keeps trying to patch it. So he's got to keep updating if we want it to keep working."

Dahl glanced over at Cassaway. "You said he looked like a yeti."

86

"He does look like a yeti," Cassaway said. "Either a yeti or Rasputin. I've heard him described both ways. Both are accurate."

"I think I met him," Dahl said. "After I went to the bridge to give Q'eeng the Box data about Kerensky's plague. He came up to me in the corridor."

"What did he say to you?" Collins asked.

"He told me to stay off the bridge," Dahl said. "And he told me to 'avoid the narrative.' What the hell does that mean?"

Mbeke opened her mouth to speak but Collins got there first. "Jenkins is a brilliant programmer, but he's also a bit lost in his own world, and life on the *Intrepid* has hit him harder than most."

"By which she means that Jenkins' wife got killed on an away mission," Mbeke said.

"What happened?" Dahl asked.

"She was shot by a Cirquerian assassin," Collins said. "The assassin was aiming at the Dub U ambassador to Cirqueria. The captain pushed the ambassador down and Margaret was standing right behind him. Took the bullet in the neck. Dead before she hit the ground. Jenkins chose to at least partly disassociate from reality after that."

"So what does he think is happening?" Dahl asked.

"Why don't we save that for another

time," Collins said. "You know what's going on now and why. I'm sorry we didn't tell you about this earlier, Andy. But now you know. And now you know what to do when either me or Ben suddenly say that we're going to get coffee."

"Hide," Dahl said.

" 'Hide' isn't a word we like to use," Cassaway said. " 'Perform alternative tasks' is the preferred term."

"Just not in the storage room," Mbeke said. "That's *our* alternative tasking place."

"I'll just alternatively task behind my work desk, then, shall I," Dahl said.

"That's the spirit," Mbeke said.

At evening mess, Dahl caught up his four friends with what he learned in the lab, and then turned to Finn. "So, did you get the information I asked you for?" he said.

"I did indeed," Finn said.

"Good," Dahl said.

"I want to preface this by saying that normally I don't do this sort of work for free," Finn said, handing his phone over to Dahl. "Normally something like this would have been a week's pay. But this shit's been weirding me out since that away mission. I wanted to see it for myself."

"What are the two of you talking about?"

Duvall said.

"I had Finn pull some records for me," Dahl said. "Medical records, mostly."

"Whose?" Duvall asked.

"Your boyfriend's," Finn said.

Dahl looked up at that. "What?"

"Duvall's dating Kerensky," Finn said.

"Shut up, Finn, I am not," Duvall said, and glanced over to Dahl. "After he recovered, Kerensky tracked me down to thank me for saving his life," she said. "He said that when he first came to in the shuttle, he thought he'd died because an angel was hovering over him."

"Oh, God," Hester said. "Tell me a line like that doesn't actually work. I might have to kill myself otherwise."

"It doesn't," Duvall assured him. "Anyway, he asked if he could buy me a drink the next time we had shore leave. I told him I'd think about it."

"Boyfriend," Finn said.

"I'm going to stab you through the eye now," Duvall said to Finn, pointing her fork at him.

"Why did you want Lieutenant Kerensky's medical records?" Hanson asked.

"Kerensky was the victim of a plague a week ago," Dahl said. "He recovered quickly enough to lead an away mission, where he lost consciousness because of a machine attack. He recovered quickly enough from that to hit on Maia sometime today."

"To be fair, he still looked like hell," Duvall said.

"To be fair, he should probably be dead," Dahl said. "The Merovian Plague melts people's flesh right off their bones. Kerensky was about fifteen minutes away from death before he got cured, and he's leading an away mission a week later? It takes that long to get over a bad cold, much less a flesh-eating bacteria."

"So he's got an awesome immune system," Duvall said.

Dahl fixed her with a look and flipped Finn's phone to her. "In the past three years, Kerensky's been shot three times, caught a deadly disease four times, has been crushed under a rock pile, injured in a shuttle crash, suffered burns when his bridge control panel blew up in his face, experienced partial atmospheric decompression, suffered from induced mental instability, been bitten by two venomous animals and had the control of his body taken over by an alien parasite. That's before the recent plague and this away mission."

"He's also contracted three STDs," Duvall said, scrolling through the file.

"Enjoy your drink with him," Finn said.

"I think I'll ask for penicillin on the rocks," Duvall said. She handed the phone back to Dahl. "So you're saying there's no way he could be walking around right now."

"Forget the fact that he should be dead," Dahl said. "There's no way he could be alive and *sane* after all this. The man should be a poster boy for post-traumatic stress disorder."

"They have therapies to compensate for that," Duvall said.

"Yeah, but not for this many times," Dahl said. "This is seventeen major injuries or trauma in three years. That's one every two months. He should be in a constant fetal position by now. As it is, it's like he has just enough time to recover before he gets the shit kicked out of him again. He's unreal."

"Is there a point to this," Duvall said, "or are you just jealous of his physical abilities?"

"The point is there's something weird about this ship," Dahl said, scrolling through more data. "My commanding officer and lab mates fed me a bunch of nonsense about it today, with the away teams and Kerensky and everything else. But I'm not buying it."

"Why not?" Duvall asked.

"Because I don't think they were buying it either," Dahl said. "And because it doesn't

91

explain away something like this." He frowned and looked over at Finn. "You couldn't find anything on Jenkins?"

"You're talking about the yeti you and I encountered," Finn said.

"Yeah," Dahl said.

"There's nothing on him in the computer system," Finn said.

"We didn't imagine him," Dahl said.

"No, we didn't," Finn agreed. "He's just not in the system. But then if he's the programming god your lab mates suggest he is, and he's currently actively hacking into the computer system, I don't think it should be entirely surprising he's not in the system, do you?"

"I think we need to find him," Dahl said.

"Why?" Finn asked.

"Because I think he knows something that no one else wants to talk about," Dahl said.

"Your friends in your lab say he's crazy," Hester pointed out.

"I don't think they're actually his friends," said Hanson.

Everyone turned to him. "What do you mean?" said Hester.

Hanson shrugged. "They said the reason they didn't tell him about what was going on is that he wouldn't have believed it before he had experienced some of it himself. Maybe that's right. But it's also true that if he didn't know what was going on, he wouldn't be able to do what they do: avoid Commander Q'eeng and the other officers, and manage not to get on away team rosters. Think about it, guys: all five of us were on the same away team at one time, on a ship with thousands of crew. What do we all have in common?"

"We're the new guys," Duvall said.

Hanson nodded. "And none of us were told any of this by our crewmates until now, when it couldn't be avoided anymore."

"You think the reason they didn't tell us wasn't because we didn't know enough to believe them," Dahl said. "You think it was because that way, if someone had to die, it would be us, not them."

"It's just a theory," Hanson said.

Hester looked at Hanson admiringly. "I didn't think you were that cynical," Hester said.

Hanson shrugged again. "When you're the heir to the third largest fortune in the history of the universe, you learn to question people's motivations," he said.

"We need to find Jenkins," Dahl said again. "We need to know what he knows."

"How do you suggest we do that?" Duvall asked.

"I think we start with the cargo tunnels," Dahl said.

CHAPTER SIX

"Dahl, where are you going?" Duvall said. She and the others were standing in the middle of the Angeles V space station corridor, watching Dahl unexpectedly split off from the group. "Come on, we're on shore leave," she said. "Time to get smashed."

"And laid," Finn said.

"Smashed *and* laid," Duvall said. "Not necessarily in that order."

"Not that there's anything wrong with doing it in that order," Finn said.

"See, I bet that's why you don't get a lot of second dates," Duvall said.

"We're not talking about *me*," Finn reminded her. "We're talking about Andy. Who's ditching us."

"He is!" Duvall said. "Andy! Don't you want to get smashed and laid with us?"

"Oh, I do," Dahl assured her. "But I need to make a hyperwave first."

"You couldn't have done that on the *In-*

trepid?" Hanson asked.

"Not this wave, no," Dahl said.

Duvall rolled her eyes. "This is about your current obsession, isn't it," she said. "I swear, Andy, ever since you got a bug in your ass about Jenkins you're no fun anymore. Ten whole days of brooding. Lighten up, you moody bastard."

Dahl smiled at this. "I'll be quick, I promise. Where will you guys be?"

"I've got us a suite at the station Hyatt," Hanson said. "Meet us there. We'll be the ones quickly losing our sobriety."

Finn pointed to Hester. "And in his case, his virginity."

"Nice," Hester said, but then actually grinned.

"Be there in a few," Dahl promised.

"Better be!" Hanson said, and then he and the rest wandered down the corridor, laughing and joking. Dahl watched them go and then headed to the shopping area of the station, looking for a wave station.

He found one wedged between a coffee shop and a tattoo parlor. It was barely larger than a kiosk and had only three wave terminals in it, one of which was out of service. A drunken crewman of another ship was loudly arguing into one of the others. Dahl took the third.

"Welcome to SurfPoint Hyperwave," the monitor read, and then listed the per-minute cost of opening a wave. A five-minute wave would eat most of his pay for the week, but this was not entirely surprising to Dahl. It took a large amount of energy to open up a tunnel in space/time and connect in real time with another terminal light-years away. Energy cost money.

Dahl took out the anonymous credit chit he kept on hand for things he didn't want traced directly to his own credit account and placed it on the payment square. The monitor registered the chit and opened up a "send" panel. Dahl spoke a phone address back at Academy and waited for the connection. He was pretty sure that the person he was calling would be awake and moving about. The Dub U kept all of its ships and stations on Universal Time because otherwise the sheer number of day lengths and time zones would make it impossible for anyone to do anything, but the Academy was in Boston. Dahl couldn't remember how many time zones behind that was.

The person on the other end of the line picked up, audio only. "Whoever you are, you're interrupting my morning jog," she said.

Dahl grinned. "Morning, Casey," he said. "How's my favorite librarian?"

"Shit! Andy!" Casey said. A second later the video feed kicked in and Casey Zane popped up, smiling, the USS *Constitution* behind her.

"Jogging the Freedom Trail again, I see," Dahl said.

"The bricks make it easy to follow," Casey said. "Where are you?"

"About three hundred light-years away, and paying for every inch of it on this hyperwave," Dahl said.

"Got it," Casey said. "What do you need?"

"The Academy Archive would have blueprints of every ship in the fleet, right?" Dahl asked.

"Sure," Casey said. "All the ones that the Dub U wants to acknowledge exist, anyway."

"Any chance they'd be altered or tampered with?"

"From the outside? No," Casey said. "The archives don't connect to outside computer systems, partly to avoid hacking. All data has to go through a live librarian. That's job security for you."

"I suppose it is," Dahl said. "Is there any chance I can get you to send me a copy of the *Intrepid* blueprints?"

"I don't think they're classified, so it shouldn't be a problem," Casey said. "Although I might have to redact some information about the computer and weapons systems."

"That's fine," Dahl said. "I'm not interested in those anyway."

"That said, you're actually on the *Intrepid*," Casey said. "You should be able to get the blueprints out of the ship's database."

"I can," Dahl said. "There have been some changes to a few systems on board and I think it'll be useful to have the original blueprints for compare and contrast."

"Okay," Casey said. "I'll do it when I get back to the archives. A couple of hours at least."

"That's fine," Dahl said. "Also, do me a favor and send it to this address, not my Dub U address." He recited an alternate address, which he had created anonymously on a public provider while he was at the Academy.

"You know I have to record the information request," Casey said. "That includes the address to which I'm sending the information."

"I'm not trying to hide from the Dub U," Dahl said. "No spy stuff, I swear."

"Says the man using an anonymous public hyperwave terminal to call one of his best friends, rather than routing it through his own phone," Casey said.

"I'm not asking you to commit treason," Dahl said. "Cross my heart."

"All right," Casey said. "We're pals and all, but espionage isn't in my job description."

"I owe you one," Dahl said.

"You owe me dinner," Casey said. "The next time you're in town. The life of an archive librarian isn't that horribly exciting, you know. I need to live vicariously."

"Trust me, at this point I'm seriously considering taking up the life of a librarian myself," Dahl said.

"Now you're just pandering," Casey said. "I'll wave you the stuff when I get in the office. Now get off the line before you don't have any money left."

Dahl grinned again. "Later, Casey," he said.

"Later, Andy," she said, and disconnected.

There was a guest in the suite when Dahl got there.

"Andy, you know Lieutenant Kerensky," Duvall said, in a curiously neutral tone of voice. She and Hester were on either side of

Kerensky, who had an arm around each of them. They seemed to be propping him up.

"Sir," Dahl said.

"Andy!" Kerensky said, slurringly. He disengaged from Duvall and Hester, took two stumbling steps and clapped Dahl on the shoulder with the hand that was not holding his drink. "We are on shore leave! We leave rank behind us. To you, right now, I am just Anatoly. Go on, say it."

"Anatoly," Dahl said.

"See, that wasn't so hard, was it?" Kerensky said. He drained his drink. "I appear to be out of a drink," he said, and wandered off. Dahl raised an eyebrow at Duvall and Hester.

"He spotted us just before we entered the hotel and attached himself like a leech," Duvall said.

"A drunken leech," Hester said. "He was blasted before we got here."

"A drunken horny leech," Duvall said. "The reason he has his arm around my shoulder is so he can grope my tit. Lieutenant or not, I'm about to kick his ass."

"Right now the plan is to get him drunk enough to pass out before he attempts to molest Duvall," Hester said. "Then we dump him down a laundry chute."

"Shit, here he comes again," Duvall said.

Kerensky was indeed stumbling back toward the trio. His progress was more lateral than forward. He stopped to get his bearings.

"Why don't you leave him to me," Dahl said.

"Seriously?" Duvall said.

"Sure, I'll baby-sit him until he passes out," Dahl said.

"Man, I owe you a blowjob," Duvall said.

"What?" Dahl said.

"What?" Hester said.

"Sorry," Duvall said. "In ground forces, when someone does you a favor you tell them you owe them a sex act. If it's a little thing, it's a handjob. Medium, blowjob. Big favor, you owe them a fuck. Force of habit. It's just an expression."

"Got it," Dahl said.

"No actual blowjob forthcoming," Duvall said. "To be clear."

"It's the thought that counts," Dahl said, and turned to Hester. "What about you? You want to owe me a blowjob, too?"

"I'm thinking about it," Hester said.

"What's this I hear about *blowjobs*?" Kerensky said, finally wobbling up.

"Okay, yes, one owed," Hester said.

"Excellent," Dahl said. "See the two of you later, then." Hester and Duvall backed away precipitately.

"Where are they going?" Kerensky asked, blinking slowly.

"They're planning a birthday party," Dahl said. "Why don't you have a seat, sir." He motioned to one of the couches in the suite.

"Anatoly," Kerensky said. "God, I hate it when people use rank on shore leave." He fell heavily onto the couch, miraculously not spilling his drink. "We're all brothers in the service, you know? Well, except those of us who are sisters." He peered around, looking for Duvall. "I like your friend."

"I know," Dahl said, also sitting.

"She saved my life, you know," Kerensky said. "She's an angel. You think she likes me?"

"No," Dahl said.

"Why not?" Kerensky blithered, hurt. "Does she like women or something?"

"She's married to her job," Dahl said.

"Oh, well, *married,*" Kerensky said, apparently not hearing the rest of what Dahl said. He drank some more.

"You mind if I ask you a question?" Dahl said.

With the hand not holding his drink, Kerensky made little waving motions as if to say, *Go ahead.*

"How do you heal so quickly?" Dahl asked.

103

"What do you mean?" Kerensky asked.

"Remember when you got the Merovian Plague?"

"Of course," Kerensky said. "I almost *died.*"

"I know," Dahl said. "But then a week later you were leading the away team I was on."

"Well, I got *better,* you see," Kerensky said. "They found a cure."

"Yes," Dahl said. "I was the one who brought the cure to Commander Q'eeng."

"That was *you*?" Kerensky said, and then lunged at Dahl, enveloping him in a bear hug. Kerensky's drink slopped up the side of the glass and deposited itself down the back of Dahl's neck. "You saved my life too! This room is filled with people who saved my life. I love you all." Kerensky started weeping.

"You're welcome," Dahl said, prying the sobbing lieutenant off his body as delicately as he could. He was aware of everyone else in the room studiously ignoring what was happening on the couch. "My point was, even with a cure, you healed quickly. And then you were seriously injured on the away mission I was on. And yet a couple of days later you were fine."

"Oh, well, you know, modern medicine is

really good," Kerensky said. "Plus, I've always been a fast healer. It's a family thing. We've got stories about one of my ancestors, in the Great Patriotic War? He was in Stalingrad. Took, like, twenty shots from Nazi bullets and still kept coming at them. He was *unreal,* man. So I inherited that gene, maybe." He looked down at his drink. "I know I had more drink than this," he said.

"It's a good thing you heal so fast, considering how often you get hurt," Dahl ventured.

"I *know!*" Kerensky said, suddenly and forcefully. "*Thank* you! No one else notices! I mean, what the hell is up with that? I'm not stupid, or clumsy, or anything. But every time I go on an away mission I get all fucked up. Do you know how many times I've been, like, *shot?*"

"Three times in the last three years," Dahl said.

"Yes!" Kerensky said. "Plus all the *other* shit that happens to me. You know what it is. Fucking captain and Q'eeng have a voodoo doll of me, or something." He sat there, brooding, and then showed every sign of being about to drift into sleep.

"A voodoo doll," Dahl said, startling Kerensky back into consciousness. "You think so."

"Well, no, not literally," Kerensky said. "Because that's just *stupid,* isn't it. But it *feels* like it. It feels like whenever the captain and Q'eeng have an away mission they know is going to be all fucked up they say, 'Hey, Kerensky, this is a *perfect* away mission for you,' and then I go off and, like, get my *spleen* punctured. And half the time it's some stupid thing I have no idea about, right? I'm an astrogator, man. I am a fucking brilliant astrogator. I wanna just . . . *astrogate.* Right?"

"Why don't you point that out to the captain and Q'eeng?" Dahl asked.

Kerensky sneered, and his lip quivered at the effort. "Because what the hell am I going to say?" he said, and started making Humpty-Dumpty movements. " 'Oh, I can't go on this mission, Captain, Commander Q'eeng. Let someone else get stabbed through the eyeball for a change.' " He stopped with the movements and was quiet for a second. "Besides, I don't know. It seems to make sense at the time, you know?"

"No, I don't know," Dahl said.

"When the captain tells me I'm going to be on an away mission, it's like some other part of my brain takes over," Kerensky said. He sounded like he was trying to puzzle through something. "I get all confident and it seems like there's a perfectly good reason for a goddamn astrogator to take medical samples, or fight killer machines or whatever. Then I get back on the *Intrepid* and I think to myself, 'What the *fuck* was I just doing?' Because it doesn't make sense, does it?"

"I don't know," Dahl said again.

Kerensky looked lost in thought for a second, and then waved it all away. "Anyway, fuck it, right?" he said, brightening up. "I lived another day, I'm on shore leave, and I'm with people who saved my life." He lunged at Dahl again, even more sloppily. "I love you, man. I do. Let's get another drink and then go find some hookers. I want a blowjob. You want a blowjob?"

"I've already got two on order," Dahl said. "I'm good."

"Oh, okay," Kerensky said. "That's good." And then he began to snore, his head nestled on Dahl's shoulder.

Dahl looked up and saw his four friends staring down at him.

"You *all* owe me blowjobs," he said.

"How about a drink instead," Finn said.

"Deal," Dahl said. He glanced down at

Kerensky. "What do we do about Sleeping Beauty here?"

"There's a laundry chute outside," Hester said, hopefully.

CHAPTER SEVEN

"Here are the blueprints to the *Intrepid* that I downloaded from the ship's database," Dahl said to Finn and Duvall at midday mess, showing them a printout. He laid down a second printout. "And here are the blueprints I received from the Academy Archive. Notice anything?"

"Nope," said Finn, after a minute.

"Nope," said Duvall, shortly thereafter.

Dahl sighed and pointed. "It's the cargo tunnels," he said. "We use them to transport cargo throughout the ship, but there's no reason a human couldn't go into them. The ship maintenance crew goes into them all the time to physically access ship systems. They're designed that way so ship maintenance doesn't get in the way of the rest of the crew."

"You think Jenkins is in there," Duvall said.

"Where else is he going to be?" Dahl said.

"He only comes out when it suits him; no one ever sees him otherwise. Think how populated this ship is. The only way you can disappear is if you stay in a place other crew don't usually go."

"The flaw in this reasoning is that the cargo tunnels are *tunnels,*" Finn said. "And even if people aren't there, they're still crawling with those autonomous delivery carts. If he stayed in any one place for long he'd be blocking their traffic or he'd get run over."

Dahl waggled a finger. "See, that's what you two aren't seeing. Look . . ." He pointed to a square inside the maze of cargo tunnels. "When the carts aren't delivering something, they have to go somewhere. They're not hanging out in the corridors. Where they go is to one of these distribution hubs. The hubs are more than large enough for a person to hole up in."

"As long as there's not a bunch of carts cluttering it up," Duvall said.

"Exactly," Dahl said. "And look. In the blueprints of the *Intrepid* we have on ship, there are six cart distribution areas. But in the ones from the archives, there are seven." He tapped the seventh distribution hub. "This distribution hub is away from major systems in the ship, which means that maintenance crews have no reason to get near it. It's as far away as you can be from anyone and still be on the ship. That's where Jenkins is. The ghost in the machine. That's where we find him."

"I don't see why you don't ask your boss to make an introduction," Duvall said. "You said that Jenkins was technically under her anyway."

"I tried that and got nowhere with it," Dahl said. "Collins finally told me that Jenkins only appears when he wants to appear and otherwise they leave him alone. He's helping them keep track of the captain, Q'eeng, and the others. They don't want to piss him off and leave themselves vulnerable."

"Speaking of which," Finn said, and motioned with his head.

Dahl turned around to see Science Officer Q'eeng coming up to him. He started to get up.

Q'eeng waved him back down. "At ease, Ensign." He noticed the blueprints. "Studying the ship?"

"Just looking for ways to do my job more efficiently," Dahl said.

"I admire that initiative," Q'eeng said. "Ensign, we're about to arrive at the Eskridge system to answer a distress call from a colony there. The reports from the colony are sketchy but I suspect a biological agent may be involved, so I'm assembling a team from your department to accompany me. You're on it. Meet me in the shuttle bay in half an hour."

"Yes, sir," Dahl said. Q'eeng nodded and headed off. He turned back to Duvall and Finn. They were looking at him oddly. "What?" he said.

"An away team with Q'eeng," Duvall said.

"A sudden, oddly coincidental away team with Q'eeng," Finn said.

"Let's try not to be too paranoid," Dahl said.

"That's funny, considering," Finn said.

Dahl pushed the blueprints at Finn. "While I'm away, Finn, find a way for us to sneak up on Jenkins without him being aware of it. I want to talk to him, but aside from that warning I don't think he wants to talk to us. I don't want to give him that choice."

"This is all *your* fault, you know," Cassaway hissed at Dahl. He, Cassaway and Mbeke constituted the away team with Q'eeng and a security team member named Taylor. Q'eeng was piloting the shuttle to the colony; Taylor took the co-pilot seat. The xenobiologists were in the back. The two other xenobiologists had been coldly silent to him during the mission briefing and for most of the shuttle ride down to the planet. These were the first words either of them had spoken to him the entire trip.

"How is this my fault?" Dahl said. "I didn't tell the captain to take the ship here."

"It's your fault for asking about Jenkins!" Cassaway said. "You're pissing him off with all your questions about him."

"I can't ask questions about him now?" Dahl said.

"Not questions that make him retaliate against us," Mbeke said.

"Shut up, Fiona," Cassaway said. "It's your fault too."

"My fault too?" said Mbeke, incredulous. "I'm not the one asking all these stupid questions!"

Cassaway jabbed a finger in Dahl's direction. "You're the one who brought up Jenkins in front of him! Twice!"

"It slipped," Mbeke said. "I was just making conversation the first time. The second time I didn't think it would matter. He already knew."

"Look where we are, Fiona." Cassaway waved to indicate the shuttle. "Tell me it doesn't matter. You never told Sid Black about Jenkins."

"Sid Black was an asshole," Mbeke said.

"And this one isn't?" Cassaway said, pointing at Dahl again.

"I'm right here, you know," Dahl said.

"Fuck you," Cassaway said, to Dahl. He looked at Mbeke again. "And fuck you too, Fiona. You should have known better."

"I was just making conversation," Mbeke said again, brokenly, her eyes on her hands, which were in her lap.

Dahl looked at the two of them for a moment. "You didn't know Q'eeng was coming to see you, did you," he said, finally. "No time for you or Collins and Trin to get coffee or for you to hide out in the storage room. Q'eeng just showed up at the lab and you were all caught flat-footed. And when he told Collins he needed an away team —"

"She volunteered us," Mbeke said.

"And you," Cassaway said, spitting out the words. "Q'eeng wanted her or Ben to come too, but she sold you out. Reminded him you had solved the Merovian Plague. Said you were one of the best xenobiologists she's ever had on staff. It's a lie, of course. You're not. But it worked because you're here and not her or Ben."

"I see," Dahl said. "I don't suppose that's unexpected, because I'm the new guy. The low man on the totem pole. The guy that's meant to be replaced every couple of months anyway, right? But you two," he said, nodding to the both of them. "You thought that you were protected. You survived long enough that you thought Collins wouldn't push you at Q'eeng if she had to. You thought she might even pick one of you over Ben Trin, didn't you."

Cassaway looked away from Dahl; Mbeke started crying quietly.

"It came as a surprise to find out just where you sat on the totem pole, didn't it?" Dahl said.

"Shut up, Dahl," Cassaway said, not looking at him.

They were quiet all the rest of the way down to the planet.

They found no colonists, but they found parts of them. And a lot of blood.

"Pulse guns on full power," Q'eeng said. "Cassaway, Mbeke, Dahl, I want you to follow the blood trails into the woods. We still might find someone alive, or find a dead one of whatever it is that did this. I'm going to check out the administrative office and see if there's anything there that can explain this. Taylor, you're with me." Q'eeng strode off toward a large, blocky trailer with Taylor following.

"Come on," Cassaway said, and led Dahl and Mbeke toward the woods.

A couple hundred meters in, the three of them found a ruined corpse.

"Give me the sampler," Dahl said to Mbeke, who was carrying that piece of equipment. She unslung the device and gave it to Dahl, who knelt and pushed the sampling tool into what remained of the corpse's abdomen.

"It'll be a couple of minutes for this thing to give me a result," Dahl said, not looking up from the corpse. "The sampler's got to go through the DNA library of the entire colony. Make sure that whatever got this guy doesn't get me while we're waiting."

"I'm on it," he heard Cassaway say. Dahl returned to his work.

"It's someone named Fouad Ali," Dahl said, a couple of minutes later. "Looks like he was the colony doctor." Dahl looked up and past Ali's corpse, into the woods. "The blood trail continues off that direction. Do we want to keep looking?"

"What are you doing?" Dahl heard Mbeke ask.

"What?" Dahl said, and turned around to see Cassaway pointing his pulse gun at him, and Mbeke staring at Cassaway, confused.

116

Cassaway grimaced. "Damn it, Fiona, can't you ever just shut up?"

"I'm with Fiona," Dahl said. "What are you doing?" He tried to stand up.

"Don't move," Cassaway said. "Don't move or I'm going to shoot you."

"It looks like you're going to shoot me anyway," Dahl said. "But I don't know why."

"Because one of us has to die," Cassaway said. "That's how it works on the away teams. If Q'eeng's leading the away team, someone is going to die. Someone always dies. But if someone dies, then whoever's left is safe. That's how it works."

"The last person who explained this idea to me got chopped up into little pieces even after someone else died," Dahl said. "I don't think it works the way you think it does."

"Shut up," Cassaway said. "If you die, Fiona and I don't have to. You'll be the sacrifice. Once the sacrifice is made, the rest are safe. We'll be safe."

"That's not the way it works," Dahl said. "When was the last time you were on an away team, Jake? I was on one a couple of weeks ago. It's not how it works. You're missing details. Killing me isn't going to mean you're safe. Fiona . . ." Dahl glanced over at Mbeke to try to reason with her. She was in the process of raising her own

117

pulse gun.

"Come on, guys," Dahl said. "Two pulse gun blasts are going to be hard to miss."

"Put your gun on low power," Cassaway said to Mbeke. "Aim for the center mass. When he's down, we cut him up. That'll cover us. We can explain the blood by saying we were trying to save —" And that's as far as he got before the things dropped out of the tree above and onto him and Mbeke.

The two of them fell, screaming as they tried to fight off the things now tearing into their flesh. Dahl gaped for a second then ran in a burst toward the colony, sensing rather than seeing that his sudden movement had only barely saved him from being jumped on himself.

Dahl weaved through the trees, screaming for Q'eeng and Taylor. Some part of his brain wanted to know if he was running in the right direction; another part wanted to know why he wasn't using his phone to contact Q'eeng. A third part reminded him that he had a pulse gun of his own, which might be effective against whatever was currently eating Cassaway and Mbeke.

A fourth part of his brain was saying, *This is the part where you run and scream a lot.*

He was listening to the fourth part.

His eye caught a break in the woods, and

in that break he could see the distant trailers of the colony and the forms of Q'eeng and Taylor. Dahl screamed at the top of his lungs and ran in a straight line toward them, waving his hands to get their attention. He saw their tiny forms jiggle, as if they heard him.

Then something tripped him and he went down.

The thing was on him instantly, biting and tearing at him. Dahl screamed and pushed and in his panic saw something that looked like it could be an eye and jammed his thumb into it. The thing roared and reared back and Dahl pushed himself back from the thing, and it was on him again and Dahl could feel teeth on his shoulder and a burning sensation that let him know that whatever had just bit him was also venomous. Dahl looked for the eye again, jabbed it a second time and got the thing to reel back again, but this time Dahl was too dizzy and sick to move.

One sacrifice and whoever's left is safe, my ass, he thought, and the last thing he saw was the thing's very impressive set of teeth coming down around his head.

Dahl woke up to see his friends surrounding him.

"Ack," he said.

"Finn, give him some water," Duvall said. Finn took a small container with a straw from the holder at the side of the medical bay cot and put it to Dahl's lips. He sipped gingerly.

"I'm not dead," he eventually whispered.

"No," Duvall said. "Not that you didn't make an effort. What was left of you should have been dead when they brought you back to the ship. Doc Hartnell says it's only luck that Q'eeng and Taylor got to you when they did, otherwise that thing would have eaten you alive."

The last phrase jogged something in Dahl's memory. "Cassaway," he said. "Mbeke."

"They're dead," Hanson said. "There wasn't much left of them to get back, either."

"You're the only one from the away team still alive," Hester said. "Besides Q'eeng."

"Taylor?" Dahl croaked.

"He got bit," Duvall said, correctly interpreting the question. "The things have a venom. It doesn't kill people, it turns them psychotic. He went crazy and started shooting up the ship. He killed three of the crew before they brought him down."

"That's what they think happened at the

colony," Finn said. "The doctor's record shows that a hunting party got bit by these things, went back to the colony and started shooting up the place. Then the creatures came in, took the dead and killed off the survivors."

"Q'eeng was bit too, but Captain Abernathy had him isolated until they could make an antivenom," Hanson said.

"From your blood," Hester said. "You were unconscious so you couldn't go crazy. That gave your body time to metabolize and neutralize the venom."

"He was lucky you survived," Duvall said.

"No," Dahl said, and lifted his arm to point at himself. "Lucky he needed me."

CHAPTER EIGHT

"What are these?" Dahl asked from his bed, taking one of the buttonlike objects that Finn held in his hand.

"Our way to sneak up on Jenkins," Finn said, passing out the rest. "They're delivery cart ID transponders. I pried them off disabled carts in the refuse hold. The cargo tunnel doors register each time they're opened and closed and look for identification. If you're a crew member, your phone IDs you. If you're a cart, one of these do."

"Why not just leave our phones behind and have no ID?" Hanson asked, holding his button up to the light.

"Because then there's an unexplained door opening," Finn said. "If this Jenkins is as paranoid and careful as Andy here thinks he is, that's not going to escape his notice."

"So we leave our phones behind, take one of these, and go on after him," Dahl said.

"That's the plan I came up with," Finn

said. "Unless you have a better one."

"I just spent two weeks doing nothing but healing," Dahl said. "This works for me."

"So when do we go find this guy?" Duvall asked.

"If he's tracking the captain and the senior officers, then he's going to be active when they are," Dahl said. "That means first shift. If we go in right after the start of third shift, we have a chance to catch him while he's asleep."

"So he's going to wake up with five people hovering over him and staring," Hester said. "*That's* not going to make him any more paranoid than he already is."

"He might not be asleep, and if he catches sight of us, he might try to run," Dahl said. "If just one of us goes, he might get past us. He's less likely to get past five of us, each coming in from a different corridor."

"Everybody be ready to take down a yeti," Finn said. "This guy is big and hairy."

"Besides that, whatever the hell is happening on this ship, I think we all want to know about it sooner than later," Dahl said.

"So, right after third shift," Duvall said. "Tonight?"

"Not tonight," Dahl said. "Give me a day or two to get used to walking again." He stretched and winced.

"When do you get off medical leave?" Hanson asked, watching his movements.

"Last day today," Dahl said. "They're going to do a final checkup after you all leave. I'm all healed, just stiff from lying around on my ass," he said. "A couple of days, I'll be ready to go. The only things I have to do between now and then is get discharged from here and go by the Xenobiology Lab to find out why neither of my superior officers has bothered to come see me since I've been in sick bay."

"It might have something to do with two of your colleagues getting eaten," Hester said. "That's just a guess."

"I don't doubt that," Dahl said. "But I need to find out what else it is, too."

"Don't bother," Lieutenant Collins said, as Dahl walked through the door of the Xenobiology Lab. "You don't work in this lab anymore. I've had you transferred."

Dahl paused and looked around. Collins was in front of him, antagonistic. Trin, at a workstation behind her, was resolutely focused on whatever was on his work tablet. From other workstations, two new faces gawked openly at him.

"The new Cassaway and Mbeke?" Dahl asked, turning his attention back to Collins.

"Jake and Fiona aren't *replaceable,*" Collins said.

"No, just expendable," Dahl said. "At least when it came down to them being on an away team." He motioned with his head to the new crew members. "Told them yet about Q'eeng? Or the captain? Have you explained your sudden absences when one of them shows up? Hauled out the Box yet, Lieutenant?"

Collins was visibly making an effort to control herself. "None of that is your concern, Ensign," she said, finally. "You're not part of this lab anymore. Ensign Dee, the junior science officer on the bridge, fell to her death a week ago, on an away mission. I recommended you to Q'eeng as her replacement. He agreed. You start tomorrow. Technically, it's a promotion. Congratulations."

"Someone once told me to stay off the bridge," Dahl said, and then nodded over at Trin. "Two people did, actually. But one of them was more forceful about it."

"Nonsense," Collins said. "The bridge is the perfect place for someone like you. You'll be in contact with senior officers on a daily basis. They'll get to know you very well. And there will be lots of opportunities for adventure. You'll be going on away missions weekly. Sometimes even more often than that." She smiled thinly.

"Well," Dahl said. "You putting me in for this promotion certainly shows what you think of me, Lieutenant."

"Think nothing of it," Collins said. "It's no more than you deserve. And now, I think you better run along, Ensign. You'll need your rest for your first day on the bridge."

Dahl straightened and saluted crisply. Collins turned away without acknowledgment.

Dahl turned and headed for the door but then changed his mind and stalked up to the new crew. "How long have you been here?" he asked the closest one of them.

She looked at the other crewman and then back at Dahl. "Four days," she said. "We transferred in from the *Honsu*."

"No away teams yet," Dahl said.

"No, sir," she said.

Dahl nodded. "A piece of advice for you." He pointed back at Collins and Trin. "When they suddenly go for coffee, that's a very good time for you to do an inventory on the storage room. Both of you. I don't think those two were going to bother to tell you that. I don't think they're going to bother to tell that to anyone who works in this lab ever again. So I'm telling you. Watch them.

126

Don't let them sell you out."

Dahl turned and walked out, leaving two very confused crewmen and two very pissed-off officers.

"Slow down, Andy," Duvall said, moving faster herself to keep up. "You just got out of sick bay."

Dahl snorted and stomped down the corridor. Duvall came up even to him.

"You think she got you assigned to the bridge to get back at you for your lab mates," she said.

"No," Dahl said. "She got me assigned to the bridge because when she had to assign Jake and Fiona, it rubbed her face in it."

"In it?" Duvall said. "In what?"

Dahl glanced at Duvall. "That she's *afraid,*" he said. "Everyone on this entire ship is afraid, Maia. They hide and they disappear and they find ways to *not think* about how much time they spend hiding. And then comes the moment when they can't hide and they have to face themselves. And they hate that. *That's* why Collins assigned me to the bridge. Because otherwise every time she looked at me she'd be reminded that she's a coward." He sped up again.

"Where are you going?" Duvall asked.

"Leave me alone, Maia," Dahl said. Duvall

127

stopped in her tracks. Dahl left her behind.

In fact Dahl had no idea where he was going; he was burning off frustration and anger, and being on the move was the closest thing the jam-packed *Intrepid* offered to being alone.

This was why, when the crew presence finally thinned and Dahl felt the fatigue his disused muscles had been trying to alert him about, he was surprised to find himself outside the cargo tunnel door closest to Jenkins' secret hideaway.

He stood outside the door for a long minute, remembering the plan to sneak up on Jenkins as a team and find out what he knew.

"Fuck it," he said. He smacked the access panel to open the corridor door.

A yeti was standing directly on the other side. It grabbed him and pulled him into the corridor. Dahl yelled in surprise but was too weak to resist. He stumbled into the corridor. The yeti, whom Dahl now recognized as Jenkins, closed the door behind them.

"Stop yelling," Jenkins said, and stuck a finger in his ear, twisting it. "Jesus, that's annoying."

Dahl looked at the closed door and then back at Jenkins. "How did you *do* that?" he asked. "How did you know?"

"Because I am a student of the human condition," Jenkins said. "And as humans go, you're pretty predictable. And because I have you under constant surveillance through your phone, you dumbass."

"So you know —"

"About your overly complicated plan to sneak up on me, yes," Jenkins said. "Your friend Finn gets partial credit for the cart ID thing. What he doesn't know is that when decommissioned cart IDs get scanned, I get an immediate alert. He's not the first person to think of that to access these corridors. And you're not the first person to try to find me."

"I'm not," Dahl said.

Jenkins snapped his fingers, as if to focus Dahl's attention. "What did I just say? Redundant conversation isn't going to do us any good."

"Sorry," Dahl said. "Let me try again. Others have tried to find you and failed."

"That's right," Jenkins said. "I don't want to be found, and those who use my services don't want me to be found either. Between us we managed to avoid anyone I don't want to see."

"So you want to see me," Dahl said, carefully.

"It's more accurate to say *you* want to see *me,* and I'm willing to let myself be seen by you," Jenkins said.

"Why me?" Dahl asked.

"You just got assigned to the bridge," Jenkins said.

"I did," Dahl said. "And I remember you telling me very specifically to stay off the bridge."

"And that's why you came looking for me," Jenkins said. "Even though it would ruin the plan you made with your friends."

"Yes," Dahl said.

"Why?" Jenkins asked.

"I don't know," Dahl said. "I wasn't thinking clearly."

"Wrong," Jenkins said. "You *were* thinking clearly, but you weren't thinking consciously. Now think about it consciously, and tell me why. But hurry. I'm feeling exposed here."

"Because you know *why,*" Dahl said. "Everyone else in the *Intrepid* knows something's fucked up about this ship. They've got their ways to avoid getting sucked into it. But they don't know *why.* You do."

"Maybe I do," Jenkins said. "But why would it matter?"

"Because if you don't know why something is the way it is, then you don't know anything about it at all," Dahl said. "All the tricks and superstitions aren't going to do a damn bit of good if you don't know the reason for them. The conditions could change and then you're screwed."

"That's all very blandly logical," Jenkins said. "It doesn't explain why you decided to track me down now."

"Because someone's actively trying to *kill* me now," Dahl said. "Collins got me assigned to the bridge because she's decided she wants me dead."

"Yes, death by away team. Very effective on this ship," Jenkins said.

"I'm on the bridge tomorrow," Dahl said. "After that, it's not a matter of *if* I get killed, it's when. I'm out of time. I need to know *now.*"

"So you can avoid dying," Jenkins said.

"It would be nice," Dahl said.

"Collins wants to avoid death and you just called her a coward for it," Jenkins said.

"That's not why she's a coward," Dahl said.

"No, I suppose not," Jenkins said.

"If I can understand why, maybe I can keep myself from getting killed, and maybe I can keep others from being killed too," Dahl said. "I have people I care about here. I'd like to see them live."

"Well, then," Jenkins said. "Let me ask you one more question, Dahl. What if I tell you what I think, and it sounds insane to you?"

"Is that what happened?" Dahl asked. "Collins and Trin. You worked for them. You told them you had a theory. They heard it and they didn't believe it."

Jenkins chuckled at that. "I said insane, not unbelievable," he said. "And I think Collins, for one, believes it just fine."

"How do you know?" Dahl asked.

"Because it's what's made her a coward," Jenkins said, then looked at Dahl appraisingly. "But maybe not you. No, maybe not at all. And maybe not your friends. So gather them up, Ensign Dahl. Meet me in my hidey-hole tonight. Same time you were going to invade. I'll see you then." He turned to go.

"May I ask you a question?" Dahl asked.

"You mean, besides that one?" Jenkins asked.

"Two, actually," Dahl said. "Cassaway said they got on that away mission because you didn't tell them Q'eeng was coming to see them. He said it was retaliation for me trying to find out about you. Was it?"

"No," Jenkins said. "I didn't tell them Q'eeng was on the way because at the time

I was taking a dump. I can't watch everything all the time. What's your second question?"

"You told me to stay off the bridge," Dahl said. "Me and Finn. Why did you do that?"

"Well, I told your friend Finn because he just happened to be there, and I didn't think it would hurt, even if he's a bit of an asshole," Jenkins said. "But as for you, well. Let's just say I have a special interest in the Xenobiology Lab. Call it a sentimental attachment. And let's also just say I guessed that your response to what happens here on the *Intrepid* would go beyond the usual fear response. So I figured offering you a warning and piece of advice in person couldn't hurt."

Jenkins moved his hand as if to say, *See.* "And look where we are now. At the very least you're still alive. So far." He reached over to the access panel and slapped open the door to return Dahl to the *Intrepid.* Then he walked off.

CHAPTER NINE

"Come *on,*" Jenkins said, and pounded on the display table. Above the table, a holographic image flickered and then died. Jenkins pounded the table again. Dahl looked over to Duvall, who with Hanson, Finn and Hester was jammed into Jenkins' tiny living space. She rolled her eyes.

"Sorry," Jenkins muttered, ostensibly to the five crewmen jammed into his living space, but mostly to himself. "I get equipment when everyone else throws it out. The carts bring it to me. Then I have to repair it. It's a little buggy sometimes."

"It's all right," Dahl said. His eyes took a visual tour of his surroundings. Along with Jenkins and the five of them, the delivery cart storage area was jammed with Jenkins' possessions: the large holographic table, situated between him and the five crew members, a thin cot, a small wardrobe with boxes of hygienic wash wipes piled on it, a pallet of Universal Union away team rations and a portable toilet. Dahl wondered how the toilet was emptied and serviced. He wasn't sure that he really wanted to know.

"Is this going to start anytime soon?" asked Hester. "I thought we'd be done by now, and I kind of have to pee."

Jenkins motioned to the toilet. "Be my guest," he said.

"I'd rather *not*," Hester said.

"You can just tell us what you want us to know," Dahl suggested. "We don't have to have a slide show presentation."

"Oh, but you *do*," Jenkins said. "If I just *tell* you, it'll sound crazy. Graphs and images make it . . . well, *less* crazy, anyway."

"Swell," Finn said, and looked over at Dahl, as if to say *Thanks for getting us into this.* Dahl shrugged.

Another table pound by Jenkins, and the holographic image stabilized. "Ha!" Jenkins said. "Okay, I'm ready."

"Thank God," Hester said.

Jenkins fiddled his hands over the table, accessing a display of flat images parallel to the top of the display table. He found one he wanted and flipped it up into the view of the rest of them.

"This is the *Intrepid*," Jenkins said, motioning to the rotating graphic that now

135

hovered atop the holographic table. "The flagship of the Universal Union Space Fleet, and one of the fleet's largest ships. But for all that, one of just thousands of ships in the fleet. For the first nine years of its existence, aside from being appointed the flagship, there was nothing particularly special about it, from a statistical point of view."

The *Intrepid* shrank and was replaced by a graph showing two closely conforming lines plotted across time, one representing the ship, the other representing the fleet as a whole.

"It had a general mission of exploration and from time to time engaged in military actions, and in both scenarios suffered crew losses consistent with Dub U average, if slightly lower, because the Dub U sees the flagship as a symbol, and generally gave it less strenuous missions. But then, five years ago, this."

The graph scrolled to include the last five years. The *Intrepid*'s line spiked violently and then plateaued at a substantially higher level than the rest of the fleet.

"Whoa," Hanson said.

" 'Whoa' is right," Jenkins said.

"What happened?" Dahl asked.

"Captain Abernathy is what happened," Duvall said. "He took command of the *In-*

trepid five years ago."

"Close but wrong," Jenkins said, and waved his hands over the table, rooting through visual elements to find the one he wanted. "Abernathy did take command of the *Intrepid* five years ago. Before that he was captain of the *Griffin* for four years, where he developed a reputation of being an unconventional and risk-taking but effective leader."

" 'Risk-taking' could be a euphemism for 'getting crew killed,' " Hester said.

"Could be but isn't," Jenkins said, and threw an image of a battle cruiser into the view. "Here's the *Griffin,*" he said. A graph scrolled out behind it, like the one that scrolled out behind the *Intrepid* earlier. "And as you can see, despite Abernathy's 'risk-taking' reputation, the crew fatality rate is on average no worse than any other ship in the line. That's impressive considering the *Griffin* is a battle cruiser — a Dub U warship. It's not until Abernathy gets to the *Intrepid* that fatalities for crew under his command spike so massively."

"Maybe he's gone nuts," Finn said.

"His psychological reviews for the last five years are clean," Jenkins said.

"How do you know —" Finn stopped and held up his hand. "You know, never mind.

Dumb question."

"He's not insane and he's not purposefully putting his crew at risk, is what you're saying," Dahl said. "But I remember Lieutenant Collins saying to me that when people complained about the high crew death rate on the *Intrepid,* they were told that as the flagship it engaged in riskier missions." He pointed at the screen. "You're telling us that it's not true."

"It's true that away missions result in higher deaths now," Jenkins said. "But it's not because the missions themselves are inherently more risky." He fiddled and threw several ship images up on the screen. "These are some of our combat and infiltration ships," he said. "They routinely take on high-risk missions. Here are their average crew fatalities over time." Graphs spewed out behind their images. "You can see their fatalities are higher than the Dub U baseline. But" — Jenkins dragged over the image of the *Intrepid* — "their crew fatalities are still *substantially* lower than the *Intrepid*'s, whose missions are generally classified as having far less risk."

"So why do people keep dying?" Duvall asked.

"The missions themselves are generally not risky," Jenkins said. "It's just that something always goes *wrong* on them."

"So it's a competence issue," Dahl said.

Jenkins tossed up a scrolling image featuring the *Intrepid*'s officers and section heads and their various citations and awards. "This is the flagship of the Dub U," he said. "You don't get to be on it if you're an incompetent."

"Then it's bad luck," Finn said. "The *Intrepid* has the worst karma in the known universe."

"That second part might be true," Jenkins said. "But I don't think luck has anything to do with it."

Dahl blinked and remembered saying the same thing, after he dragged Kerensky into the shuttle. "There's something going on with the officers here," he said.

"Five of them, yes," Jenkins said. "Abernathy, Q'eeng, Kerensky, West and Hartnell. Statistically speaking there's something highly aberrant about them. When they're on an away mission, the chance of the mission experiencing a critical failure increases. When two or more of them are on the same away mission, the chance of a critical failure increases exponentially. If three or more are on the mission, it's almost certain someone is going to die."

"But never any of *them,*" Hanson said.

"That's right," Jenkins said. "Sure, Kerensky gets the shit kicked out of him on a regular basis. Even the other four are occasionally knocked around. But death? Not for them. Never for them."

"And none of this is normal," Dahl prompted.

"Of course not!" Jenkins said. He flipped up pictures of the five officers, with graphs behind them. "Each of them has experienced exponentially higher fatality rates on away missions than any other officers in the same positions on other ships. That's across the *entire* fleet, and across the *entire existence* of the fleet, back to the formation of the Dub U nearly two hundred years ago. You have to go back to the blue water fleets for the same types of fatalities, and even the officers themselves didn't escape mortality. Captains and senior officers were dropping dead all the time."

"That's what scurvy and plague will do," Hester said.

"It's not just *scurvy,*" Jenkins said, and waved at the officers' pictures. "Officers die today too, you know. Having rank changes mortality patterns somewhat but doesn't eliminate them. Statistically speaking, all five of these guys should be dead two or three times over. *Maybe* one or two of them

140

would have survived all the experiences they've had so far. But all five of them? The odds are better that one of them would get struck by lightning."

"Which they would survive," Finn said.

"But not the crewman next to him," Duvall said.

"Now you're getting it," Jenkins said.

"So what you're saying is all this is impossible," Dahl said.

Jenkins shook his head. "Nothing's impossible," he said. "But some things are pretty damned unlikely. This is one of them."

"How unlikely?" Dahl asked.

"In all my research there's only one spaceship I've found that has even remotely the same sort of statistical patterns for away missions," Jenkins said. He rummaged through the graphic elements again, and then threw one onto the screen. They all stared at it.

Duvall frowned. "I don't recognize this ship," she said. "And I thought I knew every type of ship we had. Is this a Dub U ship?"

"Not exactly," Jenkins said. "It's from the United Federation of Planets."

Duvall blinked and focused her attention back at Jenkins. "Who are they?" she asked.

"They don't exist," Jenkins said, and pointed back at the ship. "And neither does this. This is the starship *Enterprise*. It's fictional. It was on a science fictional drama series. And so are we."

"Okay," Finn said, after a moment. "I don't know about anyone else here, but I'm ready to label this guy officially *completely fucking insane.*"

Jenkins looked over to Dahl. "I told you it would sound insane," he said. He waved at the display. "But here are the stats."

"The stats show that there's something screwed up with this ship," Finn said. "It doesn't suggest we're stars in a fucked-up science fiction show."

"I never said you were the *stars,*" Jenkins said. He pointed at the floating images of Abernathy, Q'eeng, Kerensky, West and Hartnell. "*They're* the stars. You're extras."

"Perfect," Finn said, and stood up. "Thank you *so* much for wasting my time. I'm going to get some sleep now."

"Wait," Dahl said.

" 'Wait'? Seriously, Andy?" Finn said. "I know you've been obsessed with this for a while now, but there's being on the edge and then there's going all the way *over* the edge, and our hairy friend here is so far over the edge that the edge doesn't even know him anymore."

"You know how I hate to agree with Finn," Hester said. "But I do. This isn't right. It's not even wrong."

Dahl looked at Duvall. "I'm voting for nuts, too, Andy," she said. "Sorry."

"Jimmy?" Dahl asked, looking at Hanson.

"Well, he's *definitely* nuts," Hanson said. "But he thinks he's telling the truth."

"Of course he does! That's why he's *nuts,*" Finn said.

"That's not what I mean," Hanson said. "When you're nuts, your reasoning is consistent with your own internal logic, but it's *internal* logic, which doesn't make any sort of sense outside your own head." He pointed at Jenkins. "His logic is external and reasonable enough."

"Except the part where we're all fictional," Finn sneered.

"I never said that," Jenkins said.

"Gaaah," Finn said, and pointed to the *Enterprise.* "*Fictional,* you unmitigated asshole."

"*It's* fictional," Jenkins said. "*You're* real. But a fictional television show intrudes on our reality and warps it."

"Wait," Finn said, waving his hands in disbelief. "*Television?* Are you fucking kidding me? There hasn't been *television* in hundreds of years."

143

"Television got its start in 1928," Jenkins said. "The last use of the medium for entertainment purposes was in 2105. Sometime between those two dates there's a television series following the adventures of the crew of the *Intrepid.*"

"I really want to know what you're smoking," Finn said. "Because whatever it is, I'm betting I can make a hell of a profit on it."

Jenkins looked back at Dahl again. "I can't work like this," he said.

"Everyone shut up for a minute," Dahl said. Finn and Jenkins calmed themselves. "Look. I agree it sounds crazy. Even *he* admits it sounds crazy." Dahl pointed at Jenkins. "But think about what we've seen go on in this ship. Think of how people act here. What's messed up here isn't that this guy thinks we're on a television show. What's messed up here is that as far as I can tell, at this point, it's the *most rational explanation* for what's going on. Tell me that I'm wrong."

Dahl looked around at his friends. Everyone was silent. Finn looked like he was barely holding his tongue.

"Right," Dahl said. "So at least let's hear the rest of what he has to say. Maybe it gets more nuts from here. Maybe it starts to make more sense. Either way, it's better

144

than what we have now, which is nothing."

"Fine," Finn said, finally. "But you owe us all handjobs." He sat back down.

"Handjobs?" Jenkins asked Dahl.

"Long story," Dahl said.

"Well, anyway," Jenkins said. "You're right about one thing. It's messed up that the most rational explanation for what does go on in this ship is that a television show intrudes on our reality and warps it. But that's not the worst thing about it."

"Jesus Christ," Finn said. "If that's not the worst thing, what is?"

"That as far as I can tell," Jenkins said, "it's not actually a very good show."

CHAPTER TEN

"Red alert!" said Captain Abernathy, as the Calendrian rebel ship fired its torpedoes at the *Intrepid*. "Evasive maneuvers! Now!" Dahl, standing at his science post on the bridge, positioned his feet for stability as the ship yawed widely, moving its bulk to avoid the nimble guided projectiles headed for it.

You'll notice that the Intrepid*'s inertial dampeners don't work as well in crisis situations,* Dahl remembered Jenkins telling them. *The ship could do hairpin turns and loop-de-loops any other time and you'd never notice. But whenever there's a dramatic event, there goes your footing.*

"They're still coming right at us!" yelled Ensign Jacobs, at the weapons station, tracking the torpedoes.

Abernathy pounded the button on his chair that opened a broadcast channel. "All hands! Brace for impact!"

Dahl and everyone else on the bridge grabbed on to their stations and braced themselves. *This would be a good time for a restraint system,* Dahl thought.

There was a far crump as the torpedoes hit the *Intrepid.* The bridge deck swayed from the impact.

"Damage report!" barked Abernathy.

Decks six through twelve will almost always sustain damages during an attack, Jenkins had said. *It's because these are the decks the show has sets for. They can cut away from the bridge for shots of explosions and crew being flung backward.*

"Decks six, seven and nine have sustained heavy damages," Q'eeng said. "Decks eight and ten have moderate damage."

"More torpedoes!" cried Jacobs. "Four of them!"

"Countermeasures!" yelled Abernathy. "Fire!"

Why didn't you use countermeasures in the first place? Dahl thought.

In his head, Jenkins answered. *Every battle is designed for maximum drama,* he said. *This is what happens when the Narrative takes over. Things quit making sense. The laws of physics take a coffee break. People stop*

*thinking logically and start thinking dramati-
cally.*

"The Narrative" — Jenkins' term for
when the television show crept into their
lives, swept away rationality and physical
laws and made people know, do and say
things they wouldn't otherwise. *You've had
it happen to you already,* Jenkins had said. *A
fact you didn't know before just pops into your
head. You make a decision or take an action
you wouldn't otherwise make. It's like an irresistible impulse because it is an irresistible
impulse — your will isn't your own, you're just
a pawn for a writer to move around.*

On the view screen, three orange blossoms
burned brightly as the *Intrepid*'s countermeasures took out torpedoes.

Three, not four, Dahl thought. *Because
having one get through will be more dramatic.*

"One's still heading our way!" Jacobs said.
"It's going to hit!"

There was a violent bang as the torpedo
smacked against the hull several decks
below the bridge. Jacobs screamed as his
weapons station exploded in a shower of
sparks, flinging him backward to the deck
of the bridge.

Something will explode on the bridge, Jenkins said. *That's where the camera spends*

nearly all its time. There has to be damage there, whether it makes sense or not.

"Reroute weapons controls!" yelled Abernathy.

"Rerouted!" said Kerensky. "I have them."

"Fire!" Abernathy said. "Full spread!"

Kerensky smashed his fingers into the buttons of his station. The view screen lit up as pulse beams and neutrino missiles blasted toward the Calendrian rebel, exploding in a constellation of impacts seconds later.

"Direct hits!" Kerensky said, looking at his station for information. "It looks like we cracked their engine core, Captain. We've got about a minute before she blows."

"Get us out of here, Kerensky," Abernathy said, and then turned to Q'eeng. "Additional damages?"

"Deck twelve heavily damaged," Q'eeng said.

The door to the bridge opened and Chief Engineer West came through. "And our engines are banged up pretty good," he said, as though he would have been able to hear Abernathy and Q'eeng's conversation, through a door, while red alert sirens were blaring. "We're lucky we didn't crack our own core, Captain."

"How long until it's repaired?" Abernathy asked.

Just long enough to introduce a plot complication, Dahl thought.

"Ten hours would be pushing it," West said.

"Damn it!" Abernathy said, pounding his chair again. "We're supposed to be escorting the Calendrian pontifex's ship to the peace talks by then."

"Clearly there are those among the rebels still opposed to the talks," Q'eeng said, looking toward the view screen. In it, the rebel ship blew up impressively.

"Yes, clearly," Abernathy said. "But they were the ones who asked for the talks to begin with. Why jeopardize them *now*? And why attack *us*?" He looked off, grimly.

Every once in a while Abernathy or one of the other officers will say something dramatic, or rhetorical, or leading, and then he and everyone else will be quiet for a few seconds, Jenkins told them. *That's a lead-out to a commercial break. When that happens, the Narrative goes away. Watch what they do next.*

After several seconds Abernathy blinked, relaxed his posture and looked at West. "Well, you should probably have your people start fixing those engines, then." His voice was notably less tense and drama-filled.

"Right," West said, and went right back

150

out of the door. As he did so he looked around, as if wondering why he felt it necessary to come all the way to the bridge to deliver a piece of information he could have easily offered by phone.

Abernathy turned to Q'eeng. "And, let's get repair crews to those damaged decks."

"Will do," Q'eeng said.

"And while you're at it, get someone up here to repair the weapons station," Abernathy said. "And see if we can't find some power spike dampeners or something. There's not a damn reason why everything on the bridge has to go up in sparks anytime we have a battle."

Dahl made a small choking sound at this.

"Is there a problem, Ensign?" Abernathy said, seeing Dahl for what seemed like the first time in all of this.

"No, sir," Dahl said. "Sorry, sir. A little post-combat nervousness."

"You're Dill," Abernathy said. "From Xenobiology."

"Dahl, sir," Dahl said. "That was my former posting, yes."

"First day on the bridge, then," Abernathy said.

"It is," Dahl said.

"Well, don't worry, it's not always like

151

this," Abernathy said. "Sometimes it's worse."

"Yes, sir," Dahl said.

"Okay," Abernathy said, and then nodded at the prone figure of Jacobs, who was now moaning softly. "Why don't you make yourself useful and take Jackson here to sick bay. He looks like he could use it."

"Right away, sir," Dahl said, and moved to help Jacobs.

"How is he?" Abernathy asked, as Dahl lifted him.

"Banged up," Dahl said. "But I think he'll live."

"Well, good," Abernathy said. "That's more than I can say for the last weapons specialist. Or the one before that. Sometimes, Dill, I wonder what the hell is going on with this ship. It's like it has a god-damned curse."

"It doesn't prove anything," Finn said, after Dahl recounted the events of the attack. The five of them were huddled around a table in the crew lounge, with their drinks.

"How much more proof do you want?" Dahl asked. "It was like going down a checklist. Wonky inertial dampeners? Check. Exploding bridge stations? Check. Damage to decks six through twelve? Check. Mean-

152

ingful pause before dropping to commercial? Check."

"No one died," Hanson pointed out.

"Nobody *had* to die," Dahl said. "I think this battle is just an opener. It's what you have before the first commercial break. It's the setup for whatever's supposed to happen next."

"Like what?" Duvall asked.

"I don't know," Dahl said. "*I'm* not writing this thing."

"Jenkins would know," Hester said. "He's got that collection of 'episodes.' "

Dahl nodded. Jenkins had splayed out a timeline of the *Intrepid* that featured glowing hash marks at near regular intervals. *Those are where the Narrative intrudes,* he said, zooming into one of the hash marks, which in detail branched out like a root structure. *It comes and goes, you can see. Each of these smaller events is a scene. They all tie into a narrative arc.* Jenkins zoomed out. *Six years. Twenty-four major events a year, on average. Plus a couple minor ones. I think those are tie-in novels.*

"Not *you,* now," Finn complained to Hester, breaking Dahl's reverie. "It's bad enough Andy is all wrapped up in this. Now you're going over to the crazy side, too."

"Finn, if the shoe fits, I'm going to call it

153

a shoe, all right?" Hester said. "I don't believe his *conclusions,* but his knowledge of the *details* is pretty damn impressive. This last engagement went down like Jenkins said it would. He called the thing right down to the exploding bridge station. Now, maybe we're not actually being *written,* and maybe Jenkins is off his medication. But I bet he's got a good guess where this adventure with that rebel ship takes us."

"So you're going to go running to him every time something happens to find out what you should do next?" Finn asked. "If you really want to follow a cult leader, there are better ones than a guy who hasn't eaten anything but away rations for four years and shits in a portable potty."

"How do *you* explain it, then?" Hester asked Finn.

"I *don't,*" Finn said. "Look. This is a weird damn ship. We all agree on that. But what you're trying to do is impose causality on random events, just like everyone else here has been doing."

"The suspension of the laws of physics isn't a random event, Finn," Hester said.

"And you're a physicist now?" Finn countered, and looked around. "People, we're on a goddamned *spaceship.* Can any of us really explain how the thing works? We encounter all types of alien life on planets we've just discovered. Should we be surprised we don't understand it? We're part of a civilization that spans light-years. That's inherently weird if you give it any thought. It's all inherently unlikely."

"You didn't say any of this when we met with Jenkins," Dahl said.

"I was *going* to," Finn said. "But then you were all 'let's hear what he has to say,' and there was no *point.*"

Dahl frowned, irritated.

"Look, I'm not disagreeing there's something off here," Finn said. "There is. We all know it. But maybe that's because this whole ship is on some sort of insanity feedback loop. It's been feeding on itself for years now. In a situation like that, if you're looking for patterns to connect unlikely events, you're going to find them. It doesn't help there's someone like Jenkins, who is crazy but just coherent enough to whip up an explanation that makes some sort of messed-up sense in hindsight. Then he goes rogue and starts tracking the officers for the rest of the crew, which just feeds the insanity. And into this comes Andy, who is trained to believe this sort of mumbo jumbo."

"What does that mean?" Dahl said, stiffening.

"It means you spent years in a seminary, neck-deep in mysticism," Finn said. "And not just run-of-the-mill human mysticism but genuinely *alien* mysticism. You stretched your mind out there, my friend, just wide enough to fit Jenkins' nut-brained theory." He put up his hands, sensing Dahl's irritation. "I like you, Andy, don't get me wrong. I think you're a good guy. But I think your history here is working against you. And I think whether you know it or not, you're leading our pals here into genuinely bugshit territory."

"Speaking of personal history, that's the thing that creeped me out most about Jenkins," Duvall said.

"That he knows about us?" asked Hanson.

"I mean how *much* he knew about each of us," Duvall said. "And what he thought it meant."

You're all extras, but you're glorified *extras,* Jenkins had told them. *Your average extra exists just to get killed off, so he or she doesn't have a backstory. But each of you do.* He pointed to each in turn. *You were a novitiate to an alien religion. You're a scoundrel who's made enemies across the fleet. You're the son of one of the richest men in the universe. You left your last ship after having an altercation with your superior officer, and you're sleeping with Kerensky now.*

"You're just pissed he told the rest of us that you were boinking Kerensky," Hester said. "Especially after you had already blown him off in front of us."

Duvall rolled her eyes. "I have needs," she said.

"He's had three STDs in his recent history," Finn said.

"I had him get a new round of shots, trust me," Duvall said, and then looked over at Dahl. "And anyway, don't get on me for scratching an itch. None of *you* were exactly stepping up."

"Hey, I was in sick bay when you started with Kerensky," Dahl said. "Don't blame me."

Duvall smirked at that. "And it wasn't that part that bothered me, anyway," she said. "It was the other part."

You're not just going to get killed off, Kerensky told them. *It's not enough for a television audience just to kill off some poor random bastard every episode. Every once in a while they have to make it seem like a real person is dying. So they take a smaller character, build them up long enough for the*

157

*audience to care about them, and then snap
them off. That's you guys. Because you come
with backstories. You're probably going to
have an entire episode devoted to your death.*

"More complete bullshit," Finn said.

"Easy for you to say," Hester said. "I'm
the only one of us without an interesting
backstory. I've got nothing. The next away
team I'm on, I'm fucking *doomed*."

Finn pointed at Hester and looked at
Dahl. "See, this is what I'm talking about
right here. You've overwhelmed a weak and
febrile mind."

Dahl smiled at this. "And you're the lone
voice of sanity."

"Yes!" Finn said. "I want you to think
about what it means when *I* am the person
in a group who is making the case for reality. I'm the least responsible person I
know. I resent having to be the voice of
reason. I resent it a lot."

" 'Weak and febrile,' " Hester muttered.

"You were the one calling a shoe a shoe,"
Finn said.

Duvall's phone pinged and she stepped
away for a moment. When she returned, she
was pale. "All right," she said. "That was al-
together too *damned* coincidental for my
tastes."

Dahl frowned. "What is it?"

158

"That was Kerensky," she said. "I'm wanted for a senior officer briefing."

"What for?" Hanson asked.

"When the *Intrepid* was attacked by that rebel ship, our engines got knocked out, so they sent another ship to escort the Calendrian pontifex's ship to the peace talks," Duvall said. "That ship just attacked the pontifex's ship and crippled it."

"What ship is it?" Dahl asked.

"The *Nantes*," Duvall said. "The last ship I was stationed on."

CHAPTER ELEVEN

"Trust me, Andy," Finn said, walking with Dahl toward Duvall's barracks. "She doesn't want to talk to you."

"You don't know that," Dahl said.

"I do know that," Finn said.

"Yeah?" Dahl asked. "How?"

"When I saw her just after she came out of her briefing, she said to me, 'If I see Andy, I swear to God I'm going to break his nose,' " Finn said. Dahl smiled.

The two of them reached Duvall's barracks and entered the room, which was empty except for Duvall, sitting on her bunk.

"Maia," Dahl began.

"Andy," Duvall said, stood, and punched Dahl in the face. Dahl collapsed to the deck, holding his nose.

"I told you," Finn said to Dahl, on the deck. He looked over to Duvall. "I *did* tell him."

"I thought you were kidding!" Dahl said from the deck.

"Surprise," Finn said.

Dahl pulled his hand back from his face to see if there was any blood on it; there wasn't. "What was that for?" he asked Duvall.

"It's for your conspiracy theories," Duvall said.

"They're not my theories," Dahl said. "They're Jenkins' theories."

"For Christ's sake, it doesn't matter who thought up the fucking things!" Duvall snapped. "I'm in that goddamned meeting today, telling them what I know about the *Nantes,* and all the time I'm doing that I'm thinking, 'This is it, this is the episode where I die.' And then I look over at Kerensky, and he's making cow eyes at me, like we're married instead of just screwing. And then I know I'm doomed, because if that son of a bitch has a crush on me, it makes it perfect if I get killed off. Because then he can be *sad* at the end of the episode."

"It doesn't have to work that way, Maia," Dahl said, and started to get up. She pushed him back down.

"Shut *up,* Andy," she said. "Just shut up. You're not getting it. It doesn't *matter* if it's going to work that way. What matters is now

161

I'm buying into your paranoia. Now some part of my brain is thinking about buying it on an away mission. It's thinking about it all the time. It's like waiting for the other shoe to drop. And you fucking did it to me. Thank you so *very* much." Duvall sat down on her bunk, pissed.

"I'm sorry," Dahl said, after a minute.

"Sorry," Duvall said, and laughed a small laugh. "Jesus, Andy."

"What went on in the officer briefing?" Finn asked.

"I briefed them about the *Nantes* and its crew," Duvall said. "The Calendrian rebels have a spy or turncoat in the crew, someone who could hack into the weapons systems and fire on the pontifex's ship, and then shut down communications. We've heard nothing from the *Nantes* since the attack."

"Why would they put a spy on the *Nantes*?" Finn asked. "It was the *Intrepid* that was supposed to escort the pontifex's ship."

"They must have known the *Nantes* was the backup ship for this mission," Duvall said. "And it's easier to sneak a spy on the *Nantes* than on the flagship of the Universal Union. So they send a ship to attack us, knock us out of the mission, and then the *Nantes* is in a perfect position to take a shot at the pontifex's ship. And that's the *other* thing —" Duvall pointed at Dahl. "Because when we're being told this in the briefing, I'm thinking 'How far ahead would you have to plant a spy? How could they have known the *Nantes* would be the backup ship for a mission that was just assigned a couple of days ago? How *likely* is that?' And then I think 'This episode needs to be better edited.' " She looked down at Dahl. "And that's when I decided I was going to punch you in the head the next time I saw you."

"Jenkins did say he didn't think the show was very good," Dahl said.

Duvall cocked back her arm. "Don't make me do it again, Andy," she said.

"Is there an away team?" Finn asked.

"Yes," Duvall said. "And I'm on it. The *Nantes* is silent and it isn't moving, so the *Intrepid* has been ordered to investigate the situation on the *Nantes* and to defend the pontifex's ship from any further attack. I was stationed on the *Nantes* and I was a ground trooper, so that makes me the guide for the away team. And I'm likely to get everyone on the team killed now, since thanks to Andy I'm convinced this is when it makes *dramatic sense* for me to get shot between the eyes."

"When do we arrive?" Finn asked.

"About two hours," Duvall said. "Why?"

Finn fished in his pocket and pulled out a small blue oblong pill. "Here, take this."

Duvall peered at it. "What is it?"

"It's a mood leveler made from the orynx plant," Finn said. "It's very mild."

"I don't need a mood leveler," Duvall said. "I just need to smack Andy again."

"You can do both," Finn said. "Trust me, Maia. You're a wreck right now, and you know it. And like you said, that's going to put your away team at risk."

"And taking a drug won't?" Duvall said.

"Not this one," Finn said. "Like I said, it's very mild. You'll hardly notice the effect. All you'll notice is that you'll *unclench* a little. Just enough to focus on your job and not on your state of mind. It won't affect anything else. You'll still be sharp and aware." He held the pill closer to Duvall.

She peered at it again. "There's lint on it," she said.

Finn dusted the lint off. "There," he said.

"All right," Duvall said, taking the pill. "But if I start seeing talking lizards, I'm going to punch you."

"Fair enough," Finn said. "Should I get you some water?"

"I'm fine," Duvall said, and dry swallowed. Then she leaned over and smacked

164

Dahl across the face with an open palm slap.

"What was that one for?" Dahl asked.

"Finn said I could take the pill *and* slap you," Duvall said, and then frowned. She looked up at Finn. "What was this pill made of?"

"The orynx plant," Finn said.

"And its effects are mild," Duvall said.

"Usually," Finn said.

"Because I'll tell you what, I'm getting some pretty strong effects all of a sudden," Duvall said, and then slumped off her bunk. Dahl caught her before she collapsed onto the deck.

"What did you do?" Dahl asked Finn, struggling with Duvall's unconscious body.

"Quite obviously, I knocked her out," Finn said, walking over to assist Dahl.

"I thought you said that pill was *very mild,*" Dahl said.

"I lied," Finn said, and took Duvall's legs. The two of them maneuvered her back onto her bunk.

"How long is she going to be out?" Dahl asked

"A dose like that will knock out a good-sized man for about eight hours," Finn said, "so she'll probably be down for at least ten."

"She'll miss her away team," Dahl said.

"Yes, she will. That's the *point,*" Finn said,

and then nodded down at Duvall. "Andy, you've got Duvall and our other friends so fucked up about this television thing that it's messing with their heads. If you want to go down that road, that's fine. I'm not going to stop you. But I want to make sure the rest of them see a counterargument in action."

"By drugging Maia?" Dahl said.

"That's the means to an end," Finn said. "The end is making the point that even without Maia, the away team is going to go over to the *Nantes* and do their job. Life goes on even when Jenkins' 'Narrative' is supposed to apply. Once Maia, Jimmy and Hester see that, maybe they'll stop freaking out. And who knows? Maybe you'll come to your senses, too."

Dahl nodded to Duvall. "She's still going to get in trouble for missing her mission," he said. "That's a court-martial offense. I'm not sure she'll appreciate that."

Finn smiled. "I like how you think I didn't plan for that," he said.

"And just how did you plan for that?" Dahl said.

"You're about to find out," Finn said. "Because you're part of it."

"Where's Maia?" Kerensky asked.

166

"Who?" Finn said, innocently.

"Duvall," Kerensky said somewhat impatiently. "She's supposed to be on this away team."

"Oh, her," Finn said. "She's been waylaid with Orynxian Dropsy. She's out for a couple of days. Dahl here and I are replacing her on the team. Check your orders, sir."

Kerensky looked at Finn appraisingly, then pulled out his phone and checked the away team order. After a moment he grunted and motioned them toward the shuttle. Finn and Dahl got on. Dahl didn't know how Finn had forged the away team order and didn't feel the need to ask too deeply about it.

Inside the shuttle were Captain Abernathy, Commander Q'eeng and an extraordinarily nervous-looking ensign whom Dahl had never seen before. The ensign had undoubtedly noted the presence of the three senior officers on the away team, had calculated his own odds of survival and didn't like the result. Dahl smiled at the ensign as he sat down; the ensign looked away.

Several minutes later, with Kerensky at the controls, the shuttle was out of its bay and headed toward the *Nantes.*

"Some of you are late additions to this

party," Captain Abernathy said, nodding to Finn and Dahl, "so let me review the situation and our plan of attack. The *Nantes* has been out of communication since just before it attacked the pontifex's ship. We think the Calendrian rebel spy was somehow able to take over some systems, cut off communications and fire on the pontifex, but afterward the crew must have been able to get back some control of the ship, otherwise the *Nantes* would have blown the pontifex out of the sky by now. Our job is to get onto the *Nantes,* ascertain the situation and if necessary assist in the capture of the rebel."

"Do we have any information on who this rebel might be, sir?" Dahl heard himself ask, surprised to hear the sound of his own voice. *Oh, shit,* he thought.

"An excellent question, Ensign Dahl," Q'eeng said. "Just before we left the *Intrepid* I requested a crew manifest for the *Nantes.* The crew of the ship has been stable for months, but there was a recent addition to its crew, a Crewman Jer Weston. He's a primary person of interest."

"Wait," Finn said, interrupting the commander. "Did you say Jer Weston?"

"Yes," Q'eeng said, irritated at being interrupted.

"Previously stationed on the *Springfield*?"

168

Finn asked.

"That was his posting prior to the *Nantes,* yes," Q'eeng said. "Why?"

"I know this guy," Finn said. "I knew him on the *Springfield.*"

"My God, man," Abernathy said, leaning forward to Finn. "Tell us about him."

"There's not much to say," Finn said, looking at the captain and then Q'eeng. "He and I worked in the cargo hold together."

"He was your friend?" Q'eeng asked.

"Friend might be a little much, sir," Finn said. "Jer is a dick. 'Friend' isn't part of his vocabulary. But I worked with him for more than a year. I spent time with him. He never seemed like a traitor."

"If spies seemed like traitors they wouldn't be good spies," Q'eeng said.

"Finn, we need to know everything you know about Weston," Abernathy said, intensely. "Anything we can use. Anything that can help us take back control of the *Nantes* before more Calendrian rebel ships converge on this sector. Because if they arrive before the *Nantes* is back in action, the *Intrepid* won't be enough to keep the pontifex safe. And then it won't just be the Calendrians fighting themselves. The whole galaxy will be at war."

There was a long, tense second of silence.

169

"Uh, okay, sir," Finn said, eventually.

"Great, thanks," Abernathy said. His demeanor was suddenly more relaxed. "Wow. A last-minute replacement for this away team, and you just happen to know the crewman we think is the spy. That's amazing. What are the odds of that?"

"Pretty big odds," Finn said.

"I'll say," Abernathy said.

"Captain, before Crewman Finn briefs us on Weston, I want to discuss the layout of the *Nantes* with you," Q'eeng said. He and Abernathy fell into a discussion.

Dahl turned to Finn. "You okay?" he asked.

"I'm fine," Finn said.

"You're sure," Dahl said.

"Andy, quit it," Finn said. "It's a co-incidence, is all it is. I'm going to get through this. You are going to get through this. We're going to get back to the *Intrepid,* we're going to get a drink, and then I'm going to go to Medical when Maia wakes up and kicks my ass. That's my prediction. I'll put money on it if you want."

Dahl smiled. "Okay," he said, and sat back. He looked over at Abernathy and Q'eeng, still in their conversation. Then he looked over to the other ensign. He was looking at Finn with an expression that

Dahl couldn't quite read.

After a moment, it came to him. The other ensign looked relieved.

And he looked guilty about it.

CHAPTER TWELVE

The *Nantes* bay was empty except for several automated cargo carts rolling about. "Finn and Dahl, you're with me," Captain Abernathy said, and then pointed at the remaining ensign. "Grover, you're with Kerensky and Q'eeng."

"Yes, sir," Ensign Grover said, and then was flung backward against the shuttle as a pulse beam hit him, fired from one of the automated carts. As he fell, Dahl caught a glimpse of confusion in his eyes.

And then Dahl was running, with Finn and Kerensky, looking for cover under fire. They found it several meters away, behind storage bins. Several armed cargo carts were now rolling toward them, with the others heading toward where Kerensky and Q'eeng had taken cover.

"Anyone have any ideas?" Abernathy asked.

"Those carts are being controlled from a

distance," Finn said. "If we can get to the quartermaster's office here in the bay, we can override their signal for the ones in here."

"Yes," Abernathy said, and pointed to a far wall. "If this bay is laid out anything like the *Intrepid*'s, it's over there."

"I can do it," Finn said.

Abernathy held up his hand. "No," he said. "We've already lost one crew member today. I don't want to risk another."

As opposed to risking our captain? Dahl thought, but kept silent.

Abernathy raised his pulse gun. "You two cover me as I run for it. I'm going on three." He started counting. Dahl glanced over to Finn, who shrugged and then readied his pulse gun.

At the three count, Abernathy burst from behind the storage bins like a startled quail and ran in a broken, diving pattern across the bay. The cargo carts abandoned their previous targets and fired at the captain, narrowly missing him each time. Dahl and Finn aimed and knocked out one cart each.

Abernathy made it to the quartermaster's office, blasting the window and jumping through rather than wasting time opening the door. Several seconds later, the cargo carts noisily deactivated.

"All clear," Abernathy said, coming into view and hoisting himself over the remains of the window. The members of the *Intrepid* crew reassembled by the fallen corpse of Grover, whose face still had a look of disbelief on it.

"Finn, it looks like your friend Jer Weston is now a murderer," Abernathy said, grimly.

"He's not my friend, sir," Finn said.

"But you do *know* him," Abernathy said. "If you find him, will you be ready to take him down? Alive?"

"Yes, sir," Finn said.

"Good," Abernathy said.

"Captain, we need to move," Q'eeng said. "There may be others of these carts. In fact, I'm willing to bet that Weston is using the carts as his own robot army to keep the crew members bottled up."

"Yes, precisely," Abernathy said, and nodded at Q'eeng. "You and I will make our way to the bridge to see if we can find Captain Bullington, and then assist her in taking back the ship. Kerensky, you take Finn and Dahl here and find Weston. Capture him alive."

"Yes, sir," Kerensky said.

"Good," Abernathy said. "Then let's move." He and Q'eeng jogged off toward the bay entrance, to wander the crew corridors, where they would no doubt encounter and fight more armed cargo carts.

Finn turned to Kerensky. "So, what's the plan?" he asked.

"Plan?" Kerensky said, and blinked.

"If there really is a Narrative, it's not on him right now," Dahl said, about Kerensky.

"Right," Finn said, and turned to Dahl. "How about you?"

"You know what I think," Dahl said, and motioned to the cargo carts.

"You think Jer's pulling a Jenkins," Finn said. "Hiding in the walls."

"Bingo," Dahl said.

"A what?" Kerensky said. "What are you two talking about?"

Dahl and Finn didn't answer but instead went about separate tasks — Dahl accessing the ship records while Finn salvaged from the dead cargo carts.

"There," Finn said, holding out his hand after he was done. "Three cart IDs. We're going to have to leave our phones behind so we're not ID'd when we go into the cargo tunnels, and so the armed carts think we're one of them and don't try to kill us."

"Jenkins knew about this trick," Dahl said.

"Yeah, but I took the IDs from deactivated carts," Finn said. "These carts are just recently killed. Their IDs are still in the system. I don't think Jer had time to figure this one out."

"Figure what out?" Kerensky asked.

"I think you're right," Dahl said, and pulled up on his phone a map of the cargo tunnels. "It doesn't look like he's had time to make his hidey-hole disappear from the ship records either, since all of the cart distribution nodes are still on the map."

"So that's seven nodes," Finn said. "Which one do you want to try first?"

Dahl pulled up Weston's information. "His station was here in the bay complex, so I'd say we try the node closest to it," he said, and then returned to the map and highlighted a node. "Let's start here."

"Looks good," Finn said.

"I order you to tell me what you're planning," Kerensky said, plaintively.

"We're about to help you capture Jer Weston," Finn said. "That'll probably get you promoted."

"Oh," Kerensky said, and stood up a bit straighter. "We should definitely do that, then."

"And avenge the death of Grover here," Dahl added, nodding to Grover's still surprised body.

"Yes, that too," Kerensky said, and looked down at the body. "Poor man. This was his last away mission."

"Well, yes," Finn said.

"No, I mean that his term of duty was over in just a couple of days," Kerensky said. "I assigned him to this mission specifically so he could have one more away experience. A last hurrah. He tried to beg off of it, but I insisted."

"That was deeply malicious of you," Dahl said.

Kerensky nodded, either not knowing what *malicious* meant or simply not hearing it, apparently lost in reverie. "A shame, really. He was going to be married, too."

"Oh, please, *stop,*" Finn said. "Otherwise I'm going to have to frag you."

"What?" Kerensky said, looking up at Finn.

"I think he means we should probably get going, sir," Dahl said, smoothly.

"Right," Kerensky said. "So, where are we going?"

"You two wait here," Kerensky whispered at a bend in the corridor, after which came the distribution node they were sneaking up on. "I'll surprise him and stun him, and then we'll contact the captain."

"We can't contact him, we left our phones in the shuttle bay," Finn said.

"And we should probably deactivate all the armed carts first," Dahl said.

"Yes, yes," Kerensky said, mildly irritated. "But *first,* I'll take him down."

"A fine plan," Dahl said.

"We're right behind you," Finn said.

Kerensky nodded and readied his weapon, and then leapt out into the corridor, calling Jer Weston's name. There was an exchange of pulse gun fire, each blast going wide. From the top of the corridor there was a shower of sparks as a pulse gun blast ricocheted through the duct work, which collapsed on Kerensky, pinning him. He groaned and passed out.

"He really *is* completely useless," Finn said.

"What do you want to do now?" Dahl asked.

"I have a plan," Finn said. "Come on." He stood and walked forward, pulse gun behind his back. Dahl followed.

After a few steps the curve of the corridor revealed a disheveled Jer Weston, standing on the distribution node, pulse gun in hand, clearly considering whether or not to kill Kerensky.

"Hey, Jer," Finn said, walking up to him. "It's me, Finn."

Weston squinted. "Finn? Seriously?

Here?" He smiled. "Jesus, man. What are the odds?"

"I know!" Finn said, and then shot Weston with a stun pulse. Weston collapsed.

"That was your plan?" Dahl said a second later. "Hoping he'd pause in recognition before he shot you?"

"In retrospect, the plan has significant logistical issues," Finn admitted. "On the other hand, it worked. You can't argue with success."

"Sure you can," Dahl said, "when it's based on stupidity."

"Anyway, this makes my point to you," Finn said. "If I was going to die on this mission, this probably would have been the moment, right? Me squaring off against my former fellow crew member? But I'm alive and he's stunned and captured. So much for 'the Narrative' and dying at dramatically appropriate moments. I hope you take the lesson to heart."

"Fine," Dahl said. "Maybe I've been weirding myself out. I'm still not following you into battle anymore."

"That's probably wise," Finn said, and then glanced over to the small computer at the distribution node, which Weston was probably using to control the cargo carts. "Why don't you disable the killer carts and

I'll figure out how we're going to get Jer out of here."

"You could use a cart," Dahl said, going to the computer.

"There's an idea," Finn said.

Dahl disabled the carts across the ship and then heard a groan from Kerensky's direction. "Sounds like someone is up," he said to Finn.

"I'm busy trussing Jer like a turkey," Finn said. "Handle it, if you would."

Dahl walked over to Kerensky, who was still pinned under duct work. "Morning, sir," he said, to Kerensky.

"Did I get him?" Kerensky asked.

"Congratulations, sir," Dahl said. "Your plan worked perfectly."

"Excellent," Kerensky said, and wheezed a bit as the debris on top of him compressed his lungs.

"Would you like some help with your duct work, sir?" Dahl asked.

"Please," Kerensky said.

"There's nothing in Crewman Weston's file that indicates any sympathy for the Calendrian rebel cause," said Sandra Bullington, captain of the *Nantes.* "I requested a hyperwaved report from the Dub U Investigative Service. Weston isn't religious or political.

He doesn't even vote."

Bullington, Abernathy, Q'eeng, Finn and Dahl stood in front of a windowed room in the brig, in which Jer Weston sat. He was confined to a stasis chair, which was itself the only piece of furniture in the room. He looked groggy but was smiling. Kerensky was in sick bay with bruised ribs.

"What about family and friends?" Q'eeng asked.

"Nothing there, either," Bullington said. "He comes from a long line of Methodists from on the other side of the Dub U. None of his known associates have any link to Calendria or its religious or political struggles."

Abernathy looked through the glass at Weston. "Has he explained himself at all?" he asked.

"No," Bullington said. "That son of a bitch killed eighteen crew members and he won't say why. So far he's invoked his right to non-incrimination. But he says he's willing to confess everything under one condition."

"What's that?" Abernathy said.

"That you're the one he gets to confess to," Bullington said.

"Why me?" Abernathy asked.

Bullington shrugged. "He wouldn't say," she said. "If I had to guess, I would say it's

181

because you're the captain of the flagship of the fleet and your exploits are known through the Union. Maybe he just wants to be brought in by a celebrity."

"Sir, I recommend against it," Q'eeng said.

"We've had him physically searched," Bullington said. "There's nothing in his cavities, and even if there were, he's in a stasis chair. He can't move anything below his neck at the moment. If you stay out of biting range, you'll be fine."

"I still recommend against it," Q'eeng said.

"It's worth the risk to get to the bottom of this," Abernathy said, and then looked over to Dahl and Finn. "I'll have these two come in with me, armed. If something happens, I trust one of them will take him down."

Q'eeng looked unhappy but didn't say anything more.

Two minutes later Abernathy, Dahl and Finn came through the door. Weston smiled and addressed Finn.

"Finn, you shot me," he said.

"Sorry," Finn said.

"It's all right," Weston said. "I figured I would get shot. I just didn't know it would be you who did it."

"Captain Bullington said you were ready to confess, but that you wanted to confess to me," Abernathy said. "I'm here."

"Yes you are," Weston said.

"Tell us what your relationship is with the Calendrian rebels," Abernathy said.

"The who what now?" Weston said.

"The Calendrian rebels," Abernathy repeated.

"I have no idea what you're talking about," Weston said.

"You fired on the pontifex's ship after the *Intrepid* was disabled by the rebels," Abernathy said. "You can't honestly expect us to believe that the two were unrelated."

"They are related," Weston said. "Just not that way."

"You're wasting my time," Abernathy said, and turned to go.

"Don't you want to know what the connection is?" Weston asked.

"We know what the connection is," Abernathy said. "It's the Calendrian rebels."

"No," Weston said. "The connection is you."

"What?" Abernathy said, squinting.

Weston turned to Finn. "Sorry you had to be here," he said, and then started blinking one eye at a time, first two left, then three right, then one left, then three right.

183

"Bomb!" Finn yelled, and Dahl flung himself at the captain as Weston's head exploded. Dahl felt the uniform and skin on his back fry in the heat as the blast wave pushed him into Abernathy, crushing the two of them against the wall.

Some indeterminate time later Dahl heard someone shout his name, looked up and saw Abernathy grabbing and shaking him. Abernathy had burns on his hands and arms but appeared largely fine. Dahl had shielded him from the worst of the blast. Upon realizing that, the whole of Dahl's back seared into painful life.

Dahl pushed Abernathy away from him and crawled over to Finn, on the floor, his face and front burned. He had been closest to the blast. As Dahl made it to his friend, he saw that the one eye Finn had remaining had looked over to him. Finn's hand twitched and Dahl grabbed it, causing Finn to spasm in pain. Dahl tried to break contact but Finn grabbed on. His lips moved.

Dahl moved to his friend's face to hear what he had to say.

"This is just ridiculous," is what Finn whispered.

"I'm sorry," Dahl said.

"Not your fault," Finn eventually said.

"I'm still sorry," Dahl said.

Finn gripped Dahl's hand tighter. "Find a way to stop this," he said.

"I will," Dahl said.

"Okay," Finn breathed, and died.

Abernathy came over to pull Dahl away from Finn. Despite the pain, Dahl took a swing at Abernathy. He missed and lost consciousness before his fist had swung all the way around.

CHAPTER THIRTEEN

"Tell me how to stop this," Dahl said to Jenkins.

Jenkins, who of course knew Dahl was coming to his secret lair, looked him over. "You look healed," he said. "Good. Sorry about your friend Finn."

"Did you know what was going to happen to him?" Dahl asked.

"No," Jenkins said. "It not like whoever is writing this crap sends me the scripts in advance. And this one was particularly badly written. Jer Weston walking around for years with a biological bomb in his head, waiting for an encounter with Captain Abernathy, who he blamed for the death of his own father on an away team twenty years ago, and taking advantage of an unrelated diplomatic incident to do so? That's just hackwork."

"So tell me how to stop it," Dahl said.

"You can't *stop* it," Jenkins said. "There's

no stopping it. There's only *hiding* from it."

"Hiding isn't an option," Dahl said.

"Sure it is," Jenkins said, and opened his arms as if to say, *See?*

"*This* is not an option for anyone else but you," Dahl said. "We can't all sneak around in the bowels of a spaceship."

"There are other ways to hide," Jenkins said. "Ask your former boss Collins."

"She's only safe as long as you're around," Dahl said. "And not using the toilet."

"Find a way off this ship, then," Jenkins said. "You and your friends."

"That won't help either," Dahl said. "Jer Weston killed eighteen members of the *Nantes* crew with his armed cargo carts. *They* weren't safe against what happens here on the *Intrepid,* were they? An entire planet suffered a plague so that we could create a last-minute vaccine for Kerensky. They weren't safe, either. Even you're not safe, Jenkins."

"I'm pretty safe," Jenkins said.

"You're *pretty safe* because your wife was the one who died, and all you were was part of her backstory," Dahl said. "But what happens to you when one of the writers on whatever television show this is thinks about you?"

"They're not going to," Jenkins said.

"Are you sure?" Dahl said. "On the *Nantes,* Jer Weston was using your trick of hiding in the cargo tunnels. That's where we found him. That's where we caught him. Whatever hack thought up that last episode now has it in his brain that the cargo tunnels can be used as hiding spaces. How long until he starts thinking about you?"

Jenkins didn't say anything to this, although Dahl couldn't tell if it was because he was considering the idea of being in a writer's crosshairs or because he mentioned Jenkins' wife.

"None of us are safe from this thing," Dahl said. "You lost your wife to it. I just lost a friend. You say I and all my friends are going to end up dying for dramatic purposes. I say whatever happens to us is going to happen to you, too. All your hiding doesn't change that, Jenkins. It's just delaying it. And meanwhile, you live your life like a rat in the walls."

Jenkins looked around. "I wouldn't say a rat," he said.

"Are you happy living this way?" Dahl asked.

"I haven't been happy since my wife died," Jenkins said. "It was her death that got me on to all of this anyway. Looking at the statistics of deaths on this ship, seeing

188

how events on this ship played themselves out. Figuring that the most logical explanation was that we were part of a television show. Realizing my wife died simply to be a *dramatic moment* before a commercial. That in this television show, she was a bit player. An extra. She probably had about ten seconds of airtime. No one watching that episode probably has any memory of her now. Don't know her first name was Margaret. Or that she liked white wines more than red. Or that I proposed to her in her parents' front yard during a family reunion. Or that we were married for seven years before some hack decided to kill her. But I remember her."

"Do you think she'd be happy with how you're living?" Dahl asked.

"I think she'd understand why I do it," Jenkins said. "What I do on this ship keeps people alive."

"Keeps *some* people alive," Dahl said. "It's a zero-sum game. Someone is always going to have to die. Your alert system keeps the old hands here alive, but makes it more likely the new crew get killed."

"It's a risk, yes," Jenkins said.

"Jenkins, how long were you and your wife stationed on the *Intrepid* before she died?" Dahl asked.

189

Jenkins opened his mouth to respond and then shut it like a trap.

"It wasn't very long, was it?" Dahl asked.

Jenkins shook his head to say no, and then looked away.

"People on this ship figured it out before you came on it," Dahl said. "Maybe they didn't come to the same conclusions you did, but they saw what was happening and guessed their odds of survival. Now you're giving them better tech to do the same thing to new crew that they did to your wife."

"I think you should leave now," Jenkins said, still turned away from Dahl.

"Jenkins, listen to me," Dahl said, leaning in. "There's no way to hide from this. There's no way to run from it. There's no way to avoid fate. If the Narrative exists — and you and I know it does — then in the end we don't have free will. Sooner or later the Narrative will come for each of us. It'll use us however it wants to use us. And then we'll die from it. Like Finn did. Like Margaret did. Unless we stop it."

Jenkins looked back over at Dahl, eyes wet. "You're a man of faith, aren't you, Dahl?" he said.

"You know my history," Dahl said. "You know I am."

"How can you still be?" Jenkins said.

190

"What do you mean?" Dahl asked.

"I mean that you and I know that in this universe, God is a *hack,*" he said. "He's a writer on an awful science fiction television show, and He can't plot His way out of a box. How do you have faith when you know that?"

"Because I don't think that's actually God," Dahl said.

"You think it's the show's producer, then," Jenkins said. "Or maybe the president of the network."

"I think your definition of what a god is and what my definition is probably differ," Dahl said. "But I don't think any of this is the work of God, or of a god of any sort. If this is a television show, then it was made by people. Whatever and however they're doing this to us, they are just like us. And that means we can stop them. We just have to figure out how. *You* have to figure it out, Jenkins."

"Why me?" Jenkins asked.

"Because you know this television show we're trapped in better than anyone else," Dahl said. "If there's a solution or a loop-hole, you're the only one who can find it. And soon. Because I don't want any more of my friends to die because of a hack writer. And that includes you."

■ ■ ■ ■

"We could just blow up the *Intrepid,*" said Hester.

"It wouldn't work," said Hanson.

"Of course it would work," Hester said. "Ka-plooey, there goes the *Intrepid,* there goes the show."

"The show's not about the *Intrepid,*" Hanson said. "It's about the characters on it. Captain Abernathy and his crew."

"Some of them, anyway," Duvall said.

"The five main characters," Hanson amended. "If you blow up the ship, they'll just get another ship. A better ship. They'll just call it the *Intrepid-A* or something like that. It's happened on other science fiction shows."

"You've been studying?" Hester said, mockingly.

"Yes, I have," Hanson said, seriously. "After what happened to Finn, I went and learned about every science fiction television show I could find."

"What did you find out?" Dahl asked. He had already briefed his friends on his latest encounter with Jenkins.

"That I think Jenkins is right," Hanson said.

"That we're on a television show?" Duvall asked.

"No, that we're on a *bad* one," Hanson said. "As far as I can tell, the show we're on is pretty much a blatant rip-off of that show Jenkins told us about."

"Star Wars," Hester said.

"Star Trek," Hanson said. "There was a *Star Wars,* though. It was different."

"Whatever," Hester said. "So not only is this show we're on bad, it's plagiarized. And now my life is even more meaningless than it was before."

"Why would you make a show a knockoff of another show?" Duvall asked.

"Star Trek was very successful in its time," Hanson said. "So someone else came along and just reused the basic ideas. It worked because it worked before. People would still be entertained by the same stuff, more or less."

"Did you find our show in your research?" Dahl asked.

"No," Hanson said. "But I didn't think I would. When you create a science fiction show, you create a new fictional timeline, which starts just before the production date of that television show. That show's 'past' doesn't include the television show itself."

"Because that would be recursive and

meta," Duvall said.

"Yes, but I don't think they thought about it that hard," Hanson said. "They just wanted the shows to be realistic in their own context, and you can't be realistic if there's a television show version of you in your own past."

"I hate that we now have conversations like this," Hester said.

"I don't think any of us like it," Dahl said.

"I don't know. I think it's interesting," Duvall said.

"It would be interesting if we were sitting in a dorm room, getting stoned," Hester said. "Talking about it seriously after our friend has died sort of takes the *fun* out of it."

"You're still angry about Finn," Hanson said.

"Of course I am," Hester spat. "Aren't you?"

"I recall you and him not getting along when you came on the *Intrepid*," Dahl said.

"I didn't say I always *liked* him," Hester said. "But we got better with each other while we were here. And he was one of us. I'm angry about what happened to him."

"I'm still pissed at him for knocking me out with that pill," Duvall said. "And I feel guilty about it, too. If he hadn't done that, he might still be alive."

"And you might be dead," Dahl pointed out.

"Not if I wasn't written to die in the episode," Duvall said.

"But Finn *was* written into the episode," Hanson said. "He was always going to be there. He was always going to be in that room when that bomb went off."

"Remember when I said I hated the conversations we have these days?" Hester said. "Just now? This is *exactly* the sort of conversation I'm talking about."

"Sorry," Duvall said.

"Jimmy, you said that whenever the show started, it created a new timeline," Dahl said, and ignored Hester throwing up his hands helplessly. "Do we know when that happened?"

"You think that might help us?" Hanson asked.

"I'm just curious," Dahl said. "We're an alternate timeline from 'reality,' whatever that is. I'd like to know when that branching off happened."

"I don't think we can know," Hanson said. "There's nothing that would signal where that timeline twist happened because from our perspective there's never been a break. We don't have any alternate timelines to

195

compare ourselves to. We can only see our timeline."

"We could just start looking for when completely ridiculous shit started happening in our universe," Hester said.

"But define 'completely ridiculous shit,' " Duvall said. "Does space travel count? Contact with alien races? Does quantum physics count? Because I don't understand that crap at all. As far as I'm concerned, quantum physics could have been written by a hack."

"The first science fiction television show I found information about was something called *Captain Video,* and that was in 1949," Hanson said. "The first *Star Trek* show was twenty years after that. So, probably this show was made sometime between the late 1960s and the end of television broadcasting in 2105."

"That's a lot of time to cover," Dahl said.

"Assuming that *Star Trek* actually *exists,*" Hester said. "There are all sorts of entertainment programs today that exist only in our timeline. The timeline we exist in could go back before this *Star Trek* show was actually made, and it exists in this timeline basically to *taunt* us."

"Okay, now, *that* is recursive and meta," Duvall said.

"I think that's probably what it is," Hester said. "We've already established whoever is writing us is an asshole. This sounds like just the sort of thing an asshole writer would do."

"I have to give you that," Duvall said.

"This timeline sucks," Hester said.

"Andy," Hanson said, and motioned away from the table. A cargo cart was rolling up to the table they were sitting at. Inside of it was a note. Dahl took the note; the cargo cart rolled away.

"A note from Jenkins?" Duvall asked.

"Yeah," Dahl said.

"What does it say?" Duvall asked.

"It says he thinks he's come up with something that might work," Dahl said. "He wants to talk to us about it. All of us."

CHAPTER FOURTEEN

"I want to warn you that this sounds like a crazy idea," Jenkins said.

"I'm amazed you feel the need to say that anymore," Hester said.

Jenkins nodded, as if to say, *Point.* Then he said, "Time travel."

"Time travel?" Dahl said.

Jenkins nodded and fired up his holographic display, showing the timeline of the *Intrepid* and the tentacles branching down, signifying the collection of episodes. "Here," he said, pointing to a branching node of tendrils. "In the middle of what I think was this show's fourth season, Abernathy, Q'eeng and Hartnell took a shuttle and aimed it toward a black hole, using its gravity-warping powers to go backward in time."

"That makes no sense at all," Dahl said.

"Of course it doesn't," Jenkins said. "It's yet another violation of physics caused by the Narrative. The point is not that they violated physics in a nonsensical way. The point is they went back in time. And they went back in time to a specific time. A specific year. They went back to 2010."

"So?" Hester said.

"So, I think the reason they went back to that year was because that was the current year of this show's production," Jenkins said.

"Science fiction shows had their people going back in time all the time," Hanson said. "They were always having them meet famous historical people or take part in important events."

Jenkins pointed his finger excitedly at Hanson. "But that's just *it*," he said. "If a show goes back to a specific time in its actual past, they'll usually key it to a specific important historical person or event, because they have to give the audience something it knows about history, or else it won't care. But if the show goes back to the *present*, then it doesn't do that. It just shows that time and the characters reacting to it. It's a dramatic irony thing."

"So if the show just has them wandering around a past time, if they meet someone famous, it's the past, but if they don't, it's the present," Duvall said. "Their present."

"More or less," Jenkins said.

"That's some great show trivia," Duvall said, "but what does it have to do with us?"

"If we go back to the present, we can find a way to stop it," Dahl said suddenly.

Jenkins smiled and touched his nose.

Duvall looked at the two of them, not quite getting it. "Explain this to me, Andy," she said, "because right now it just looks like you and Jenkins are sharing a crazy moment."

"No, this makes sense," Dahl said. "We know when the present is for the show. We know how to time travel to get back to the show's present. We go back to the present, we can stop the people who are making the show."

"If we stop the show, then *everything* stops," Hester said.

"No," Dahl said. "When the Narrative doesn't need us, we still exist. And this timeline existed before the Narrative started intruding on it." He paused, and turned to Jenkins. "Right?"

"Maybe," Jenkins said.

"*Maybe?*" Hester said, suddenly very concerned.

"There's actually an interesting philosophical argument about whether this timeline exists independently, and the Narrative accesses it, or whether the creation of the

Narrative also created this timeline, causing its history to appear instantly even if to us on the inside it appears that the passage of time has actually occurred," Jenkins said. "It's very much a corollary to the Strong Anthropic Principle —"

"Jenkins," Dahl said.

"— but we can talk about that some other time," Jenkins said, getting the hint. "The point is, yes, whether it existed before the Narrative or was created by it, this timeline now exists and is persistent even when the Narrative does not impose itself."

"Okay," Hester said.

"Probably," Jenkins said.

"I really want to throw things at him," Hester said to Dahl.

"I'm going to vote for the idea we exist and will continue to exist even when this show stops," Dahl said. "Because otherwise we're all doomed anyway. All right?"

No one offered a disagreement.

"In which case, to get back to what I was saying, if we go back in time and stop the show, then the *Intrepid* stops being a focus of the Narrative," Dahl said. "It goes back to just being a ship. We stop being glorified extras in our own lives."

"So we won't die," Duvall said.

"Everybody dies," Jenkins said.

"Thank you for that news flash," Duvall said, irritated. "I mean we won't die just to give an audience a thrill."

"Probably not," Jenkins said.

"If we really are in a television series, then it's going to be hard to stop," Hanson said, and looked to Dahl. "Andy, a really successful television series could be worth a lot of money, just like a good drama series today can be. It's not just the show, it's everything around it, including things like merchandising."

"Your boyfriend has an action figure," Hester said to Duvall.

"Yeah, and you *don't,*" Duvall shot back. "In this universe that's a problem."

"I'm saying that even if we do travel back in time and find the people making this show, we might not be able to stop it," Hanson said. "There might be too much money involved."

"What other option do we have?" Dahl said. "If we stay here, the only thing to do is wait for the Narrative to kill us off. We might have a slim chance of stopping the show, but a slim chance there is better than a certainty of a dramatic death here."

"Why even bother trying to stop the show?" Hester said. "Look, if we really are extras, then we're not actually needed here.

I say we go back in time and just stay there."

"Do you really want to live in the early twenty-first century?" Duvall asked. "It wasn't exactly the most cheerful time to be alive. It's not like they had a cure for cancer then."

"Whatever," Hester said.

"Or baldness," Duvall said.

"This is my original hair," Hester said.

"You can't stay in the past," Jenkins said. "If you do, you'll dissolve."

"What?" Hester said.

"It has to do with conservation of mass and energy," Jenkins said. "All the atoms you're using now are being used in the past. If you stay in the past, then the atoms have to be in two places at the same time. This creates an imbalance and the atoms have to decide where to be. And eventually they'll choose their then-present configuration because technically speaking, you're from the future, so you don't actually exist yet."

"What's 'eventually' here?" Dahl asked.

"About six days," Jenkins said.

"That's completely idiotic!" Hester said.

"I don't make up the rules," Jenkins said. "It's just how it worked last time. It makes sense in the Narrative, though — it gave Abernathy, Q'eeng and Hartnell a reason to get their mission done in a certain, dramatic amount of time."

"This timeline sucks," Hester said.

"If you brought atoms forward, they would have the same problem," Jenkins said. "And in that case they'd choose the present, which means the thing from the past would dissolve. It's a pretty problem, actually. Mind you, that's just one of your problems."

"What else is there?" Dahl asked.

"Well, you'll need to acquire a shuttle, which will be no small matter," Jenkins said. "It's not like they'll let you borrow one for a lazy excursion. But that's not actually the hard part."

"What's the hard part?" Duvall asked.

"You're going to have to get one of the five stars of the show to come with you," Jenkins said. "Take your pick: Abernathy, Q'eeng, West, Hartnell or Kerensky."

"What do we need one of them for?" Hester asked.

"You said it yourself," Jenkins said. "You're extras. If *you* try to aim a shuttle at a black hole, you know what will happen? The gravitational forces will rip apart the shuttle, you'll spaghettify into a long stream of atoms sucking down to the singularity, and you'll die. You'll be dead long before the spaghettification, of course. That's the end event for you. But you get my point."

"And that won't happen if we have one of the main characters in the show," Dahl said.

"No, because the Narrative needs them for later," Jenkins said. "So in that case when you zoom toward a black hole you'll switch over to Narrative physics."

"And we're *sure* main characters never die," Hester said.

"Oh, they can die," Jenkins said, and Hester gave him another look like he wanted to punch him. "But not like *this*. When a main character dies they'd make a big deal out of it. The idea that the Narrative would let one of them die on a mission to go back in time to stop their own show from being made just doesn't seem very likely in the grand scheme of things."

"It's nice at least *something* is unlikely at this point," Hester said.

"So, to recap," Dahl said. "Kidnap a senior officer, steal a shuttle, fly dangerously close to a black hole, go back in time, find the people making the show, stop them from making it anymore, and then come back to our own time before our atoms divorce us and we disintegrate."

"That's what I've got for you, yes," Jenkins said.

"It's a little crazy," Dahl said.

"I told you that going in," Jenkins reminded him.

"And you didn't disappoint," Dahl said.

"So what do we do now?" Duvall asked.

"I think we have to work the problem a step at a time," Dahl said. "And the first step is: How do we get that shuttle?"

Dahl's phone rang. It was Science Officer Q'eeng, ordering him to the senior officer briefing room.

"The religious war on Forshan is heating up," Q'eeng said, with Captain Abernathy nodding beside him. "The Universal Union is trying to negotiate a cease-fire, but we're limited by a lack of live translators. Our diplomatic team has computer translators, of course, but they only translate the first dialect with any accuracy and even then it lacks the ability to handle idiom. We run the risk of unintentionally offending the Forshan at the worst possible time."

"Q'eeng here tells me you speak all four dialects," Abernathy said.

"That's correct, sir," Dahl said.

"Then there's no time to lose," Abernathy said. "We need you to go to Forshan immediately and start acting as a translator for our diplomats."

"Yes, sir," Dahl said, and felt a chill. *It's*

come for me, he thought. *The Narrative has finally come for me. Just as we figured out how to stop it.* "How long until the *Intrepid* reaches Forshan?" he asked.

"The *Intrepid* isn't," Q'eeng said. "We have a mission to the Ames system which can't be put off. You'll have to go yourself."

"How?" Dahl asked.

"You'll be taking a shuttle," Q'eeng said.

Dahl burst out laughing.

"Ensign Dahl, are you all right?" Q'eeng asked, after a moment.

"Sorry, sir," Dahl said. "I was embarrassed that I asked such an obvious question. When do I leave?"

"As soon as we assign a shuttle pilot for you," Abernathy said.

"If I may beg the captain's indulgence, I would like to select my own pilot," Dahl said. "In fact, it might be best if I selected my own team for this mission."

Abernathy and Q'eeng both frowned. "I'm not sure you need an entire away team for this mission," Q'eeng said.

"Respectfully, sir, I do," Dahl said. "As you note, this is a critical mission. I am one of the few humans who can speak all four Forshan dialects, so I expect I will be used exhaustively by our diplomats. I will need my own team for errands and to send communiqués between diplomatic teams. I'll also need to retain the pilot and shuttle in case I am called to travel on Forshan itself, between those diplomatic teams."

"How large of a team do you need?" Q'eeng asked.

Dahl paused and looked up, as if thinking. "A pilot and two aides should probably do it," he said.

Q'eeng looked at Abernathy, who nodded. "Fine," Q'eeng said. "But ensign rank and below only."

"I have just the people in mind," Dahl said. "Although I wonder if it might be useful to have a senior officer on the team as well."

"Such as?" Abernathy asked.

"Lieutenant Kerensky," Dahl said.

"I'm not sure how an astrogator would be of much use on this mission, Ensign," Q'eeng said. "We do try to have away team members have relevant skills."

Dahl paused ever so slightly at this but then moved on. "Then perhaps you, sir," he said to Q'eeng. "You have some familiarity with the Forshan language, after all."

"I know what this is about," Abernathy said.

Dahl blinked. "Sir?" he said.

"I know what this is about," Abernathy

repeated. "You were with me on the *Nantes,* Dill."

"Dahl," said Dahl.

"Dahl," Abernathy said. "You were there when your friend was killed when that madman tried to assassinate me. You saw firsthand the risks of an away team. Now you're being asked to lead an away team and you're worried about the responsibility, you're worried about someone dying on your watch."

"I'm pretty sure it's not that," Dahl said.

"I'm telling you not to worry about that," Abernathy said, not hearing Dahl. "You're an officer, Dill. Dahl. Sorry. You're an officer and you've been trained to lead. You don't need me or Q'eeng or Kerensky to tell you what you already know. Just do it. I believe in you, damn it."

"You're very inspiring, sir," Dahl said, after a moment.

"I see good things for you, Ensign," Abernathy said. "It wouldn't surprise me one day to have you as one of my senior staff."

"I should live so long," Dahl said.

"So," Abernathy said. "Assemble your team, brief them and have them ready to go in four hours. Think you can handle that?"

"I do, sir," Dahl said. "Thank you, sir."

He stood and saluted. Abernathy returned the salute. Dahl nodded to Q'eeng and then left as quickly as he could, and then called Hester as soon as he was ten steps away from the briefing room.

"So what happened?" Hester asked.

"Our schedule just got drastically tightened," Dahl said. "Listen, do you still have Finn's effects?"

"Are you talking about the same effects I think you're talking about?" Hester asked, carefully.

"Yeah," Dahl said.

"Then yes," Hester said. "It would have been awkward to hand them over."

"Find a small blue oblong effect," Dahl said. "And then meet me at Maia's barracks. As quickly as you can."

CHAPTER FIFTEEN

Three hours and thirty minutes later, Dahl knocked on the door of Lieutenant Kerensky's private berth. Hester and Hanson were behind him, storage crate and cargo cart in tow.

The berth door slid open and Duvall was inside. "For God's sake, get in here," she said.

Dahl looked into the berth. "We're not all going to fit in there," he said.

"Then *you* get in here," she said. "And bring the crate." She looked at Hester and Hanson. "You two try to look like you're not doing something that will get us shot."

"Swell," Hester said. Dahl pushed the storage crate into the berth, followed it and then closed the door behind him.

Inside was Lieutenant Kerensky, pantless and passed out.

"You couldn't put his pants back on him?" Dahl asked.

"Andy, the next time *you* want to drug into unconsciousness the person you're screwing, you can do it the way you want to," Duvall said. "Which reminds me to reiterate that this is definitely a 'you owe me a fuck' level of favor."

"That's ironic, considering," Dahl said, nodding in the direction of Kerensky.

"Very funny," Duvall said.

"How long has he been out?" Dahl asked.

"Not even five minutes," Duvall said. "It was completely unbelievable. I tried to get him to have a drink with me first — I put that little pill in his tumbler — but he just wanted to get at it. I could tell you what I had to do to get him to take a drink, but that's more about me than I think you want to know."

"I'm trying to imagine what that could even mean and I have to tell you I'm drawing a blank," Dahl said.

"It's better that way," Duvall said. "Anyway. He's out now and if I'm any indication of how effective these little pills are, he'll be down for several hours at least."

"Good," Dahl said. "Let's get to work." Duvall nodded and stripped Kerensky's bunk, lining the bottom of the crate with the sheets and blanket.

"Will he have enough air?" she asked.

"It's not airtight," Dahl said. "But maybe you should put his pants back on him now."

"Not yet," Duvall said.

"I'm not sure where this is leading," Dahl said.

"Shut up and let's get him into this thing," Duvall said.

Five minutes later, Dahl and Duvall had contorted Kerensky into the storage crate. Duvall took Kerensky's pants and jacket and stuffed them into a duffel bag.

"Where's his phone?" Dahl asked. Duvall grabbed it off Kerensky's desk and tossed it to Dahl, who opened up the text messaging function, typed a note and sent it. "There," he said. "Kerensky just sent a note that he is on sick leave for his next shift. It'll be twelve hours at least before anyone comes looking for him."

"Poor bastard," Duvall said, looking at the crate. "I do feel bad about this. He's dim and self-centered, but he's not really a bad guy. And he's decent enough in the cot."

"Don't need to know," Dahl said.

"Prude," Duvall said.

"You can make it up to him later," Dahl said, and opened the door, on the other side of which stood Hester.

"Thought you guys had started up a game of Parcheesi in there," he said.

"Don't you start," Duvall said. "Let's get him up on that cart."

A few minutes later, the four of them and their unconscious cargo were at the door of the shuttle bay.

"Get the shuttle ready," Dahl said to Hester, then turned to Hanson and Duvall. "And get the cargo into the shuttle as quietly as possible, please."

"Look who's all authoritative now," Duvall said.

"For now let's just pretend you actually respect my authority," Dahl said.

"Where are you going?" Hanson asked.

"I have one more quick stop to make," Dahl said. "Have to pick up some extra supplies." Hanson nodded and backed the cargo cart into the shuttle bay, Duvall and Hester following. Dahl walked until he found a quiet cargo tunnel and quietly opened the access door to it.

Jenkins was on the other side.

"You know that's creepy," Dahl said.

"I'm trying not to waste your time," Jenkins said. He held up a briefcase. "The leftovers from that mission Abernathy, Q'eeng and Hartnell went on," he said. "Phones and money. The phones will work with that era's communication and information networks. Those networks will be slow and rudimentary. Be patient with them. The money is physical money, which they still use where you're going."

"Will they be able to tell it's not real?" Dahl asked.

"They couldn't last time," Jenkins said.

"How much is in there?" Dahl asked.

"About ninety-three thousand dollars," Jenkins said.

"Is that a lot?" Dahl asked.

"It'll be enough to get you through six days," Jenkins said. Dahl took the suitcase and turned to go.

"One other thing," Jenkins said, and then handed him a small box.

Dahl took it. "You really want me to do this," he said.

"I'm not going with you," Jenkins said. "So you have to do it for me."

"I may not have time," Dahl said.

"I know," Jenkins said. "If you have time."

"And it won't last," Dahl said. "You know it won't."

"It doesn't have to last," Jenkins said. "It just has to last long enough."

"All right," Dahl said.

"Thanks," Jenkins said. "And now I think you better get off the ship as soon as you can. Leaving that note from Kerensky was smart, but don't tempt fate any more than you have to. You're already tempting it enough."

"You can't do this to me," Kerensky said, in a muffled fashion, from inside the crate. He had woken up five minutes earlier, after sleeping more than ten hours. Hester had been taunting him since.

"That's a funny thing to say," Hester said, "considering where you are."

"Let me out," Kerensky said. "That's an order."

"You keep saying funny things," Hester said. "From *inside a crate.* Which you can't escape from."

There was a moment of silence at that.

"Where are my pants?" Kerensky asked, plaintively.

Hester glanced over at Duvall. "I'm going to let you field that one," he said. Duvall rolled her eyes.

"I really have to pee," Kerensky said. "Really bad."

Duvall sighed. "Anatoly," she said. "It's me."

"Maia?" Kerensky said. "They got you too. Don't worry. I won't let these bastards do anything to you. Do you hear me, you sons of bitches?"

Hester looked over to Dahl disbelievingly.

Dahl shrugged.

"Anatoly," Maia said, more forcefully. "They didn't get me too."

"What?" Kerensky said. Then, after a minute, *"Oh."*

" 'Oh,' " Duvall agreed. "Now, listen, Anatoly. I'm going to open up the crate and you can come out, but I really need you not to be stupid or to panic. Do you think you can do that?"

There was a pause. "Yes," Kerensky said.

"Anatoly, that little pause you just did suggests to me that what you're really planning to do is something stupid as soon as we uncrate you," Duvall said. "So just to be sure, two of my friends here have pulse guns trained on you. If you do anything particularly idiotic, they'll just blast you. Do you understand?"

"Yes," Kerensky said, sounding somewhat more resigned.

"Okay," Duvall said. She walked over to the crate.

" 'Pulse guns'?" Dahl asked. No one had pulse guns with them. It was Duvall's turn to shrug.

"You know he's lying," Hester said.

"That's why I have his pants," Duvall said, and started unlatching the hinges.

Kerensky burst out of the crate, rolled,

spied the door and sprinted toward it, flinging it open and throwing himself through it. Everyone else in the room watched him go.

"What do we do now?" Hanson asked.

"Window," Dahl said. They stood up and walked toward the window, cranking the louvers so they were open to the outside.

"This should be good," Hester said.

Thirty seconds later Kerensky burst into view, running into the street, whereupon he stopped, utterly confused. A car honked at him to get out of the way. He backed up onto the sidewalk.

"Anatoly, come back in," Duvall said through the window. "For God's sake, you're not wearing pants."

Kerensky turned around, following her voice. "This isn't a ship," he yelled up to the window.

"No, it's the Best Western Media Center Inn and Suites," Duvall said. "In Burbank."

"Is that a planet?" Kerensky yelled. "What system is it in?"

"Oh, for Christ's sake," Hester muttered. "You're on *Earth,* you moron," he yelled at Kerensky.

Kerensky looked around disbelievingly. "Was there an apocalypse?" he yelled.

Hester looked at Duvall. "You actually have sex with this imbecile?"

218

"Look, he's had a rough day," Duvall said, and then turned her attention to Kerensky. "We went back in time, Anatoly," she said. "It's the year 2012. This is what it looks like. Now come back inside."

"You drugged me and kidnapped me," Kerensky said, accusingly.

"I know, and I'm really sorry about that," Duvall said. "I was kind of in a rush. But listen, you have to come back inside. You're half-naked. Even in 2012, you can get arrested for that. You don't want to get arrested in 2012, Anatoly. It's not a nice time to be in jail. Come back inside, okay? We're in room 215. Just take the stairs."

Kerensky looked around, looked down at his pantless lower half, and then sprinted back into the Best Western.

"I'm not rooming with him," Hester said. "I just want to be clear on that."

A minute later there was a knock on the door. Hanson went to open it. Kerensky strode into the room.

"First, I want my pants," Kerensky said.

Everyone turned to Duvall, who gave everyone a *what?* expression and then pulled Kerensky's pants out of her duffel and threw them at him.

"Second," Kerensky said, fumbling into his pants, "I want to know why we're here."

"We're here because we landed and hid the shuttle in Griffith Park, and this was the closest hotel," Hester said. "And it was a good thing it was so close, because your crated ass was *not* light."

"I don't mean the *hotel*," Kerensky spat. "I mean here. On Earth. In 2012. In *Burbank*. Someone needs to explain this to me *now*."

This time everyone turned to Dahl.

"Oh," he said. "Well, it's complicated."

"Eat something, Kerensky," Duvall said, pushing the remains of the pizza at him. They were in a booth at the Numero Uno Pizza down the street from the Best Western. Kerensky was now wearing pants.

Kerensky barely glanced at the pizza. "I'm not sure it's safe," he said.

"They did have food laws in the twenty-first century," Hanson said. "Here in the United States, anyway."

"I'll pass," Kerensky said.

"Let him starve," Hester said, and reached for the last piece. Kerensky's hand shot out and he grabbed it.

"Got it," Dahl said, and turned his phone — his twenty-first-century phone — around, showing the article to the rest of them. " '*Chronicles of the Intrepid.*' " He turned the phone back around to him. "Shows every Friday at nine on something called the Corwin Action Network, which is apparently something called a 'basic cable channel.' It started in 2007, which means it's now in its sixth season."

"This is completely ridiculous," Kerensky said, around his pizza.

Dahl looked over to him, and then pressed the screen to open up another article. "And playing Lieutenant Anatoly Kerensky on *Chronicles of the Intrepid* is an actor named Marc Corey," he said, flipping the screen around to show Kerensky the picture of a smiling doppelgänger in a stylish blazer and open-collared dress shirt. "Born in 1985 in Chatsworth, California. I wonder if that's anywhere near here."

Kerensky grabbed the phone and read the article sullenly. "This doesn't prove anything," he said. "We don't know how accurate any of this information is. For all we know, this" — he scrolled up on the phone screen to find a label — "this Wikipedia information database here is compiled by complete idiots." He handed back the phone.

"We could try to track down this Corey fellow," Hanson said.

"I want to try someone else first," Dahl

221

said, and started poking at his phone again. "If Marc Corey is a regular on a show, he's probably going to be hard to get to. I think we should probably aim lower."

"What do you mean?" Duvall said.

"I mean, I think we should start with me," Dahl said, and then turned the phone around again, to a picture of what appeared to be his own face. "Meet Brian Abnett."

Dahl's friends looked at the picture. "It's a little unsettling, isn't it?" Hanson said, after a minute. "Looking at a picture of someone who is exactly like you but isn't."

"No kidding," Dahl said. "Of course, you all have your own people, too."

At that, the rest of them started to power up their own phones.

"What does Wikipedia say about *him*?" Kerensky sneered. He did not have his own phone.

"Nothing," Dahl said. "He apparently doesn't meet the standard. I followed the link on the *Chronicles of the Intrepid* page to a database called IMDB, which had information about the actors on the series. He has a page there."

"So how do we contact him?" Duvall said.

"It doesn't have contact information on that page," Dahl said. "But let me put his name in the search field."

"I just found myself," Hanson said. "I'm some guy named Chad."

"I knew a Chad once," Hester said. "He used to beat me up."

"I'm sorry," Hanson said.

"It wasn't *you,*" Hester said. "Either of you."

"He has his own page," Dahl said.

"Chad?" Hanson asked.

"No, Brian Abnett," Dahl said. He scrolled through the page until he found a tab that said 'Contact.' " Dahl pressed it and an address popped up.

"It's for his agency," Dahl said.

"Wow, actors had agents even then," Duvall said.

"Even *now,* you mean," Dahl said, and pressed his screen again. "His agency is only a couple of miles from here. We can walk it."

"What are we going to do when we get there?" Duvall asked.

"I'm going to get his address from them," Dahl said.

"You think they'll give it you?" Hester asked.

"Of course they will," Dahl said. "I'm him."

Chapter Sixteen

"Okay, I see him," Duvall said, pointing up Camarillo Street. "He's the one on the bicycle."

"Are you sure?" Dahl asked.

"I know what you look like, even wearing a bicycle helmet," Duvall said. "Trust me."

"Now, remember not to freak him out," Dahl said. He had on a baseball cap he had bought and was holding a copy of the day's *Los Angeles Times* in his hand. The two of them were standing in front of the condominium complex Brian Abnett lived in.

"You're telling *me* not to freak him out," she said. "You're the one who's his clone."

"I don't want him freaking out *until* he sees me," Dahl said.

"Don't worry, I'm good with men," Duvall said. "Now go stand over there and try not to look . . ." She paused.

"Try not to look what?" asked Dahl.

"Try not to look so clone-y," Duvall said.

"At least not for a couple more minutes." Dahl grinned, stepped back and raised his newspaper.

"Hey," Dahl heard Duvall say a minute later. He peeked over the top of the newspaper just enough to see her walk up to Brian Abnett, who was getting off his bike and unlatching his helmet.

"Hey," Abnett said, and then took another look at her. "Wait, don't tell me," he said, smiling. "We've worked together."

"Maybe," Duvall said, coyly.

"Recently," Abnett said.

"Maybe," Duvall said again.

"That hemorrhoid cream commercial," Abnett said.

"No," Duvall said, flatly.

"Wait!" Abnett said, pointing. "*Chronicles of the Intrepid.* A few months ago. You and I did that scene together where we were being chased by killer robots. Tell me I'm right."

"It's very close to what I remember," Duvall said.

"Thank you," Abnett said. "I hate it when I forget people I've worked with. You're still doing work with them, right? I think I've seen you around the set since then."

"You could say so," Duvall said. "What about you?"

"I've got a small character arc on the show," Abnett said. "It's only been a few shots through the season, and of course they're killing off my character a couple of episodes from now, but until then it's nice work." He motioned at the condominium building. "Means I get to stay here through the year, anyway."

"So they're going to kill you off?" Duvall asked. "You're sure about that?"

"That's what the agent tells me," Abnett said. "She says they're still writing the episode, but it's pretty much a done deal. Which is fine, since she wants to put me up for a couple of film roles and staying on *Intrepid* will just get in the way of that."

"Sad about the character, though," Duvall said.

"Well, that's science fiction television for you, though," Abnett said. "Someone's got to be the red shirt."

"The what?" Duvall said.

"The red shirt," Abnett said. "You know, in the original *Star Trek,* they always had Kirk and Bones and Spock and then some poor dude in a red shirt who got vaporized before the first commercial. The moral of the story was not to wear a red shirt. Or go on away missions when you're the only one whose name isn't on the opening credits."

"Ah," Duvall said.

"You never watched *Star Trek*?" Abnett asked, smiling.

"It was a little before my time," Duvall said.

"So what brings you to my neighborhood, uh . . . ," Abnett said.

"Maia," Duvall said.

"Maia," Abnett repeated. "You aren't looking at the condo that's for sale in the building, are you? I probably shouldn't say this, but I think you might want to look at other places. The last guy in that condo I'm pretty sure was making meth in the bathtub. It's a miracle the entire building didn't go up."

"Oh, I won't be staying for very long," Duvall said. "Actually, I came looking for you."

"Really," Abnett said, with an expression that flickered between being flattered that an attractive woman came looking for him, and worry that the woman, who might be crazy, knew where he lived.

Duvall read the flicker of expression perfectly. "I'm not stalking you," she assured Abnett.

"Okay, that's a relief," Abnett said.

Duvall motioned with her head toward Dahl, still semi-obscured by the hat and newspaper. "In fact, my friend over there is a big fan of yours and he just wanted to meet you for a second. If that's okay. It would really make his day."

"Yeah, okay, sure," Abnett said, still looking at Duvall. "What's your friend's name?"

"Andy Dahl," Duvall said.

"Really?" Abnett said. "That's so weird. That's actually the name of my character on *Chronicles of the Intrepid.*"

"That's why he wants to meet you," Duvall said.

"And it's not the only thing we share in common," Dahl said. He walked up to Abnett, took off the cap and dropped the *Times.* "Hello, Brian. I'm you. In red shirt form."

"I'm still having trouble with this," Abnett said. He was sitting in the Best Western suite with the crew members of the *Intrepid.* "I mean, really really *really* having trouble with this."

"You think *you're* having trouble," Hester said. "Think about us. At least you're not *fictional.*"

"Do you know how unreal this is?" Abnett said.

"We've been living with this for a while now, yes," Dahl said.

228

"So you understand why I'm freaking out about it," Abnett said.

"We could do another freckle check if you like," Dahl said, referring to the moment, shortly after he introduced himself, where Abnett checked every visible freckle, mole and blemish on both of them to confirm that they matched exactly.

"No, I've just got to sit with this," Abnett said. Hester looked over to Dahl, quickly to Abnett and then back to Dahl, conveying the message *The other you is a flake* with his expression. Dahl shrugged. Actors were actors.

"You know what convinces me that you might be telling the truth," Abnett said.

"The fact you're sitting in a room with an exact copy of yourself?" Hester said.

"No," Abnett said. "Well, yes. *That.* But what's really helping me wrap my head around the idea you're telling the truth is *him.*" Abnett pointed at Kerensky.

"Me?" Kerensky said, surprised. "Why me?"

"Because the real Marc Corey wouldn't be caught dead in a Best Western attempting to prank an extra whose name he can't be bothered to remember," Abnett said. "No offense, but the other you is a complete asshole."

229

"So's this one," Hester said.

"Hey," Kerensky said.

"Having another me around is hard to swallow," Abnett said, and pointed to Kerensky again. "But another one of him? That's actually easier to accept."

"You believe us, then," Duvall said.

"I don't know if I *believe* you," Abnett said. "What I do know is that this is very definitely the strangest damn thing that's ever happened to me, and I want to find out what happens next."

"So you'll help us," Dahl said.

"I *want* to help you, but I don't know if I *can* help you," Abnett said. "Look, I'm just an extra. They allow me onto the set for work, but it's not like I can bring anyone else in with me. I get a few lines with the regular cast, but otherwise we're told not to bother them. And I don't talk to the show runners or other producers at all. I couldn't get you in to see any of them if I wanted to. And even if I did, I don't think any of them would believe you. This is Hollywood. We make things up for a living. And the story you're telling is completely nuts. I tell it to anyone, they'll just throw me off the set."

"That might keep you from getting killed a couple of episodes from now," Hanson said, to Dahl.

Abnett shook his head. "No, they'll just recast the part with someone who looks enough like me to work," he said. "You'll still be killed off. Unless you stay here."

Dahl shook his head. "We expire in five days."

"Expire?" Abnett asked.

"It's complicated," Dahl said. "It involves atoms."

"Five days is not a lot of time," Abnett said. "Especially if you want to kill a show."

"Tell us something we don't know," Hester said.

"Maybe you can't help us directly," Duvall said. "But do you know someone who could? Even as an extra, you know the people who work high up the food chain."

"That's what I'm telling you," Abnett said. "I don't. I don't know anyone on the show who could move you up the ladder." His gaze rested on Kerensky, and he suddenly cocked his head. "But you know what, maybe I know someone *outside* the show who could help you."

"Why are you looking at me like that?" Kerensky asked, unsettled by Abnett's gaze.

"Are those the only clothes you have?" Abnett asked.

"I wasn't given the option of packing," Kerensky said. "Why? What's wrong with the uniform?"

"There's nothing wrong with the uniform if you're at Comic-Con, but it's not going to work for the club I'm thinking of," Abnett said.

"Which club?" Dahl asked.

"What's Comic-Con?" Kerensky asked.

"The Vine Club," Abnett said. "One of those very secret clubs mere mortals can't get into. I can't get into it. But Marc Corey rates, barely."

"Barely," Dahl said.

"That means he has first-floor access but not second-floor, and definitely not basement," Abnett said. "For second-floor you have to be the star of your own show, not part of the supporting cast. For the basement, you have to make twenty million a film and get a slice of the gross."

"I still want to know what Comic-Con is," Kerensky said.

"Later, Kerensky," Hester said. "Jesus." He turned to Abnett. "So, what? We get Kerensky to pose as Marc Corey and get into the club? What does that do?"

Abnett shook his head. "He doesn't pose as Corey. You have him go to the club and do to him what Andy here did to me. Draw him out and get him interested and maybe he will help you. I wouldn't tell him you want to kill the show, since that means he'd be out of a regular job. But otherwise maybe you can get him to introduce you to Charles Paulson. He's the show's creator and executive producer. He's the one you have to talk to. He's the one you have to convince."

"So you can get us into this club," Dahl said.

"I can't," Abnett said. "Like I said, I don't rate. But I have a friend who's a bartender there, and I got him a commercial gig last summer. Kept him from going into foreclosure. So he owes me big. He can get you in." He looked at them all, and then pointed at Kerensky. "Well, get *him* in." He pointed at Duvall next. "And maybe her, too."

"You keep your friend from losing his house, and he lets two people into a club, and these are equal favors?" Hester said.

"Welcome to Hollywood," Abnett said.

"We'll take it," Dahl said. "And thank you, Brian."

"Happy to help," Brian said. "I mean, I've sort of become attached to you. Seeing that you're actually real and all."

"I'm glad to hear that," Dahl said.

"Can I ask you a question?" Abnett said.

"Sure," Dahl said.

"The future," Abnett said. "It really is like it is on the show?"

"The future really is like it is on the show," Dahl said. "But I don't know if it's really the future."

"But this is your past," Abnett said. "We're part of your past. The year 2012, I mean."

"2012 is in our past, but not *this* 2012," Dahl said. "There's no *Chronicles of the Intrepid* television show in our past. It doesn't exist in our timeline."

"So that means that *I* might not exist in your timeline," Abnett said.

"Maybe not," Dahl said.

"So you're the only part of me there," Abnett said. "The only part of me that's *ever* existed there."

"I guess that's possible," Dahl said. "Just like you're the only part of me that's ever existed here."

"Doesn't that mess with you?" Abnett asked. "Knowing that you exist, and don't exist, and are real and aren't, all at the same time?"

"Yes, and I have training dealing with deep, existential questions," Dahl said. "The way I'm dealing with it right now is this: I don't care whether I really exist or don't, whether I'm real or fictional. What I want right now is to be the person who decides my own fate. That's something I can work on. It's what I'm working on now."

"I think you might be smarter than me," Abnett said.

"That's okay," Dahl said. "I think you're better looking than me."

Abnett smiled. "I'll take that," he said. "And speaking of which, it's time to take you folks clothes shopping. Those uniforms work in the future, but here and now, they'll get you branded as geeks who don't get out of the basement enough. Do you have money?"

"We have ninety-three thousand dollars," Hanson said. "Minus seventy-eight dollars for lunch."

"I think we can work with that," Abnett said.

CHAPTER SEVENTEEN

"I hate these clothes," Kerensky said.

"You look good," Dahl said, assuring him.

"No, I don't," Kerensky said. "I look like I dressed in the dark. How did people wear this?"

"Stop whining," Duvall said. "It's not like you don't wear civvies back where we come from."

"This underwear is *itchy,*" Kerensky said, tugging.

"If I knew you were this whiny, I never would have slept with you," Duvall said.

"If I knew you were going to drug me, kidnap me and take me back to the dark ages *without my pants,* I never would have slept with *you,*" Kerensky shot back.

"Guys," Dahl said, and motioned with his eyes to the cabbie, who was studiously ignoring the weirdos in his backseat. "Not so much with the dark ages talk."

The cab, on Sunset, took a left onto Vine.

"So we're sure Marc Corey's still there, right?" Kerensky asked.

"Brian said his friend called as soon as he got there, and would call if he left," Dahl said. "Brian hasn't called me since then, so we can assume he's still in there."

"I don't think this is going to work," Kerensky said.

"It'll work," Dahl said. "I know."

"That was with your guy," Kerensky said. "This guy could be different."

"Please," Duvall said. "If he's anything like you, he'll be totally infatuated with you. It'll be like looking into a mirror he can poke."

"What is that supposed to mean?" Kerensky said.

"It means that you being fascinated with yourself isn't going to be a problem," Duvall said.

"You don't actually like me, do you?" Kerensky said, after a second.

Duvall smiled and patted his cheek. "I like you just fine, Anatoly," she said. "I really do. But right now, I need you to focus. Think of this as another away mission."

"I always get hurt on away missions," Kerensky said.

"Maybe," Duvall said. "But you always survive."

"The Vine Club," the cabbie said, pulling up to the sidewalk.

The three of them got out of the cab, Dahl pausing to pay the cabbie. From inside the club, music thumped. A line of young, pretty, studiously posed people waited outside.

"Come on," Dahl said, and walked up to the bouncer. Duvall and Kerensky followed.

"Line starts over there," the bouncer said, motioning to the pretty, posed people.

"Yes, but I was told to talk to you," Dahl said, and held out his hand with the hundred-dollar bill folded in it, like Abnett told him to do. "Mitch, right?"

Mitch the bouncer glanced down almost imperceptibly at Dahl's hand, then shook it, deftly scraping the bill out of it as he did so. "Right," Mitch said. "Talk to me, then."

"I'm supposed to tell you that these two are Roberto's friends," Dahl said, mentioning the name of Abnett's bartender friend, and nodding back to Kerensky and Duvall. "He's expecting them."

Mitch looked over at Kerensky and Duvall. If he noted Kerensky's resemblance to Marc Corey, he kept it to himself. He turned his gaze back to Dahl. "First floor only," he said. "If they try for the second floor, they're out on their ass. If they go for the basement, they're out on their ass minus teeth."

"First floor," Dahl repeated, nodding.

"And not you," Mitch said. "No offense."

"None taken," Dahl said.

Mitch motioned to Kerensky and Duvall and unlatched the rope; audible protests came from the line of pretty, posed people.

"You got this?" Dahl asked Duvall, as she walked by.

"Trust me, I got this," she said. "Stick by your phone."

"I will," Dahl said. The two of them disappeared into the dark of the Vine Club. Mitch latched the rope behind them.

"Hey," Dahl said to him. "Where can a normal human go get a drink?"

Mitch smiled at this and pointed. "Irish pub right up there," he said. "The bartender's name is Nick. Tell him I sent you."

"Thanks," Dahl said, and headed up the street.

The pub was noisy and crowded. Dahl worked his way to the bar and then fished in his pocket for money.

"Hey, Brian, right?" someone said to him.

Dahl looked up to see the bartender staring back at him, smiling.

"Finn," Dahl said.

"Nick," the bartender said.

239

"Sorry," Dahl said, after a second. "Brain freeze."

"Occupational hazard," Nick said. "You get known by your part."

"Yeah," Dahl said.

"Hey, are you all right?" Nick asked. "You seem a little" — he wiggled his hands — "dazed."

"I'm fine," Dahl said, and made the effort to smile. "Sorry. Just a little strange to see you here."

"It's the life of an actor," Nick said. "Out of work and bartending. What are you having?"

"Pick a beer for me," Dahl said.

"Brave man," Nick said.

"I trust you," Dahl said.

"Famous last words," Nick said, and then headed off to the taps. Dahl watched him working the taps and tried very hard not to freak out.

"Here you go," Nick said a minute later, handing over a pint glass. "Local microbrew. It's called a Starlet Stout."

Dahl tried it. "It's not bad," he said.

"I'll tell the brew master you said so," Nick said. "You might remember him. The three of us were in a scene together. He got killed by a swarm of robots."

"Lieutenant Fischer," Dahl said

"That's the one," Nick said, and nodded at Dahl's glass. "Real name is Jake Klein. His microbrewery's taking off, though. He's mostly doing that now. I'm thinking of joining him."

"And stop being an actor?" Dahl said.

Nick shrugged. "It's not like they're tearing down the doors to get at me," he said. "I've been out here nine years now and that gig on *Intrepid* was the best thing I've gotten so far, and it wasn't all that great. I got killed by an exploding head."

"I remember," Dahl said.

"That was what did it for me, actually," Nick said. He started washing glasses in the bar sink to give the appearance of being busy as he talked. "We did ten takes of that scene. Every time we did it I had to toss myself backward like there was an actual explosion. And around take seven I thought to myself, 'I'm thirty years old and what I'm doing with my life is pretending to die on a TV show that I wouldn't watch if I wasn't on it.' At a certain point you have to ask yourself why you do it. I mean, why do *you* do it?"

"Me?" Dahl asked.

"Yeah," Nick said.

"I do it because for a long time I didn't know I had a choice," Dahl said.

"That's just it, though," Nick said. "You do. You still on the show?"

"For now," Dahl said.

"But they're going to kill you off too," Nick said.

"In a couple of episodes," Dahl said. "Unless I can avoid it."

"Don't avoid it," Nick said. "Die and then figure out the rest of your life."

Dahl smiled. "It's not as simple as that for some of us," he said, and took a drink.

"Mortgage, huh," Nick said.

"Something like that," Dahl said.

"C'est la vie," Nick said. "So what brings you down to Hollywood and Vine? I think you told me you were in Toluca Lake."

"I had some friends who wanted to go to the Vine Club," Dahl said.

"They didn't let you in?" Nick asked. Dahl shrugged. "You should have let me know. My friend's the bouncer there."

"Mitch," Dahl said.

"That's him," Nick said.

"He's the one who told me to come down here," Dahl said.

"Ouch," Nick said. "Sorry."

"I'm not," Dahl said. "It's really good to see you again."

Nick grinned and then went to tend to other customers.

Dahl's phone vibrated. He fished it out of his pocket and answered it.

"Where are you?" Duvall asked.

"I'm at a pub down the street," Dahl said. "Having a very weird time. Why?"

"You need to come back down here. We just got kicked out of the club," Duvall said.

"You and Kerensky?" Dahl asked. "How did that happen?"

"Not just me and Kerensky," Duvall said. "Marc Corey too. He attacked Kerensky."

"What?" Dahl said.

"We walked up to Corey in his booth, he saw Kerensky and said, 'So you're the fucker whose picture is on Gawker,' and lunged at him," Duvall said.

"What the hell is a Gawker?" Dahl asked.

"Don't ask me, it's not my century," Duvall said. "We all got thrown out and now Corey's passed out on the sidewalk. He was already drunk off his ass when we got there."

"Scrape him off the sidewalk and fish through his pockets for his valet ticket," Dahl said. "Get all of you in his car and then wait for me. I'll be there in just a couple of minutes. Try not to get yourselves arrested."

"I promise nothing," Duvall said, and hung up.

"Problem?" Nick asked. He had come

243

back up while Dahl was on the phone.

"My friends got into a fight at the Vine Club and got kicked out," Dahl said. "I need to go get them before the police arrive."

"You're having an interesting night," Nick said.

"You have no idea," Dahl said. "What do I owe you for the beer?"

Nick waved him off. "On the house," he said. "Your one good thing for the evening."

"Thank you," Dahl said, and then paused, looking at his phone and then looking up at Nick. "Would you mind if I took a picture of the two of us?"

"Now you're getting weird," Nick said, but smiled and leaned in. Dahl held the phone out and took the picture.

"Thanks," Dahl said again.

"No problem," Nick said. "Now you better go before your friends are hauled away."

Dahl hurried out.

Two minutes later he was outside the Vine Club, watching Duvall and Kerensky wrestling with Marc Corey by a black, sleek automobile, while Mitch and a valet looked on. The pretty, posed people had their phones out, taking video of it all.

"Man, what the hell is this?" Mitch asked as Dahl walked up. "Your pals are in there not ten minutes and this chump tries to wreck the place getting at them."

"Sorry about that," Dahl said.

"And this clone action is just freaky," Mitch said.

"My friends were in there to get Marc," Dahl lied, and pointed at Kerensky. "That's his public double. They use him for publicity sometimes. We heard he was getting a little rowdy and came to get him because he's got to be on set tomorrow."

"He wasn't rowdy until your friends showed up," Mitch said. "And what does that dude need a double for? He's a supporting actor on a basic cable science fiction show. It's not like he's actually *famous.*"

"You should see him at Comic-Con," Dahl said.

Mitch snorted. "He better enjoy that, then, because he's banned here," he said. "When your friend is coherent tell him that if he shows up again, he'll achieve warp speed thanks to my foot in his ass."

"I'll use those words exactly," Dahl said.

"Do that," Mitch said, and turned back to his duties.

Dahl walked over to Duvall. "What's the problem?" he asked.

"He's drunk and has no bones," Duvall said, struggling with Corey. "And he's woken up enough to argue with us."

"You can't handle a boneless drunk?" Dahl asked.

"Of course I can," Duvall said. "But you said you didn't want us to get arrested."

"A little help here would be nice," Kerensky said, as Corey's drunken hand stabbed a finger up his nose.

Dahl nodded, opened the door to the black car and pulled the front seat forward. Duvall and Kerensky got a better grip on Corey, steadied him and then hurled him into the backseat. Corey jammed in, head into the far corner of the backseat, ass in the air. He whimpered for a second and then made a flabby exhaling sound. He was out again.

"I'm not sitting with him," Kerensky said.

"No you're not," Dahl agreed, reached into the car and pulled Corey's wallet out of his pants. He held it out to Kerensky. "You're driving."

"Why am I driving?" Kerensky asked.

"Because then if we get pulled over, you're him," Dahl said.

"Right," Kerensky said, taking the wallet.

"I'll pay the valet," Duvall said.

"Tip well," Dahl said.

A minute later Kerensky figured out what "D" meant on the shift column and the four of them were driving up Vine.

"Keep to the speed limit," Dahl said.

"I have no idea where I'm going," Kerensky said.

"You're an astrogator," Duvall said.

"This is a *road,*" Kerensky said.

"Hold on," Duvall said, and pulled out her phone. "This thing's got a map function. Let me get it working." Kerensky grunted and kept driving.

"Well, we had a fun evening," Duvall said to Dahl, as she entered the address of the Best Western into her phone. "What did you do?"

"I saw an old friend," Dahl said, and showed Duvall the picture of him and Nick.

"Oh," Duvall said, taking the phone. She reached into the backseat and grabbed his hand. "Oh, Andy. You okay?"

"I'm okay," he said.

"He looks just like him," Duvall said, looking at the picture again.

"He would," Dahl said, and looked out the window.

CHAPTER EIGHTEEN

"He's slept long enough," Dahl said, nodding to Marc Corey's unconscious form on the bed. "Wake him up."

"That would mean touching him," Duvall said.

"Not necessarily," Hester said. He reached over and took one of the pillows Corey wasn't using, and then hit him on the head with it. Corey woke up with a start.

"Nicely done," Hanson said, to Hester. He nodded in acknowledgment.

Corey sat up and looked around, disoriented. "Where am I?" he asked, to no one in particular.

"In a hotel," Dahl said. "The Best Western in Burbank."

"Why am I here?" Corey said.

"You passed out at the Vine Club after you attacked a friend of mine," Dahl said. "We got you in your car and drove you here."

Corey looked down and furrowed his brow. "Where are my *pants*?" he said.

"We took them from you," Dahl said.

"Why?" Corey said.

"Because we need to talk to you," Dahl said.

"You could do that without taking my pants," Corey said.

"In a perfect world, yes," Dahl said.

Corey peered at Dahl, groggily. "I know you," he said after a minute. "You're an extra on my show." He looked at Duvall and Hanson. "So are you two." His gaze turned to Hester. "You I've never seen before."

Hester looked slightly exasperated at this. "We had a scene together," he said to Corey. "You were attacked by swarm bots."

"Dude, I have a lot of scenes with extras," Corey said. "That's why they're called 'extras.' " He turned his attention back to Dahl. "And if any of you ever want to work on the show again, you will give me my pants and my car keys, right now."

"Your pants are in the restroom," Hanson said. "Drying."

"You were so drunk you pissed yourself," Hester said.

"Besides taking your pants for discussion purposes, we figured you might not want to go into work with clothes that smelled like

249

urine," Dahl said.

Corey looked puzzled at this, glanced down at the underwear on his body, and then bent over at the waist, sniffing. Both Duvall and Hester gave up looks of mild disgust; Dahl watched impassively.

"I smell fine," Corey said.

"New underwear," Dahl said.

"Whose?" Corey said. "Yours?"

"No, mine," Kerensky said. All this time he had been sitting silently in a suite chair with its back to the bed. Now he stood and turned to face Corey. "After all, you and I are the same size."

Corey gazed up at Kerensky, dumbly. "You," he said, finally.

"Me," Kerensky agreed. "Who is also 'you.' "

"It's you I saw on Gawker yesterday," Corey said.

"I don't know what that means," Kerensky said.

"There was a video of someone who looked like me standing in the street without pants," Corey said. "Someone took the video on their phone and sent it to the Gawker Web site. Our show had to confirm I was on the set before anyone would believe it wasn't me. It was you."

"Yes, it was probably me," Kerensky said.

"Who are you?" Corey asked.

"I'm you," Kerensky said. "Or who you pretend to be, anyway."

"That doesn't make any sense," Corey said.

"Well, you talking about this Gawker thing doesn't make any sense to me, either, so we're even," Kerensky said.

"Why were you running around in the street without pants?" Corey asked.

Kerensky motioned to the others in the room. "They took my pants," he said.

"Why?" Corey asked.

"Because we needed to talk to him," Dahl said.

Corey tore his eyes away from Kerensky. "What is wrong with you people?" he asked.

"You're still here," Dahl pointed out.

But Corey was ignoring him again. He got out of the bed and walked over to Kerensky, who stood there, watching him. Corey looked him all over. "It's amazing," Corey said. "You look exactly like me."

"I *am* exactly like you," Kerensky said. "Down to the last detail."

"That's not possible," Corey said, staring into Kerensky's face.

"It's possible," Kerensky said, and stepped closer to Corey. "Take a closer look." The two of them stood an inch apart while

251

Corey examined Kerensky's body.

"Okay, *this* is getting creepy," Hester said, quietly, to Dahl.

"Marc, we need your help," Dahl said to Corey. "We need you to get us in to talk to Charles Paulson."

"Why?" Corey said, not taking his eyes off Kerensky.

"There's something about the show we need to discuss with him," Dahl said.

"He's not seeing people right now," Corey said, turning. "A month ago his son was in a motorcycle accident. Son's in a coma right now and they don't think he's going to pull through. Paulson gave his son the bike for a birthday gift. The rumor is Paulson goes to his office in the morning, sits down and stares at the walls until six o'clock and then goes home again. He's not going to see you." He turned back to Kerensky.

"We need to try," Dahl said. "And that's why we need you. He can avoid dealing with nearly everyone else, but you're a star on his show. He has to see you."

"He doesn't have to see anybody," Corey said.

"You could make him see you," Duvall said.

Corey glanced over, and then broke away from Kerensky to step over to her. "And why would I do that?" he asked. "You're right, if I threw a fit and demanded to see Paulson, he'd make time to see me. But if I saw him and wasted his time, he might kick me off the show. He might have my character killed off in some horrible way just to get a quick ratings boost out of it. And then I'd be out of a job. Do you know how hard it is to get a regular series gig in this town? I was a waiter before I got this. I'm not going to do anything for you people."

"It's important," Dahl said.

"*I'm* important," Corey said. "My career is important. It's more important than whatever *you* want."

"If you help us, we can give you money," Hanson said. "We've got ninety thousand dollars."

"That's less than what I make an episode," Corey said, and looked back toward Kerensky. "You'll have to do better than that."

Dahl opened his mouth to speak.

"I'll handle this," Kerensky said, and looked at the others. "Let me talk to Marc."

"So talk," Hester said.

"Alone," Kerensky said.

"Are you sure?" Dahl said.

"Yes," Kerensky said. "I'm sure."

"All right," Dahl said, and motioned to Duvall, Hanson and an incredulous Hester

253

to clear the room.

"Tell me I'm not the only one who thinks something *unseemly* is about to happen in there," Hester said, in the hall.

"It's only you," Dahl said.

"No it's not," Duvall said. Hanson also shook his head. "You can't tell me you weren't seeing how Corey was responding to Anatoly, Andy," Duvall said.

"I must have missed it," Dahl said.

"Right," Hester said.

"You really *are* a prude, aren't you," Duvall said to Dahl.

"I just prefer to think there is a sober, reasoned discussion going on in there and that Kerensky is making some very good points."

From the other side of the door there was a muffled *thump*.

"Yes, *that's* it," Hester said.

"I think I'm going to wait in the lobby," Dahl said.

Two hours later, as dawn broke, a tired-looking Kerensky came down to the lobby.

"Marc needs his keys," he said. "He's got a six-thirty makeup call."

Dahl dug in his pocket for the keys. "So he'll help us?" he asked.

Kerensky nodded. "He's going to put in a

call as soon as he gets to the set," he said. "He'll tell Paulson that unless he schedules a meeting today, he's going to quit."

"And just how did you manage to get him to agree to that?" Hester said.

Kerensky fixed Hester with a direct stare. "Are you actually interested?"

"Uh," Hester said. "Actually, no. No, I'm not."

"Didn't think so," Kerensky said. He took the keys from Dahl.

"I am," Duvall said.

Kerensky sighed, and turned to Duvall. "Tell me, Maia: Have you ever met someone who you know so completely, so exactly and so perfectly that it's like the two of you share the same body, thoughts and desires? And had that feeling compounded by the knowledge that how you feel about them is exactly how they feel about you, right down to the very last atom of your being? Have you?"

"Not really," Duvall said.

"I pity you," he said, and then headed back to the hotel room.

"You *had* to ask," Hester said to Duvall.

"I was curious," Duvall said. "Sue me."

"Now I have *images*," Hester said. "They are in my *mind*. They will never leave me. I blame you."

"It's certainly a side of Kerensky we

255

haven't seen before," Dahl said. "I never saw him being interested in men."

"It's not that," Hanson said.

"Did you *miss* the last couple of hours?" Hester said. "And the thumping?"

"No, Jimmy's right," Duvall said. "He's not interested in men. He's interested in himself. Always has been. Now he's gotten the chance to follow through on that."

"Ack," Hester said.

Duvall looked over at him. "Wouldn't you, if you had the chance?" she asked.

"I didn't," Dahl pointed out.

"Yes, but we already established you're a prude," Duvall said.

Dahl grinned. "Point," he said.

The elevator opened and Corey came out, followed by Kerensky. Corey walked up to Dahl. "I need your phone number," he said. "So I can call you when I set up the meeting today."

"All right," Dahl said, and gave it to him. Corey added it to his contacts and then looked at them all.

"I want you to appreciate what I'm doing for you," he said. "By getting you this meeting, I'm putting my ass on the line. So if you do anything that puts me or my career at risk, I swear I will find you and make you miserable for the rest of your lives. Are you all clear on this?"

"We're clear," Dahl said. "Thank you."

"I'm not doing it for you," Corey said, and then nodded over to Kerensky. "I'm doing it for him."

"Thank you anyway," Dahl said

"Also, if anyone asks, the reason you guys were helping me into my car last night is because I had an allergic reaction to the tannins in the wine I was drinking at the Vine Club," Corey said.

"Of course," Dahl said.

"That's the truth, you know," Corey said. "People are allergic to all sorts of things."

"Yes," Dahl said.

"You didn't see if anyone was taking video while you were putting me into the car, did you?" Corey asked.

"There might have been a couple," Dahl allowed.

Corey sighed. "Tannins. Remember it."

"Will do," Dahl said.

Corey nodded at Dahl, and then walked over to Kerensky and enveloped him in a passionate hug. Kerensky reciprocated.

"I wish we had more time," Corey said.

"So do I," Kerensky said. They hugged again and separated. Corey walked out of the lobby. Kerensky watched him go.

"Wow," Hester said. "You've got it bad,

Kerensky."

Kerensky wheeled around. "What is *that* supposed to mean?"

Hester held up his hands. "Look, I'm not judging," he said.

"Judging what?" Kerensky said, and looked at the others. "What? You all think I had *sex* with Marc?"

"Didn't you?" Duvall asked.

"We *talked,*" Kerensky said. "The most amazing conversation I have ever had with anyone in my entire life. It was like meeting the brother I never had."

"Come on, Anatoly," Hester said. "We heard *thumps.*"

"Marc was putting on his pants," Kerensky said. "I gave him back his pants, and he was still unsteady, and he fell over. That was *it.*"

"All right," Hester said. "Sorry."

"Jesus," Kerensky said, looking around. "You people. I have one of the most incredible experiences I'll *ever* have, talking with the one person who really gets me — who really *understands* me — and you're all down here thinking I'm performing some sort of time-traveling incestuous masturbation thing. Thanks so very much for crapping on my amazing, life-altering experience. You all make me sick." He stormed off.

"Well, that was interesting," Duvall said.

Kerensky stormed back in and pointed at Maia. "And we're through," he said.

"Fair enough," Duvall said. Kerensky stormed off a second time.

"I'd just like to point out that I was right," Dahl said, after a minute. Duvall walked over and smacked him on the head.

CHAPTER NINETEEN

Charles Paulson's private offices were in Burbank, off the studio lot, in a building that housed three other production companies, two agencies, a tech start-up and a nonprofit dedicated to fighting thrush. Paulson's offices filled the third floor; the group took the elevator.

"I shouldn't have eaten that last burrito," Hester said as they entered the elevator, a pained look on his face.

"I told you not to," Hanson said.

"You also said that the twenty-first century had food safety laws," Hester said.

"I don't think food safety laws are going to protect you from a third carnitas burrito," Hanson said. "That's not about food safety. It's about pork fat overload."

"I need a bathroom," Hester said.

"Can this wait?" Dahl said, to Hester. The elevator reached the third floor. "This is kind of an important meeting."

260

"If I don't find a bathroom, you're not going to want me at the meeting," Hester said. "Because what would happen would be grim."

The elevator doors opened and the five of them stepped off. Down the hallway to the right was a sign for the men's bathroom. Hester made his way toward it, quickly but stiffly, and disappeared through its door.

"How long do you think this is going to take?" Duvall asked Dahl. "Our meeting is in about a minute."

"Have you ever had a carnitas incident?" Dahl asked Duvall.

"No," Duvall said. "And from the looks of it I should be glad."

"He'll probably be in there a while," Dahl said.

"We can't wait," Kerensky said.

"No," Dahl said.

"You guys go ahead," Hanson said. "I'll stay and make sure Hester's all right. We'll wait for you in the office lobby when he's done."

"You're sure?" Dahl asked.

"I'm sure," Hanson said. "Hester and I were just going to be spectators in the meeting anyway. We can wait in the lobby just as easily, and read magazines. It's always fun to catch up on three-hundred-and-fifty-

261

year-old gossip."

Dahl smiled at this. "All right," he said. "Thanks, Jimmy."

"If Hester's intestines explode, you let us know," Duvall said.

"You'll be the first," Hanson said, and headed toward the bathroom.

The receptionist at Paulson Productions smiled warmly at Kerensky as he, Dahl and Duvall entered the office lobby. "Hello, Marc," she said. "Good to see you again."

"Uh," Kerensky said.

"We're here to see Mr. Paulson," Dahl said, stepping into Kerensky's moment of awkwardness. "We have an appointment. Marc set it up."

"Yes, of course," the receptionist said, glancing at her computer screen. "Mr. Dahl, is it?"

"That's me," Dahl said.

"Have a seat over there and I'll let him know you're here," she said, smiling at Kerensky again before picking up her handset to call Paulson.

"I think she was flirting with you," Duvall said to Kerensky.

"She thought she was flirting with Marc," Kerensky pointed out.

"Maybe there's a history there," Duvall said.

"Stop it," Kerensky said.

"Just trying to help you rebound after the breakup," Duvall said.

"Mr. Dahl, Marc, ma'am," the receptionist said. "Mr. Paulson will see you now. Follow me, please." She led them down the corridor to a large office, in which sat Paulson, behind a large desk.

Paulson looked at Kerensky, severely. "I'm supposed to be talking to these people of yours, not you," he said. "You're supposed to be at work."

"I am at work," Kerensky said.

"This is not work," Paulson said. "Your work is at the studio. On the set. If you're not there, we're not shooting. If we're not shooting, you're wasting production time and money. The studio and the Corwin are already riding me because we're behind on production this year. You're not helping."

"Mr. Paulson," Dahl said, "perhaps you should call your show and see if Marc Corey is there."

Paulson fixed on Dahl, seeing him for the first time. "You look vaguely familiar. Who are you?"

"I'm Andrew Dahl," he said, sitting on one of the chairs in front of the desk, and then motioned to Duvall, who sat on the other. "This is Maia Duvall. We work on

Intrepid."

"Then you should be on set as well," Paulson said.

"Mr. Paulson," Dahl repeated. "You should really call your show and see if Marc Corey is there."

Paulson pointed at Kerensky. "He's right *there,*" he said.

"No, he's not," Dahl said. "That's why we're here to talk to you."

Paulson's eyes narrowed. "You people are wasting my time," he said.

"Jesus," Kerensky said, exasperated. "Will you just call the damn set? Marc's *there.*"

Paulson paused to stare at Kerensky for a moment, and then picked up his desk phone and punched a button. "Yeah, hi, Judy," he said. "You on the set? . . . Yeah, okay. Tell me if you see Marc Corey there." He paused, and then looked at Kerensky again. "Okay. How long has he been there? . . . Okay. He been acting weird today? Out of character? . . . Yeah, okay. . . . No. No, I don't need to speak to him. Thanks, Judy." He hung up.

"That was my show runner, Judy Melendez," Paulson said. "She says Marc's been on set since the six-thirty makeup call."

"Thank you," Kerensky said.

"All right, I'll bite," Paulson said, to Kerensky. "Who the hell are you? Marc obviously *knows* you, or he wouldn't have set up this meeting. You could be his identical twin, but I know he doesn't have any brothers. So, what? Are you his cousin? Do you want to be on the show? Is this what this is about?"

"Do you put family members on the show?" Dahl asked.

"We don't go out of our way to advertise it, but sure," Paulson said. "A season ago I gave my uncle a part. He was about to lose his SAG insurance, so I put him in for the part of an admiral who tried to have Abernathy court-martialed. I also put in a small role for my son —" He stopped speaking, abruptly.

"We heard about your son," Dahl said. "We're very sorry."

"Thank you," Paulson said, and paused again. His demeanor had transformed from aggressive producer to something more tired and small. "Sorry," he said, after a moment. "It's been difficult."

"I can't imagine," Dahl said.

"Be glad that you can't," Paulson said, and reached over on his desk for a picture frame, looked at it, and held it in his hand. "Stupid kid. I told him to be careful handling the bike in the rain." He turned the frame briefly, showing a picture of him and a younger man, dressed in motorcycle leathers, smiling at the camera. "He never did listen to me," he said.

"Is that your son?" Duvall asked, reaching out for the frame.

"Yes," Paulson said, handing over the picture. "Matthew. He had just gotten his master's in anthropology when he tells me he wants to try being an actor. I said to him, if you wanted to be an actor, why did I just pay for you to get a master's in anthropology? But I put him on the show. He was an extra on a couple of episodes before . . . well."

"Andy," Duvall said, handing the picture to Dahl. He started at it.

Kerensky came over and looked at the picture Dahl was holding. "You have *got* to be kidding me," he said.

"What?" Paulson said, looking at the three of them. "Do you know him? Do you know Matthew?"

All three of them looked at Paulson.

"Matthew!" screamed a woman's voice, from out of the room and down the hall.

"Oh, shit," Duvall said, and launched herself out of her chair and out of the room. Dahl and Kerensky followed.

In the lobby, the receptionist had attached

herself to Hester, sobbing in joy. Hester stood there, wearing a receptionist, deeply confused.

Hanson saw his three crewmates and came over to them. "We walked into the lobby," he said. "That's all we did. We walked into the lobby, and she screams a name and then almost leaps over her desk to get at Hester. What's going on?"

"I think we found the actor who plays Hester," Dahl said.

"Okay," Hanson said. "Who is he?"

"Matthew?" Paulson said, from the hall. He had followed his three guests out of the room to find out what was going on. "Matthew! *Matthew!*" He rushed to Hester, hugged him furiously and started kissing him on the cheek.

"He's Charles Paulson's kid," Duvall said to Hanson.

"The one who's in a coma?" Hanson said.

"That's the one," Dahl said.

"Oh, wow," Hanson said. "Wow."

All three of them looked at Hester, who whispered, "Help me."

"Someone's going to have to tell them who Hester really is," Kerensky said. He, Hanson and Duvall all looked at Dahl.

Dahl sighed, and moved toward Hester.

■ ■ ■ ■

"Are you all right?" Dahl asked Hester. They were in a private hospital room, in which Matthew Paulson lay on a bed, tubes keeping him alive. Hester was staring at his comatose double.

"I'm better off than he is," Hester said.

"Hester," Dahl said, and looked out the doorway, where he was standing, to see if Charles Paulson was close enough in the hall to have heard Hester's comment. He wasn't. He was in the waiting area with Duvall, Hanson and Kerensky. Matthew Paulson could have only two visitors at a time.

"Sorry," Hester said. "I didn't mean it to be an asshole. It's just . . . well, now it all makes sense, doesn't it?"

"What do you mean?" Dahl asked.

"About me," Hester said. "You and Duvall and Hanson and Finn all are *interesting*, because you had to have interesting back-stories, so you could all get killed off in a contextual way. Finn getting killed by someone he knew, right? You, about to be killed when you go back to Forshan. But I didn't have anything unusual about me. I'm just some guy from Des Moines who had a

B minus average in high school, who joined the Dub U Fleet to see some of the universe before he came back home and stayed. Before I came on the *Intrepid* I was just another sarcastic loner.

"And now that makes sense, because I was never *meant* to do anything special, was I? I really was an extra. A placeholder character who Paulson could pour his kid into until his kid got bored with playing actor and went back to school to get a doctorate. Even the one thing I can do — pilot a shuttle — is just something that got stuck in because the show needed someone in that seat, and why not give it to the producer's kid? Make him feel *special*."

"I don't think it's like that," Dahl said.

"It's *exactly* like that," Hester said. "I'm meant to fill a spot and that's it."

"That's not true at all," Dahl said.

"No?" Hester looked up at Dahl. "What's my first name?"

"What?" Dahl asked.

"What's my first name?" Hester repeated. "You're Andy Dahl. Maia Duvall. Jimmy Hanson. Anatoly Kerensky, for Christ's sake. What's *my* first name, Andy? You don't know, do you?"

"You *have* a first name," Dahl said. "I could look on my phone and find it."

"But you don't *know* it," Hester said. "You never used it. You never call me by it. We're *friends,* and you don't even know my full name."

"I'm sorry," Dahl said. "I just never thought about calling you anything other than 'Hester.' "

"My point exactly," Hester said. "If even my *friends* never think about what my first name might be, that points out my role in the universe pretty precisely, doesn't it?" He went back to looking at Matthew Paulson, in his coma.

"So, what *is* your first name?" Dahl finally asked.

"It's Jasper," Hester said.

"Jasper," Dahl said.

"Family name," Hester said. "Jasper Allen Hester."

"Do you want me to call you Jasper from now on?" Dahl asked.

"Fuck, no," Hester said. "Who wants to be called Jasper? It's a ridiculous fucking name."

Dahl tried to stifle a laugh and failed. Hester smiled at this.

"I'll keep calling you Hester," Dahl said. "But I want you to know that inside, I'll be saying Jasper."

"If it makes you happy," Hester said.

270

"Jasper Jasper Jasper," Dahl said.

"All right," Hester said. "Enough. I'd hate to kill you in a hospital."

They returned their attention to Matthew Paulson.

"Poor kid," Hester said.

"He's your age," Duvall said.

"Yeah, but I'm likely to outlive him," Hester said. "There's a change for one of us."

"I suppose it is," Dahl said.

"That's the problem with living in the twenty-first century," Hester said. "In our world, if he got in the same accident, we could fix him. I mean, hell, Andy, think of all the horrible things that happened to you, and you survived."

"I survived because it wasn't time for me to die yet," Dahl said. "It's like Kerensky and his amazing powers of recovery. It's all thanks to the Narrative."

"Does it matter why?" Hester said. "I mean, really, Andy. If you're just about dead and you survive and are healed by entirely fictional means, do you really give a shit? No, because you're not dead. The Narrative knocks us off when it's convenient. But it's not all bad."

"You were just talking about how it all made sense you were a nobody," Dahl said.

271

"That didn't sound like you were in love with the Narrative."

"I didn't say I was," Hester said. "But I think you're forgetting that this meant I was the only one of us not absolutely fated to die horribly for the amusement of others."

"This is a good point," Dahl said.

"This show we're on, it's crap," Hester said. "But it's crap that sometimes works to our advantage."

"Until it finally kills us," Dahl said.

"Kills *you*," Hester reminded him. "*I* might survive, remember." He motioned to Matthew Paulson. "And if he lived in our world, he might have been saved, too."

Dahl was silent at this. Hester looked up at him eventually to see Dahl looking at him curiously. "What?"

"I'm thinking," Dahl said.

"About what?" Hester said.

"About using the Narrative to our advantage," Dahl said.

Hester squinted. "This involves me in some way, doesn't it," he said.

"Yes, Jasper," Dahl said. "Yes it does."

CHAPTER TWENTY

Charles Paulson opened the door to the conference room where the five of them sat, waiting, followed by another man. "Sorry about the wait," he told them, and then motioned to the other man. "You wanted to see the show's head writer, here he is. This is Nick Weinstein. I've explained to him what's going on."

"Hello," Weinstein said, looking at the five of them. "Wow. Charles really wasn't kidding."

"Now, *that's* funny," Hester said, breaking up the slack-jawed staring four of the five of them were doing.

"What's funny?" Weinstein asked.

"Mister Weinstein, were you ever an extra on your show?" Dahl asked.

"Once, a few seasons ago," Weinstein said. "We needed a warm body for a funeral scene. I happened to be on the set. They threw a costume on me and told me to act sad. Why?"

"We know the man you played," Dahl said. "His name is Jenkins."

"Really?" Weinstein said, and smiled. "What's he like?"

"He's a sad, crazed shut-in who never got over the loss of his wife," Duvall said.

"Oh," Weinstein said, and stopped smiling. "Sorry."

"You're better groomed, though," Hanson said, encouragingly.

"That's probably the first time anyone's ever said that about me," Weinstein said, motioning at his beard.

"You said you had something you wanted to talk to me and Nick about," Paulson said, to Dahl.

"I do," Dahl said. "We do. Please sit."

"Who is Jenkins?" Kerensky whispered to Dahl, as Paulson and Weinstein took their chairs.

"Later," Dahl said.

"So," Paulson said. His eyes flickered involuntarily over to Hester every few seconds.

"Mister Paulson, Mister Weinstein, there's a reason we came back to your time," Dahl said. "We came to convince you to stop your show."

"What?" Weinstein said. "Why?"

"Because otherwise we're dead," Dahl said. "Mister Weinstein, when you kill off an extra in one of your scripts, the actor playing the extra eventually walks off the set and goes to get lunch. But where we are, that person stays dead. And people are killed off in just about every episode."

"Well, not every episode," Weinstein said.

"Jimmy," Dahl said.

"*Chronicles of the Intrepid* has aired one hundred twenty-eight episodes over six seasons to date," Hanson said. "One or more *Intrepid* crew members have died in ninety-six of those episodes. One hundred twelve episodes have death portrayed in one way or another. You've killed at least four hundred *Intrepid* crew members overall in the course of the series, and when you add in episodes where you've had other ships destroyed or planets attacked or suffering from diseases, your total death count reaches into the millions."

"Not counting enemy deaths," Dahl said.

"No, those would bump up the figure incrementally," Hanson said.

"He's read up a lot on the show," Dahl said to Weinstein, about Hanson.

"All of those deaths aren't my fault," Weinstein said.

"You *wrote* them," Duvall said.

"I didn't write *all* of them," Weinstein said. "There are other writers on staff."

"You're the head writer," Hester said. "Everything in the scripts goes through you for approval."

"The point is not to pin these deaths on you," Dahl said, cutting in. "You couldn't have known. From your point of view you're writing fiction. From our point of view, though, it's real."

"How does that even work?" Weinstein said. "How does what we write here affect your reality? That doesn't make any sense."

Hester snorted. "Welcome to our lives," he said.

"What do you mean?" Weinstein said, turning his attention to Hester.

"Do you think our lives make any sense at all?" Hester said. "You've got us living in a universe where there are killer robots with harpoons walking around a space station, because, sure, it makes perfect sense to have harpoon-launching killer robots."

"Or ice sharks," Duvall said.

"Or Borgovian Land Worms," Hanson said.

Weinstein held up a finger. "I was not responsible for those land worms," he said. "I was out for two weeks with bird flu. The writer who did that script loved *Dune*. By

276

the time I got back, it was too late. The Herbert estate flayed us for those."

"We dove *into a black hole* to get here," Hester said, and jerked a thumb at Kerensky. "And we made sure to kidnap this sad bastard to make sure it would work, because he's a main character on your show and won't die offscreen. Think about that — physics *alters around him*."

"Not that it keeps me from having the crap beaten out of me on a regular basis," Kerensky said. "I used to wonder why bad things kept happening to me. Now I know it's because at least one of your main characters has to be made to suffer. That just sucks."

"You even make him heal super quickly so you can beat him up again," Duvall said. "Which now that I think about it seems cruel."

"And there's the Box," Hanson said, motioning to Dahl.

"The Box?" Weinstein said, looking at Dahl.

"Whenever you write bad science into the show, the way it gets resolved is that we feed the problem into the Box, and then when it's dramatically appropriate it spits out an answer," Dahl said.

"We never wrote a Box into the series,"

Weinstein said, confused.

"But you do write bad science into the series," Dahl said. "All the time. So there's a Box."

"Did they teach you science in school?" Hester asked. "I'm just wondering."

"I went to Occidental College," Weinstein said. "It has really good science classes."

"Yeah, but did you *go* to any?" Duvall said. "Because I have to tell you, our universe is a mess."

"Other science fiction shows had science advisers and consultants," Hanson pointed out.

"It's science *fiction*," Weinstein said. "The second part of that phrase matters too."

"But you're making it *bad* science fiction," Hester said. "And *we* have to live in it."

"Guys," Dahl said, interrupting everyone again. "Let's try to stay on target here."

"What *is* the target?" Paulson asked. "You said you had an idea you wanted to talk about, and all I'm hearing so far is a bitch session at my head writer."

"I'm feeling a little defensive," Weinstein said.

"Don't," Dahl said. "Again: You couldn't have known. But now you know where we are coming from, and why we came back to stop your show."

Paulson opened his mouth at this, probably to object and offer any number of reasons why that would be impossible. Dahl held up his hand to forestall the objection. "Now that we're here, I know that just stopping the show can't happen. It was a long shot anyway. But now I don't want the show to end, because I can see a way for it to work to our advantage. Both ours and yours."

"Get to it, then," Paulson said.

"Charles, your son's in a coma," Dahl said.

"Yes," Paulson said.

"There's no chance for him ever coming out of it," Dahl said.

"No," Paulson said after a minute, and looked around, eyes wet. "No."

"You didn't say anything about this," Weinstein said. "I thought there was still a chance."

"No," Paulson said. "Doctor Lo told me yesterday that the scans show his brain function continuing to deteriorate, and that it's the machines keeping his body alive at this point. We're waiting until we have the family together so we can say good-bye. We'll have him taken off the machines then." He looked over at Hester, who sat there silently, and then back at Dahl. "Unless you have another idea."

"I do," Dahl said. "Charles, I think we can save your son."

"Tell me how," Paulson said.

"We take him with us," Dahl said. "Back to the *Intrepid.* We can cure him there. We have the technology there to do it. And even if we didn't" — he pointed at Weinstein — "we have the Narrative. Mister Weinstein here writes an episode in which Hester is injured but survives and is taken to sick bay to be healed. It gets done. Hester survives. Your son survives."

"Take him into the show," Paulson said. "That's your plan."

"That's the idea," Dahl said. "Sort of."

"Sort of," Paulson said, frowning.

"There are some logistical issues," Dahl said. "As well as some that are, for lack of a better word, teleological."

"Like what?" Paulson said.

Dahl turned to Weinstein, who was also frowning. "I'm guessing you're thinking of a few right now," he said.

"Yeah," Weinstein said, and motioned to Hester. "The first is that you'll have two of him in your universe."

"You can make up an excuse for that," Paulson said.

"I could, yes," Weinstein said. "It would be messy and nonsensical."

"This is a problem for you?" Hester asked.

"But the thing is that two of him in their universe means none of him in this one," Weinstein said, ignoring Hester's comment. "You had — have, sorry — your son playing this character here. If they both go, there's no one to play the character."

"We'll recast the role," Paulson said. "Someone who looks like Matthew."

"But then the problem is which of the —" Weinstein looked at Hester.

"Hester," he said.

"Which of the Hesters the new one back here affects," Weinstein said. "Besides that, and I'm the first to admit that I have no idea how this screwy voodoo works, but if I were trying to do this, I wouldn't be using a substitute Hester, because who knows how that would affect your son's healing process. He might not end up himself."

"Right," Dahl said. "Which is why we offer the following solution."

"I stay behind," Hester said.

"So, you stay behind, pretend to be my son," Paulson said. "You make a miraculous recovery, then we make the episode where you play my son, and we make you well."

"Sort of," Hester said.

281

"What is it with these 'sort ofs'?" Paulson snapped. "What's the problem?"

Dahl looked over at Weinstein again. "Tell him," he said.

"Oh, shit," Weinstein said, straightening up in his chair. "This is about that atom thing, isn't it?"

"Atom thing?" Paulson said. "What 'atom thing'?"

Weinstein grabbed his head. "So *stupid,*" he said to himself. "Charles, when we wrote the episode where Abernathy and the others came back in time, we did this thing where they could only be here six days before their atoms reverted to their current positions in the timeline."

"I have no idea what that means, Nick," Paulson said. "Talk normal human to me."

"It means that if we stay in this timeline for six days, we die," Dahl said. "And we're already on day three."

"It also means that if Matthew goes to their timeline, he only has six days before the same thing happens to him," Weinstein said.

"What a stupid fucking idea!" Paulson exploded at Weinstein. "Why the fuck did you do that?"

Weinstein held his hands out defensively. "How was I supposed to know one day I'd

282

be here talking about this?" he said, plaintively. "Jesus, Charles, we were just trying to get through the damn episode. We needed them to have a reason to get everything done on a schedule. It made sense at the time."

"Well, change it," Paulson said. "New rule: People traveling through time can take as much fucking time as they want."

Weinstein looked over at Dahl, pleadingly. "It's too late for that," Dahl said, interpreting Weinstein's look. "The rule was in effect when we came through time, and besides, this isn't an episode. We're acting outside the Narrative, which means that even if you could change it, it wouldn't have an effect because it's not being recorded. We're stuck with it."

"They're right," Paulson said to Weinstein, motioning at the *Intrepid* crew. "The universe you've written sucks." Weinstein looked cowed.

"He didn't know," Dahl said to Paulson. "You can't blame him. And we need him, so please don't fire him."

"I'm not going to fire him," Paulson said, still staring at Weinstein. "I want to know how we *fix* this."

Weinstein opened his mouth, then closed it, then turned to Dahl. "Help would be appreciated," he said.

"This is where it gets a little crazy," Dahl said.

"Gets?" Weinstein said.

Dahl turned to Paulson. "Hester stays behind," he said. "We take your son with us. We go back to our time and our universe, but he" — Dahl pointed at Weinstein — "writes that the person in the shuttle is Hester. We don't try to sneak him in or have him be another extra. He has to be central to the plot. We call him out by name. His full name. Jasper Allen Hester."

"Jasper?" Duvall said, to Hester.

"Not now," Hester said.

"So we call him Jasper Allen Hester," Paulson said. "So what? He'll still be my son, not your friend."

"No," Dahl said. "Not if we say he isn't. If the Narrative says it's Hester, then it's Hester."

"But —" Paulson cut himself short and looked at Weinstein. "This makes no fucking sense to me at all, Nick."

"No, it doesn't," Weinstein said. "But that's the thing. It doesn't *have* to make sense. It just has to *happen*." He turned to Dahl. "You're using the shoddy world building of the series to your advantage."

"I wouldn't have put it that way, but yes,"

284

Dahl said.

"What about this atom thing?" Paulson said. "I thought this was a problem."

"If it was Hester here and your son there, then it would be," Weinstein said. "But if it's definitely Hester there, then it will definitely be your son here, and all their atoms will be where they should be." He turned to Dahl. "Right?"

"That's the idea," Dahl said.

"I *like* this plan," Weinstein said.

"And we're sure this will work," Paulson said.

"No, we're not," Hester said. Everyone looked at him. "What?" he said. "We don't know if it will work. We could be wrong about this. In which case, Mister Paulson, your son will still die."

"But then you will die, too," Paulson said. "You don't have to die."

"Mister Paulson, the fact of the matter is that if your son hadn't gone into his coma, you would have eventually killed me off as soon as he got bored being an actor," Hester said, and then pointed at Weinstein. "Well, *he* would kill me off. Probably by being eaten by a space badger or something else completely asinine. Your son is in a coma now, so it's possible I'll live, but then again one day I might be on deck six when the

285

Intrepid gets into a space battle, in which case I'll be just some anonymous bastard sucked into space. Either way, I would have died pointlessly."

He looked around the table. "I figure this way, *if* I die, I die trying to do something useful — saving your son," he said, looking back at Paulson. "My life will actually be good for something, which it's avoiding being so far. And if this works, then both your son and I get to live, which wasn't going to happen before. Either way I figure I'm better off than I was before."

Paulson got up, crossed the room to where Hester was sitting and collapsed into him, sobbing. Hester, not quite knowing what to do with him, patted him on the back gingerly.

"I don't know how I can make this up to you," Paulson said to Hester, when he finally disengaged. He looked over to the rest of the crew. "How I'm going to make it up to all of you."

"As it happens," Dahl said, "I have some suggestions on that."

286

CHAPTER TWENTY-ONE

The taxi turned off North Occidental Boulevard onto Easterly Terrace and slowed to a stop in front of a yellow bungalow.

"Your stop," the taxi driver said.

"Would you mind waiting?" Dahl asked. "I'm only going to be a few minutes."

"I have to run the meter," the driver said.

"That's fine," Dahl said. He got out of the car and walked up the brick walkway to the house door and knocked.

After a moment a woman came to the door. "I don't need any more copies of *The Watchtower,*" she said.

"Pardon?" Dahl said.

"Or the Book of Mormon," she said. "I mean, thank you. I appreciate the thought. But I'm good."

"I do have something to deliver, but it's neither of those things," Dahl said. "But first, tell me if you're Samantha Martinez."

"Yes," she said.

"My name is Andy Dahl," Dahl said. "You could say that you and I almost have a friend in common." He held out a small box to her.

She didn't take it. "What is it?" she said.

"Open it," Dahl suggested.

"I'm sorry, Mister Dahl, but I am a little suspicious of strange men coming to my door on a Saturday morning, asking my name and bearing mysterious packages," Martinez said.

Dahl smiled at this. "Fair enough," he said. He opened the package, revealing a small black hemisphere that Dahl recognized as a holographic image projector. He activated it; the image of someone who looked like Samantha Martinez appeared and hovered in the air over the projector. She was in a wedding dress, smiling, standing next to a man who looked like a clean-shaven version of Jenkins. Dahl held it out for her to see.

Martinez looked at the image quietly for a minute. "I don't understand," she said.

"It's complicated," Dahl admitted.

"Did you Photoshop my face into this picture?" she asked. "And how are you doing this?" She motioned to the floating projection. "Is this some new Apple thing?"

"If you're asking if I've altered the image,

the answer is no," Dahl said. "And as for the projector, it's probably best to say it's something like a prototype." He touched the surface of the projector and the image shifted, to another picture of Jenkins and Martinez's double, looking happily at each other. After a few seconds the picture changed to another.

"I don't understand," Martinez said again.

"You're an actress," Dahl said.

"Was an actress," Martinez said. "I did it for a couple of years and didn't get anywhere. I'm a teacher now."

"When you were an actress, you had a small role on *Chronicles of the Intrepid,*" Dahl said. "Do you remember?"

"Yes," Martinez said. "My character got shot. I was in the episode for about a minute."

"This is that character," Dahl said. "Her name was Margaret. The man in the picture is her husband." He held the projector out to Martinez. She took it, looked at it again and then set it down on a small table on the other side of the door. She turned back to Dahl.

"Is this some kind of a joke?" she said.

"No joke," Dahl said. "I'm not trying to trick you or sell you anything. After today, you won't see me again. All I'm doing is delivering this to you."

"I don't understand," Martinez said again. "I don't understand how you have all these pictures of me, with someone I don't even know."

"They're not my pictures, they're his," Dahl said, and held out the box the projector came in to Martinez. "Here. There's a note in the box from him. It'll explain things better than I can, I think."

Martinez took the box and took out a folded sheet, dense with writing. "This is from him," she said.

"Yes," Dahl said.

"Why isn't he here?" Martinez asked. "Why didn't he deliver it himself?"

"It's complicated," Dahl repeated. "But even if he could have been, I think he would have been afraid to. And I think seeing you might have broken his heart."

"Because of her," Martinez said.

"Yes," Dahl said.

"Does he want to meet me?" Martinez asked. "Is this his way of introducing himself?"

"I think it's his way of introducing himself, yes," Dahl said. "But I'm afraid he can't meet you."

"Why?" Martinez asked.

"He has to be somewhere else," Dahl said.

"That's the easiest way to put it. Maybe his letter will explain it better."

"I'm sorry I keep saying this, but I still don't understand," Martinez said. "You show up at my door with pictures of someone who looks just like me, who you say is the person I played for a minute in a television show, who is dead and who has a husband who sends me gifts. You know how crazy that sounds?"

"I do," Dahl said.

"Why would he do this?" Martinez said. "What's the point of it?"

"Are you asking my opinion?" Dahl asked.

"I am," Martinez said.

"Because he misses his wife," Dahl said. "He misses his wife so much that it's turned his life inside out. In a way that's hard to explain, you being here and being alive means that in some way his wife's life continues. So he's sending her to you. He wants to give you the part of her life he had with her."

"But why?" Martinez said.

"Because it's his way of letting her go," Dahl said. "He's giving her to you so he can get on with the rest of his life."

"He said this to you," Martinez said.

"No," Dahl said. "But I think that's why he did it."

Martinez stepped away from the door, quickly. When she came back a minute later, she had a tissue in her hand, with which she had dried her eyes. She looked up at Dahl and smiled weakly.

"This is definitely the strangest Saturday morning I've had in a while," she said.

"Sorry about that," Dahl said.

"No, it's fine," Martinez said. "I still don't understand. But I guess I'm helping your friend, aren't I?"

"I think you are," Dahl said. "Thank you for that."

"I'm sorry," Martinez said, and stepped aside slightly. "Would you like to come in for a minute?"

"I would love to, but I can't," Dahl said. "I have a taxi running its meter, and I have people waiting for me."

"Going back to your mysterious, complicated place," Martinez said.

"Yes," Dahl said. "Which reminds me. That projector and that letter will probably disappear in a couple of days."

"Like, vaporize?" Martinez said. "As in 'this letter will self-destruct in five seconds'?"

"Pretty much," Dahl said.

"Are you a spy or something?" Martinez said, smiling.

"It's complicated," Dahl said once more. "In any event, I suggest making copies of everything. You can probably just project the pictures against a white wall and take pictures of them, and scan the letter."

"I'll do that," Martinez said. "Thanks for telling me."

"You're welcome," Dahl said, and turned to go.

"Wait a second," Martinez said. "Your friend. Are you going to see him when you get back?"

"Yes," Dahl said.

Martinez stepped out of the doorway to Dahl and gave him a small kiss on the cheek. "Give him that for me," she said. "And tell him that I said thank you. And that I'll take good care of Margaret for him."

"I will," Dahl said. "I promise."

"Thank you." She leaned up and gave him a peck on the other cheek. "That's for you."

Dahl smiled. "Thanks."

Martinez grinned and went back into the bungalow.

"So, you're ready for this," Dahl asked Hester, in the shuttle.

"Of course not," Hester said. "If everything goes according to plan, then the moment you guys go back to our universe, I'll be transported from this perfectly functioning body to one that has severe physical and brain damage, at which point all I can hope for is that we're not wrong about twenty-fifth-century medicine being able to cure me. If everything *doesn't* go according to plan, then in forty-eight hours all my atoms go pop. I want to ask you how you think one gets *ready* for either scenario."

"Good point," Dahl said.

"I want to know how you talked me into this," Hester said.

"I'm apparently very persuasive," Dahl said.

"Then again, I'm the guy who got talked into holding Finn's drugs for him because he convinced me they were candy," Hester said.

"If I recall correctly, there *were* candied," Dahl said.

"I'm gullible and weak-willed, is what I'm saying," Hester said.

"I disagree with that assessment," Dahl said.

"Well, you *would* say that," Hester said, "now that you've talked me into your ridiculous plan."

The two of them stood over the body of Matthew Paulson, whose stretcher was surrounded by mobile life support apparatus.

Duvall was checking the equipment and the comatose body it was attached to.

"How is he?" Dahl asked.

"He's stable," Duvall said. "The machines are doing the hard work for the moment, and the shuttle has adapters I could use, so we don't have to worry about depleting any batteries. As long as he doesn't have any major medical emergencies between now and when we make the transition back, we should be fine."

"And if he does?" Hester asked.

Duvall looked at him. "Then I'll do my best with the training I have," she said. She reached over and slapped his shoulder. "Don't worry. I'm not going to let you down."

"Guys, it's time to go," Kerensky said, from the pilot seat of the shuttle. "Our trip over from Griffith Park did not go unnoticed, and I've got at least three aircraft coming our way. We've got another couple of minutes before things get messy."

"Got it," Dahl said, and looked back to Hester. "So, you're ready for this," he said.

"Yes," Hester said. The two of them walked outside, into the lawn of Charles Paulson's Malibu estate. Charles and his family were there, waiting for Hester. Hanson, who had been keeping them company, broke off and joined Dahl. Hester walked over to join Paulson's family.

"When will we know?" Paulson asked Dahl.

"We're taking the engines to maximum capacity to the black hole we're using," Dahl said. "It will be within the day. I suppose you'll know when your son starts acting like your son again."

"If it works," Paulson said.

"If it works," Dahl agreed. "Let's work on the assumption it will."

"Yes, let's," Hester said.

"Now," Dahl said, to Paulson. "We're agreed on everything."

"Yes," Paulson said. "None of your characters will be killed off going forward. The show will stop randomly killing off extras. And the show itself will wrap up next season and we won't make any new shows in the universe within a hundred years of your timeline."

"And this episode?" Dahl said. "The one where everything we planned happens."

"Nick messaged me about it just a few minutes ago," Paulson said. "He says he's almost got a rough version done. As soon as it's done he and I will work on a polish, and then we'll get it into production as soon as . . . well, as soon as we know whether or not your plan worked."

"It'll work," Dahl said.

"It's going to make hell with our production schedule," Paulson said. "I'm going to end up having to pay for this episode out of my own pocket."

"It'll be worth it," Dahl said.

"I know," Paulson said. "If everything works, it'll be a hell of a show for you."

"Of course," Dahl said. Hester rolled his eyes a little.

"I hear helicopters," Hanson said. From the shuttle came the sound of engines primed to move. Dahl looked at Hester.

"Good luck," Hester said.

"See you soon," Dahl said, and made his way to the shuttle.

They were gone before the helicopters could get to them.

"It's time," Kerensky said, as they approached the black hole. "Everyone get ready for the transition. Dahl, come take the co-pilot seat."

"I can't fly a shuttle," Dahl said.

"I don't need you to fly it," Kerensky said. "I need you to hit the automatic homing and landing sequence in case that asshole writer has something explode and knock me out."

Dahl got up and looked over to Duvall. "Hester doing okay?" he asked.

"He's fine, everything's fine," Duvall said. "He's not Hester yet, though."

"Call him Hester anyway," Dahl said. "Maybe it'll matter."

"You're the boss," Duvall said.

Dahl sat down in the co-pilot seat. "You remember how to do this," he said to Kerensky.

"Aim for the gap between the accretion disk and the Schwartzchild radius and boost engines to one hundred ten percent," Kerensky said, testily. "I've got it. Although it might have been helpful for me to observe the last time we did it. But no, you had me in a crate. Without my pants."

"Sorry about that," Dahl said.

"Not that it matters anyway," Kerensky said. "I'm your good-luck charm, remember? We'll make it through this part just fine."

"Hopefully the rest of it, too," Dahl said.

"If this plan of yours works," Kerensky said. "How will we know that it's worked?"

"When we revive Hester, and he's Hester," Dahl said.

A sensor beeped. "Transition in ten seconds," Kerensky said. "So we won't know until we're back on the *Intrepid*."

"Probably," Dahl said.

"Probably?" Kerensky said.

"I thought of one way we might know if the transfer didn't take," Dahl said.

"How?" Kerensky asked.

The shuttle jammed itself into the ragged edge between the accretion disk and the Schwartzchild radius and transitioned instantly.

In the view screen the planet Forshan loomed large, and above it a dozen ships, including the *Intrepid,* were locked in battle.

Every single sensor on the shuttle flashed to red and began to blare.

One of the nearby starships sparkled, sending a clutch of missiles toward the shuttle.

"When we come through, it might look like *this,*" Dahl said.

Kerensky screamed, and Dahl then felt ill as Kerensky plunged the shuttle into evasive maneuvers.

CHAPTER TWENTY-TWO

"Five missiles coming," Dahl said, fighting the sickness in his stomach from the shuttle's dive to read the co-pilot's panel.

"I know," Kerensky said.

"Engines minimal," Dahl said. "We burned them coming through."

"I *know*," Kerensky said.

"Defense options?" Dahl asked.

"It's a *shuttle*," Kerensky said. "I'm doing them." He cork-screwed the shuttle violently. The missiles changed course to follow, spreading out from their original configuration.

A message popped up on Dahl's screen. "Three missiles locked," he said. "Impact in six seconds."

Kerensky looked up, as if toward the heavens. "Goddamn it, I'm a *featured character*! Do something!"

A beam of light lanced from the *Intrepid*, vaporizing the nearest missile. Kerensky yanked the shuttle over to avoid the explosion and debris. The *Intrepid*'s pulse beam touched the four other missiles, turning them into atoms.

"Holy shit, that *worked,*" Kerensky said.

"If only you knew before, right?" Dahl said, amazed himself.

The shuttle's phone activated. "Kerensky, come in," it said. It was Abernathy on the other end.

"Kerensky here," he said.

"Not a lot of time here," Abernathy said. "Do you have the carrier?"

The carrier? Dahl thought — and then remembered that Hester carried in his body invasive cells whose DNA was a coded message detailing the final will and testament of the leader of the Forshan's rightward schism — which if unlocked could end the religious wars on Forshan — which would not be convenient to any number of leaders on either side of the conflict — which was why all those ships were out there: to bring the shuttle down.

Then Dahl remembered that until that very second, absolutely none of that was true.

But it was now.

"We have the carrier," Kerensky said. "Crewman Hester. Yes. But he's awfully

301

sick, Captain. We're barely keeping him alive."

A panel on Dahl's co-pilot screen flashed. "Three new missiles away!" he said to Kerensky, who spun the shuttle into new evasive maneuvers.

"Kerensky, this is Chief Medical Officer Hartnell," a new voice said. "Crewman Hester's immune system is fighting those cells and losing. If you don't get him to the ship now, they're going to kill him, and then the cells will die too."

"We're being fired on," Kerensky said. "It makes travel difficult."

A new pulse beam flickered out of the *Intrepid*, vaporizing the three new missiles.

"You worry about getting to the *Intrepid*, Kerensky," Abernathy said. "We'll worry about the missiles. Abernathy out."

" 'The carrier'?" Duvall said, from the back of the shuttle. "He's got cells in his body with an encoded message in his DNA? That doesn't even make sense!"

"Nick Weinstein had to write the episode really quickly," Dahl said. "Cut him a break."

"He also wrote *this*?" Kerensky said, motioning out the view screens to the space battle in front of them. "If I ever see him again I'm going to kick his ass."

"Focus," Dahl said. "We need to get to the *Intrepid* without dying."

"Do you think Paulson's son is in Hester's old body?" Kerensky said.

"What?" Dahl said.

"Do you think the switch worked?" Kerensky asked, glancing at Dahl.

Dahl looked back at the body on the stretcher. "I don't know," he said. "Maybe?"

" 'Maybe' works for me," Kerensky said, stopped the shuttle's evasive maneuvers and jammed it as fast as it would go, straight toward the *Intrepid*. All around them Forshan spacecraft fired missiles, beams and projectiles. The *Intrepid* lit up like a Christmas tree, firing all available weapons to shoot down missiles and disable beams and projectile weapons on the Forshan spacecraft.

"This is a bad idea," Dahl said to Kerensky, who was grimly staring forward, keeping the *Intrepid* squarely in his sights.

"We're going to live or die," Kerensky said. "Why fuck around?"

"I liked you better before you were a fatalist," Dahl said.

A missile erupted starboard, knocking the shuttle off its course. The shuttle's inertial dampeners flickered, hurling Hester, Duvall and Hanson around the rear of the shuttle.

"Don't fly into missiles!" Duvall shouted.

"Blame the writer!" Kerensky shot back.

"That's a shitty excuse!" Duvall said. The shuttle rocked again as another missile scored a near miss.

The shuttle ran through the gauntlet of ships, breaking through toward the *Intrepid*.

"The shuttle bay is aft," Dahl said. "We're not aimed at aft."

"Here's where we find out just how hot a shuttle pilot that writer thinks I am," Kerensky said, and threw the shuttle into a reverse Fibonacci spiral, over the top of the *Intrepid*. Dahl groaned as the *Intrepid* wheeled and grew in the view screen. Missiles vibrated the shuttle as they zoomed by, narrowly missing the arcing shuttle. Dahl was certain they were going to smash against the *Intrepid*'s hull, and then they were in the shuttle bay, slamming into the deck. The shuttle screeched violently and something fell off of it outside.

Kerensky whooped and shut down the engines. "*That's* good television," he said.

"I'm never flying with you again," Duvall said, from the back of the shuttle.

"There's no time to waste," Kerensky said, changing his demeanor so suddenly that Dahl had no doubt he'd just been gripped by the Narrative. "We've got to get

Hester to sick bay. Dahl, you're with me on the left side of the stretcher. Duvall, Hanson, take the right. Let's run, people."

Dahl unbuckled and scrambled over to the stretcher, unexpectedly giddy. Kerensky had used Hester's name while under the influence of the Narrative.

As they raced through the corridors with the stretcher, they heard the booms and thumps of the *Intrepid* under attack.

"Now that we're on board, all those ships are attacking the *Intrepid*," Kerensky said. "We need to hurry." The ship shook again, more severely.

"Took you long enough," Medical Officer Hartnell said, as the four of them wheeled the stretcher into sick bay. "Any longer and there wouldn't be a sick bay left. Or any other part of the ship."

"Can't we bug out?" Dahl heard himself say, as they maneuvered the stretcher.

"Engines have been disabled in the attack," Hartnell said. "Nowhere to run. If we don't get this message out of him fast, we're all dead. Lift!" They lifted Hester's body and put it onto a medical table. Hartnell flicked at his tablet and Hester's body stiffened.

"There, he's in stasis," Hartnell said. "He'll be stable until all of this is done." He

305

looked at his medical tablet and frowned. "What the hell are all these fractures and brain trauma?" he said.

"It was a rough shuttle ride," Kerensky said.

Hartnell looked at Kerensky as if he were going to say something, but then the entire ship lurched, throwing everyone but Hester to the deck.

"Oh, that's not good," Duvall said.

Hartnell's phone activated. "This is the captain," Abernathy said through the phone. "What's the status of the carrier?"

"Crewman Hester's alive and in stasis," Hartnell said. "I'm about to take a sample of the invasive cells to start the decoding process."

There was another violent shudder to the ship. "You're going to need to work faster than that," Abernathy said. "We're taking hits we can't keep taking. We need that decoded now."

"Now isn't going to work," Hartnell said. "How much time can you give me?"

Another shudder, and the lights flickered. "I can give you ten minutes," Abernathy said. "Try not to use them all." The captain disconnected.

Hartnell looked at them all. "We're fucked," he said.

Dahl couldn't help smiling crazily at that. *Pretty sure he wasn't in the Narrative when he said that,* he thought.

"Andy," Hanson said. "The Box."

"Shit," Dahl said. "The Box."

"What's a Box?" Hartnell said.

"Take a sample and give it to me," Dahl said to Hartnell.

"Why?" Hartnell asked.

"I'll take it to Xenobiology and run it there," Dahl said.

"We've got the same equipment here —" Hartnell said.

Dahl looked over to Kerensky for help. "Just do it, Hartnell," Kerensky said. "Before you get us all killed."

Hartnell frowned but took his sampler and jammed it into Hester's arm, then took out the sample container and gave it to Dahl. "Here. Now someone please tell me what this is about."

"Andy," Hanson said. "To get to Xenobiology from here you'll need to go through deck six."

"Right," Dahl said, and turned to Kerensky. "Come with me, please."

"Who's going to tell me what's going on?" Hartnell said, and then Dahl and Kerensky were out the door, into the corridor.

"What's with deck six?" Kerensky asked

as they ran.

"It has a tendency to blow up when we're attacked," Dahl said. "Like right now."

"You're using me as a good-luck charm again, aren't you?" Kerensky said.

"Not exactly," Dahl said.

Deck six was exploding and on fire.

"The corridors are blocked!" Kerensky said, over the noise.

"Come on," Dahl said, and slapped open an access door to the cargo tunnels. There was a gust as the heated air of deck six blew into the opened door. Kerensky went through and Dahl shut the access door as something erupted in the hall.

"This way," Dahl said, and the two fished their way around the cargo carts to an access door on the other side of the deck and then back into the main corridors.

Lieutenant Collins did not look happy to see Dahl.

"What are you doing here?" she said. Dahl ignored her and went to the storage room, pulling out the Box.

"Hey, you can't be using that around *Kerensky,*" Collins said, moving toward Dahl.

"If she tries to come near me, take her out," Dahl said to Kerensky.

"Got it," Kerensky said. Collins abruptly stopped.

"Take her tablet," Dahl said. Kerensky did.

"How much time?" Dahl asked. He set the Box on an induction pad.

"Seven minutes," Kerensky said.

"That'll work," Dahl said, slipped the sample into the Box and pressed the green button. He walked over to Kerensky, took Collins' tablet, signed her off and signed into his own account.

"Now what?" Kerensky said.

"We wait," Dahl said.

"For how long?" Kerensky said.

"As long as dramatically appropriate," Dahl said.

Kerensky peered at the Box. "So this was the thing that kept me from turning into mush when I got the Merovian Plague?"

"That's it," Dahl said.

"Ridiculous," Kerensky said.

Collins looked at Kerensky, gaping. "You *know*?" she said. "You're not supposed to know."

"At this point, I know a lot more than you," Kerensky said.

The Box pinged and the tablet was flooded with data. Dahl barely glanced at it. "We're good," he said. "Back to sick bay." They ran out of Xenobiology, back to the access corridors to return to deck six.

"Almost there," Kerensky said, as they emerged out of the access corridors into the fires of deck six.

The ship rocked violently and the main corridor of deck six collapsed onto Dahl, crushing him and slicing a jagged shard of metal through his liver. Dahl stared at it for a moment and then looked at Kerensky.

"You *had* to say 'almost there,' " he whispered, the words dribbling out between drips of blood.

"Oh, God, Dahl," Kerensky said, and started trying to move debris off of him.

"Stop," Dahl said. Kerensky ignored him. *"Stop,"* he said again, more forcefully. Kerensky stopped. Dahl pushed the tablet, still in his hands, to Kerensky. "No time. Take the results. Feed them into the sick bay computer. Don't let Hartnell argue. When the sick bay computer has the data, the Narrative will take over. It will be done. But get there. Hurry."

"Dahl —" Kerensky said.

"This is why I brought you with me," Dahl said. "Because I knew whatever happened to me, *you'd* make it back. Now go. Save the day, Kerensky. Save the day."

Kerensky nodded, took the tablet, and ran.

Dahl lay there, pinned through the liver, and in his final moments of consciousness tried to focus on the fact that Hester would live, the ship would be saved and his friends would make it through the rest of their lives without being savaged by the Narrative. And all it needed was one more dramatic death of an extra. His dramatic death.

It's a fair trade, he thought, trying to reconcile himself to how it all played out. A fair trade. Saved his friends. Saved Matthew Paulson. Saved the *Intrepid.* A fair trade.

But as everything went gray and slid into black, a final thought bubbled up from the bottom of what was left of him.

Screw this, I want to live, it said.

But then everything went to black anyway.

"Stop being dramatic," the voice said. "We know you're awake."

Dahl opened his eyes.

Hester was standing over him, along with Duvall and Hanson.

Dahl smiled at Hester. "It worked," he said. "It's you. It really worked."

"Of course it worked," Hester said. "Why wouldn't it work?"

Dahl laughed weakly at this. He tried to get up but couldn't.

"Stasis medical chair," Duvall said. "You're regrowing a liver and a lot of burned skin and healing a broken rib cage.

You wouldn't like what you'd be feeling if you moved."

"How long have I been in this thing?" Dahl asked.

"Four days," Hanson said. "You were a mess."

"I thought I was dead," Dahl said.

"You would have been dead if someone hadn't rescued you," Duvall said.

"Who rescued me?" Dahl asked.

Another face loomed into view.

"Jenkins," Dahl said.

"You were right outside a cargo tunnel," Jenkins said. "I figured, might as well."

"Thank you," Dahl said.

"No thanks necessary," Jenkins said. "I did it purely out of self-interest. If you died, I would never know if you ever delivered that message for me."

"I did," Dahl said.

"How did it go over?" Jenkins asked.

"It went over well," Dahl said. "I'm supposed to give you a kiss for her."

"Well, maybe some other time," Jenkins said.

"What are you two talking about?" Duvall asked.

"I'll tell you later," Dahl said, and then looked back to Jenkins. "So you're out of your hiding place, then."

"Yes," he said. "It was time."

"Good," Dahl said.

"And the great news is we're all heroes," Hester said. "The 'message' was extracted out of my body and broadcast by the *Intrepid,* ending the religious war on Forshan. How lucky is that."

"Amazing," Dahl said.

"Of course, none of it even begins to make sense if you think about it," Hester said.

"It never has," Dahl said.

Later in the day, after his friends had left, Dahl had another visitor.

"Science Officer Q'eeng," Dahl said.

"Ensign," Q'eeng said. "You are healing?"

"So I've been told," Dahl said.

"Lieutenant Kerensky tells me it was you who cracked the code, so the rightward schism leader's last will and testament could be broadcast," Q'eeng said.

"I suppose it was," Dahl said, "although I can't honestly take all the credit."

"Nevertheless, for your bravery and your sacrifice I have written you up for a commendation," Q'eeng said. "If it's approved, which it will be, then you will also be advanced in rank. So let me be the first to say, Congratulations, Lieutenant."

"Thank you, sir," Dahl said.

"There's one other thing," Q'eeng said.

"Just a few minutes ago I received a highly classified message from the Universal Union High Command. I was informed that I was to read it to you, and only to you, out loud."

"All right, sir," Dahl said. "I'm ready."

Q'eeng pulled out his phone, pressed the screen and read the words there. "Andy, I don't know if these words will reach you. Nick wrote this scene and we filmed it, but obviously it won't be shown on TV. I don't know if just filming it will be enough, and I guess there is no way for you to tell us if it worked. But if it does work, I want you to know two things. One, I'm sorry for everything you just got put through — Nick felt we had to really push the action in this one or the audience would start to question what was going on. Maybe that's not a great argument to you now, considering where you are. But it made sense at the time.

"Two, no words I can say will ever thank you, Jasper and all of you for what you have done for my family and for me. You gave me my son back, and by giving him back you have given us everything. We will stick to our end of the agreement. Everything we said we would do we will. I don't know what else to say, except this: Thank you for letting us live happily ever after. We will do the same for you. In love and gratitude, Charles

Paulson."

"Thank you," Dahl said to Q'eeng, after a moment.

"You are welcome," Q'eeng said, putting away his phone. "A most curious message."

"I suppose you could say it's in code, sir," Dahl said.

"Are you allowed to tell your superior officer what it's about?" Q'eeng asked.

"It's a message from God," Dahl said. "Or someone close enough to Him for our purposes."

Q'eeng looked at Dahl appraisingly. "I sometimes get the feeling there are things happening on the *Intrepid* that I'm not meant to know about," he said. "I suspect this is one of them."

"Sir, and with all due respect," Dahl said, "you don't know how right you are."

CHAPTER TWENTY-THREE

"So what now?" Duvall asked. The four of them were in the mess, picking at their midday meal.

"What do you mean?" Hester asked.

"I mean, what now?" Duvall said. She pointed to Hester. "You're transplanted into a new body" — her point changed to Dahl — "he's back from the dead, we've all come back from an alternate reality to keep ourselves from being killed for dramatic purposes. We've won. What now?"

"I don't think it works like that," Hanson said. "I don't think we've won anything, other than being in control of our own lives."

"Right," Hester said. "After everything, what it all means is that if one day we slip in the bathroom and crack our head on the toilet, our last thoughts can be a satisfied, 'Well, I and only I did this to myself.'"

"When you put it that way, it hardly seems

316

worth it," Duvall said.

"I don't mind cracking my head on the toilet," Hester said. "As long as I do it at age one hundred and twenty."

"On your one hundred and twentieth birthday, I'll come over with floor wax," Duvall promised.

"I can't wait," Hester said.

"Andy? You okay?" Hanson asked.

"I'm fine," Dahl said, and smiled. "Sorry. Was just thinking. About being fictional, and all that."

"We're over that now," Hester said. "That was the point of all of this."

"You're right," Dahl said. "I know."

Duvall looked at her phone. "Crap, I'm going to be late," she said. "I'm breaking in a new crew member."

"Oh, the burdens of a promotion," Hester said.

"It's hard, it really is," Duvall said, and got up.

"I'll walk with you," Hester said. "You can tell me more of your woes."

"Excellent," Duvall said. The two of them left.

Hanson looked back at Dahl. "Still thinking about being fictional?" he said, after a minute.

"Sort of," Dahl said. "What I've been

really thinking about is you, Jimmy."

"Me," Hanson said.

"Yeah," Dahl said. "Because while I was recuperating from our last adventure, something struck me about you. You don't really fit."

"That's interesting," Hanson said. "Tell me why."

"Think about it," Dahl said. "Think of the five of us who met that first day, the day we joined the crew of the *Intrepid*. Each of us turned out to be critical in some way. Hester, who didn't seem to have a purpose, turned out to be the key to everything. Duvall had medical training and got close to Kerensky, which helped us when we needed it and made him part of our crew when we needed him. Finn gave us tools and information we needed and his loss galvanized us to take action. Jenkins gave us context for our situation and the means to do something about it."

"What about you?" Hanson asked. "Where do you fit in?"

"Well, that's the one I had a hard time with," Dahl said. "I wondered what I brought to the party. I thought maybe I was just the man with the plan — the guy who came up with the basic ideas everyone else went along with. Logistics. But then I

318

started thinking about Kerensky, and what he is to the show."

"He's the guy who gets beat up to show that the main characters can get beat up," Hanson said.

"Right," Dahl said.

"But you can't be Kerensky," Hanson said. "We have a Kerensky. It's Kerensky."

"It's not about Kerensky getting beat up," Dahl said. "It's about Kerensky not dying."

"I'm not following you," Hanson said.

"Jimmy, how many times should I have died since we've been on the *Intrepid*?" Dahl asked. "I count at least three. The first time, when I was attacked at Eskridge colony, when Cassaway and Mbeke died. Then in the *Nantes* interrogation room with Finn and Captain Abernathy. And then on deck six when we returned to the *Intrepid* with Hester. Three times I should have been dead, no ifs, ands or buts. I should *be* dead, three times over. But I'm not. I get hurt. I get hurt really badly. But I don't die. That's when I figured it out. I'm the protagonist."

"But you're an extra," Hanson said. "We all are. Jenkins said it. Charles Paulson said it. Even the actor playing you said it."

"I'm an extra on the show," Dahl said. "I'm the protagonist somewhere else."

"Where?" Hanson said.

319

"That's what I want you to tell me, Jimmy," Dahl said.

"What?" Hanson said. "What are you talking about?"

"It's like I said: You don't fit," Dahl said. "Everyone else served a strong purpose for the story. Everyone but you. For this, you were just *around,* Jimmy. You have a back-story, but it never really entered in to what we did. You did a few useful things — you looked into show trivia, and talked about people, and occasionally you reminded people to do things. You added just enough that it seemed like you were taking part. But the more I think about it, the more I realize that you don't quite add up the way the rest of us do."

"Life is like that, Andy," Hanson said. "It's messy. We don't all add up that way."

"No," Dahl said. "We *do.* Everyone else does. Everyone else but you. The only way you fit is if the thing you're supposed to do, you haven't done yet. The only way you fit is if there's something else going on here. We're all supposed to think we were real people who found out they were extras on a television show. But I know that doesn't begin to explain me. I should be dead several times over, like Kerensky or any of the show's major characters are supposed

320

to be dead, but aren't, because the universe plays favorites with them. The universe plays favorites with me, too."

"Maybe you're lucky," Hanson said.

"No one is that lucky, Jimmy," Dahl said. "So here's what I think. I think there's no television show. No *real* television show. I think that Charles Paulson and Marc Corey and Brian Abnett and everyone else over there are just as fictional as we were supposed to be. I think Captain Abernathy and Commander Q'eeng, Medical Officer Hartnell and Chief Engineer West are the bit players here, and that me and Maia and Finn and Jasper are the people who really count. And I think in the end, you really exist for just one reason."

"What reason is that, Andy?" Hanson said.

"To tell me that I'm right about this," Dahl said.

"My parents would be surprised by your conclusion," Hanson said.

"My parents would be surprised by all of this," Dahl said. "Our parents are not the point here."

"Andy, we've known each other for years," Hanson said. "I think you know who I am."

"Jimmy," Dahl said. "Please. Tell me if I'm right."

Hanson sat there for a minute, looking at

Dahl. "I don't think it would actually make you happier to be told you were right about this," he said, finally.

"I don't want to be happy," Dahl said. "I just want to know."

"And even if you were right," Hanson said, "what do you get out of it? Aren't you better off believing that you've accomplished something? That you've gotten the happy ending you were promised? Why would you want to push that?"

"Because I need to know," Dahl said. "I've always needed to know."

"Because that's the way you are," Hanson said. "A seeker of truth. A spiritual man."

"Yes," Dahl said.

"A man who needs to know if he's really that way, or just written to *be* that way," Hanson said.

"Yes," Dahl said.

"Someone who needs to know if he's really his own man, or —"

"Tell me you're not about to make the pun I think you are," Dahl said.

Hanson smiled. "Sorry," he said. "It was there." He pushed out from his chair and stood up. "Andy, you're my friend. Do you believe that?"

"Yes," Dahl said. "I do."

"Then maybe you can believe this," Hanson said. "Whether you're an extra or the hero, this story is about to end. When it's done, whatever you want to be will be up to you and only you. It will happen away from the eyes of any audience and from the hand of any writer. You will be your own man."

"If I exist when I stop being written," Dahl said.

"There is that," Hanson said. "It's an interesting philosophical question. But if I had to guess, I'd guess that your creator would say to you that he would want you to live happily ever after."

"That's just a guess," Dahl said.

"Maybe a little more than a guess," Hanson said. "But I will say this, though: You were right."

"About what?" Dahl said.

"That now I've done what I was supposed to do," Hanson said. "But now I have to go do the other thing I'm supposed to do, which is assume my post. See you at dinner, Andy?"

Dahl grinned. "Yes," he said. "If any of us are around for it."

"Great," Hanson said. "See you then." And he wandered off.

Dahl sat there for a few more minutes, thinking about everything that had happened and everything that Hanson said.

And then he got up and went to his station on the bridge. Because whether fictional or not, on a spaceship, a television show or in something else entirely, he still had work to do, surrounded by his friends and the crew of the *Intrepid*.

And that's just what he did, until the day six months later when a systems failure caused the *Intrepid* to plow into a small asteroid, vaporizing the ship and killing everyone on board instantly.

CHAPTER TWENTY-FOUR

No, no, I'm just fucking with you.
They all lived happily ever after.
Seriously.

Coda I:
First Person

CODA I: FIRST PERSON

Hello, Internet.

There isn't any good way to start this, so let me just jump right in.

So, I am a scriptwriter for a television show on a major network who just found out that the people he's been making up in his head (and killing off at the rate of about one an episode) are actually real. Now I have writer's block, I don't know how to solve it, and if I don't figure it out soon, I'm going to get fired. Help me.

And now I just spent 20 minutes looking at that last paragraph and feeling like an asshole. Let me break it down further to explain it to you a little better.

"Hello, Internet": You know that *New Yorker* cartoon that has a dog talking to another dog by a computer and saying, "On the Internet, no one knows you're a dog"? Yeah, well, this is that.

No, I'm not a dog. But yes, I need some

anonymity here. Because *holy shit,* look what I just wrote up there. That's not something you can just say out loud to people. But on the Internet? Anonymously? Might fly.

"I am a scriptwriter . . .": I really am. I've been working for several years on the show, which (duh) has been successful enough to have been around for several years. I don't want to go into too much more detail about that right now, because remember, I'm trying to have some anonymity here to work through this thing I've been dealing with. Suffice to say that it's not going to win any major Emmys, but it's still the sort of show that you, my dear Internet, would probably watch. And that in the real world, I have an IMDB page. And it's pretty long. So there.

"Who just found out the people he's been making up in his head are real": Yes, I know. I *know.* Didn't I just say "holy shit" two paragraphs ago about it? Don't you think I know how wobbly-toothed, speed freak crazy it sounds? I do. I very very very *very* much do. If I didn't think it was completely bugfuck crazy, I'd be writing about it on my own actual blog (if I had my own actual blog, which I don't, because I work on a weekly television series, and *who*

330

has the time) and finding some way to go full Whitley Strieber on it. I don't want that. That's a lifestyle. A whacked-out, late night talking to the tinfoil-hatted on your podcast lifestyle. I don't want that. I just want to be able to get back to my own writing.

But still: The people I wrote in my scripts exist. I know because I met them, swear to God, right there in the flesh, I could reach out and touch them. And whenever I kill one of them off in my scripts, they actually die. To me, it's just putting down words on a page. To them, it's falling off a building, or being hit by a car, or being eaten by a bear or whatever (these are just examples, they're not necessarily how I've killed people off).

Think about that. Think about what it means. That just *writing down* "BOB is consumed by badgers" in a script means that somewhere in the universe, some poor bastard named Bob has just been chased down by ravenous mustelids. Sure, it sounds funny when I write it like that. But if you were Bob? It would suck. And then you would be dead, thanks to me. Which explains the next part:

"Now I have writer's block": You know, I never understood writer's block before this. You're a writer and you suddenly can't write because your girlfriend broke up with you? Shit, dude, that's the *perfect* time to write. It's not like you're doing anything else with your nights. Having a hard time coming up with the next scene? Have something explode. You're done. Filled with existential ennui about your place in the universe? Get over yourself. Yes, you're an inconsequential worm in the grand scope of history. But you're an inconsequential worm who makes shit up for a living, which means that you don't have to lift heavy boxes or ask people if they want fries with that. Grow up and get back to work.

On a good day, I can bang out a first draft of an episode in six hours. Is it good? It ain't Shakespeare, but then, Shakespeare wrote *Titus Andronicus,* so you tell me. Six hours, one script, a good day. And I have to tell you, as a writer, I've had my share of good days.

But now I have writer's block and I can't write a script because *fuck me I kill people when I write.* It's a pretty good excuse for having writer's block, if you ask me. Girlfriend leaving you? Get on with it. You send people to their deaths by typing? Might give you pause. It's given me pause. Now I sit in front of my laptop, Final Draft all loaded up, and just stare at the screen for hours.

"I'm going to get fired": My job is writing scripts. I'm not writing scripts. If I don't start writing scripts again, soon, there's no reason for me to be kept on staff. I've been able to stall a bit because I had one script in the outbox before the block slammed down, but that gives me about a week's insurance. That's not a lot of time. You see why I'm nervous.

"Help me": Look, I need help. This isn't something I can talk to with people I actually know. Because, again: *Bugshit crazy.* I can't afford to have people I work with — or other writers I know, most of whom are unemployed and would be happy to crawl over my carcass to get my television show writing staff position — think that I've lost my marbles. Gigs like this don't grow on trees. But I have to talk to someone about it, because for the life of me I haven't the first damn clue about what I should be doing about this. I need some perspective from outside my own head.

And this is where you come in, Internet. You have perspective. And I'm guessing that some of you might just be bored enough to help out some anonymous dude on the Internet, asking for advice on a completely ridiculous situation. It's either this or Angry Birds, right?

So, what do you say, Internet?

Yours,
Anon-a-Writer

So, the good news is that apparently people are reading this. The bad news is people are asking me questions instead of, you know, *helping me*. But then again when you anonymously post on the Internet that the characters you write have suddenly come alive, I suppose you have to answer a few questions first. Fine. So for those of you who need it, a quick run-through of the most common questions I've gotten so far. I'm going to paraphrase some to keep from repeating questions and comments.

Dude, are you serious?

Dude, I am serious. I am not high (being high is more fun), I am not making this up (if I was making things up, I would be getting paid for it), and I am not crazy (crazy would be more fun, too). This is for real.

Really?

Yes.

Really?

Yes.

No, really?

Shut up. Next question.

Why haven't you discussed this with your therapist?

Because contrary to popular belief, not every writer in Los Angeles has been in therapy since before they could walk. All my neuroses are manageable (or were, anyway). I suppose I could get one, but that would be a hell of a first session, wouldn't it, and I'm not entirely convinced I'd get out of there without being sedated and sent off to the funny farm. Call me paranoid.

Isn't this kind of the plot to that movie *Stranger than Fiction* ?

Maybe? That's the Will Ferrell movie where he's a character in someone's book, right? (I know I could check this on IMDB, but I'm lazy.) Except for that I'm the writer, not the character. So same concept, different spin. Maybe?

But, look, even if it is, I didn't say what was happening to me was creatively 100% *original.* I mean, there's *The Purple Rose of Cairo,* which had characters coming down off the screen. There's those Jasper Fforde books where everyone's a fairy tale or literary character. There's Denise Hogan's books where she's always arguing with her characters and sometimes they don't listen to her and mess with her plots. My mom loves those. Hell, there's *The Last Action Hero,* for God's sake. Have you seen that? You have? I'm sorry.

335

There's also the small but telling detail that those are all fictional, and this is *really happening to me.* Like I said, a subtle difference. But an important one. I'm not going for originality here. I'm trying to get this solved.

Hey, is your show [insert name of show here]?

Friend, what part of "I want to be anonymous" don't you understand? Even if you guessed right I'm still not going to tell you. Want a hint? Fine: It's not *30 Rock.* Also I am not Tina Fey. Mmmm . . . Tina Fey.

Likewise:

You know that these days the Internet *does* know if you're a dog, right?

Yes, but *this* dog opened this blog account using a throwaway e-mail address and cruises the Web using Tor.

Why don't you just write scripts where people don't get killed?

Well, I *could* do that, but two things will happen then:

1. The script gets turned in and the producers say, "The stakes need to be raised in this scene. Kill someone." And then I have to kill someone in the script, or a co-writer does, or one of the producers does a quick uncredited wash of the script, or the director zaps a character during shooting,

and someone dies *anyway.*

2. Even if I don't kill anyone, there still needs to be drama, and on a show like mine, drama usually means if someone isn't killed, then they are maimed or mutilated or given a disease that turns them into a pustule with legs. Admittedly, turning a character into a pustule is better than killing them dead, but it's still not *comfortable* for them, and it's still me doing it to them. So I still have guilt.

Believe me, there's nothing I'd like to do better than turn in scripts whether the characters do nothing but lounge on pillows, eating chocolates and having hot, cathartic sex for an hour (minus commercial time, your capitalistically inspired refractory period). I think our audience wouldn't mind either — it would be inspirational and educational! But it's not that kind of show, and there's only so edgy basic cable is going to let us be.

I have to write stuff that's actually like what gets written for our show, basically. If I don't, I'll get canned. I don't want to get canned.

You understand that if what you're saying is actually true, then the existential ramifications are astounding!

Yeah, it's pretty weird shit. I could go on for hours about it — that is, if it wasn't *also* messing with my day-to-day life in a pretty substantial way. You know what it's like? It's like waking up one morning, going outside and finding a *Tyrannosaurus rex* in your front yard, staring at you. For the first five seconds, you're completely amazed that a real live dinosaur is standing in front of you. And then you run like hell, because to a *T. rex*, you're a chewy, crunchy bite-sized snack.

Is there a *T. rex* in your front yard?

No.

Damn.

You're not helping.

For someone who says they're having writing block, aren't you writing a lot?

Yeah, but this isn't real writing, is it? I'm not doing anything creative here, I'm just answering comments and asking for help. Blogs are nice and all, but what I really need to be doing is writing scripts. And I can't do that right now. The creative lobe of my brain is completely blown out. That's where the blockage is.

You mentioned that you were using Final Draft. Have you considered that maybe your software is the problem? I use Scrivener myself. You should try it!

Wow, really? Dude, if someone's having a heart attack in front of you, do you take that opportunity to talk about your amazing low-cholesterol diet, too? Because that would be *awesome*.

The software is not the problem. The problem is that every time I write *I kill someone*. If you're going to try to help, don't suggest a particular brand of sprinkler after the house is already on fire. Grab a hose.

Related to this:

I believe everything you say and I think we should meet so we can discuss this in detail possibly in my SECRET BASEMENT LAIR AT MY MOM'S HOUSE *WHERE I LIVE*.

Oooooh, man. *That's* another reason to remain safely anonymous, isn't it.

So now that the Q&A session is done, does anyone actually have help for me? Please?

AW

Finally! An actual good idea from a comment, which I will now replicate in full:

In your last post you mentioned some movies and books in which the line between the creator and the created had been broken (or at least smudged) in some way. Have you considered that perhaps the people who wrote those movies and books might have had experiences similar to yours? It's possible that they have, and just haven't ever talked about it for the same reason you're trying to stay anonymous, which is, it sounds completely crazy. But if you approached them and your experience is similar to theirs, maybe they would talk to you in confidence. The fact you actually are a screenwriter of some note might keep them from fleeing in terror, at least at first.

The "at least at first" bit is a nice touch, thank you. And I'm glad you have the delusion that a scriptwriter on a weekly basic cable series has any sort of credibility. It warms my heart.

But to answer your question, no, it didn't occur to me at all, because, well, it's nuts, isn't it. And we live in the really real world, where stuff like this doesn't happen. But on the other hand, it happened to *me,* and — no offense to me — I'm not all *that* special, either as a writer or a human being.

So: I have to admit that it's entirely possible that what's happened to me has happened to others. And if it has happened to others, then it's entirely possible they've found some way to deal with it that doesn't involve not writing anymore. And that's the goal here. And now I have a plan: Contact those writers and find out if they've got a secret experience like mine.

Which sounds perfectly reasonable until you think about what that actually means. To give you an idea, let me present to you a quick, one-act play entitled *Anon-a-Writer Presents His Conundrum to Someone Who Is Not the Internet:*

ANON-A-WRITER
Hello! I have been visited by characters from my scripts who inform me that I kill them whenever I write an action scene. Does this happen to you too?

OTHER WRITER
Hello, Anon-a-Writer! In one hand I have a restraining order, and in the other I have a Taser. Which would you like to meet first?

Yes, I see no way that this perfect plan could ever go wrong.

But on the other hand I don't have a *better* plan, do I. So here's what I'm going to do:

Make a list of writers whose characters break the reality wall one way or another.

Contact them and find out if it's based on their actual real-world experience, without coming across like a psychotic freakbag.

Profit! Okay, not profit, but if their work *is* based on their real-life experiences, find out from them a way to keep writing.

Off to craft introductions that don't sound too creepy. Wish me luck.

AW

Guys, seriously now: Stop trying to guess which show I work for. I'm just not going to tell you. Because I don't want to get *fired*. Which is what happens when people like me talk about their jobs to people like you, i.e., the Internet. And especially when people like me are claiming their characters are coming to life and talking to them. I know it's good fun for you to be guessing, but, come on. A little charity, please. I promise you that after this is all done, if everything works out, I'll tell you. Say, in five years. Or after I win an Emmy. Whichever comes first (bet on five years).

Okay? Okay. Thank you.

Hello, Internet. You're wanting updates. Well, here we go. I've identified some creative types who have written stories similar to my situation, including those we mentioned here earlier: Woody Allen, for *Purple Rose of Cairo,* Jasper Fforde, Zak Penn and Adam Leff (*Last Action Hero*),

Zach Helm (*Stranger than Fiction*) and Denise Hogan. The plan here is to approach them credits first — to at least suggest I'm not completely insane — and then to ask them in a *very subtle way* about whether what they've written has any connection to their real-life experiences. Then off they go to the writers. And we'll see if anyone nibbles.

And, to anticipate some of you raising your hands out there in the audience, yes, I'll share with you the responses — after I snip out major identifying details. Oh, don't look at me like that. Remember that anonymity thing I'm striving for? Yeah. Too many details and I'm out of my very peculiar little closet (it's a lovely closet; it smells of pine and desperation). But on the other hand, as you've been helpful, I figure I owe you continuing updates on this thing.

Also, to make no mistake about it, I fully expect that the responses will be, "Wow, you're even crazier than most random people who write me, would you like my suggestion for antipsychotic pharmaceuticals." Because that's how I would respond to this showing up randomly in my inbox. It's how I *have* responded, in fact. You wouldn't *believe* the sort of random crazy gets sent to you when you're a writer on a successful television series. Or maybe you would. Crazy is highly distributed these days.

(insert pause to send off e-mails)

And they're off. Now we get to see how long it takes before anyone responds. Want to start a betting pool?

AW

Wow, so that didn't take long at all. The first response. E-mail posted below:

XXX XXXXX <u>via</u> gmail.com
<u>show details</u> 4:33 PM (0 minutes ago)

Dear ANON-A-WRITER:
Hello, I'm XXX XXXXXX, assistant for XXXXX XXXXX. We received your query and wanted to know whether it was some sort of creative or interview project you're doing for a major magazine or newspaper. Please let us know.

My response:

Hello, XXX XXXXXX. No, it's not for any newspaper or magazine or blog (well, it might be for my own personal blog). It's more of something I'm asking for my own information. Thank you and let me know if XXXXX XXXXX has time for a chat. It would be very useful to me.

The assistant's response:

Unfortunately XXXXX XXXXX doesn't have any availability at this time. Thanks for your interest and good luck on your project.

Translation: Your crazy would be fine if it was for *People* magazine, or maybe even *Us,* but if it's freelance crazy, we don't want anything to do with you.
Sigh. There was a time when freelance crazy was respected in this town! I think it was the early 80s. David Lee Roth was hanging out at the Whisky then. Or so I have heard. I was, like, *six* at the time.
One down, five to go. . . .

AW

New response. This is kind of awesome, actually.

To: ANON-A-WRITER
From: XXXXX X XXXX, Esq.,
    partner, XXXX, XXXXX, XXX and
    XXXXX

Dear Mr. Writer:

Your e-mail query to XXXXX XXXXXX was forwarded to us by his assistant, as is every letter for which they feel there is some concern about. Mr. XXXXXX values his privacy considerably and was greatly unsettled by your e-mail, both for its content and because it arrived in an unsolicited manner at a private e-mail.

At this time our client has decided not to escalate the matter by asking the XXXXXXX Police Department to investigate you and your e-mail. However, we request that you do not ever again attempt to contact our client in any way. If you attempt to do so, we will forward all correspondence both to the XXXXXXX Police Department and to the FBI and file for a restraining order against you. I do not need to tell you that such a request would instantly become news, severely impacting your career as a staff writer on XXXXXX XXXX.

We trust that this is the last we will hear from you.

Yours,

XXXXX X XXXX, Esq., partner,

XXXX, XXXXX, XXX and XXXXX

Whoa.

Just for the record, the e-mail I sent did *not* begin: "Dear XXXXX, as I happened to be standing over your bed last night, *watching you sleep . . .*" It really didn't. I *swear.*

Either this person gets more crazy e-mails than usual from people who dress up as their cat and then stand outside their house, or this person got spooked by this e-mail for an entirely other reason. Hmmmm.

Is it worth getting the FBI involved to find out?

No. No, it is not.

Not *yet,* anyway. Still curious.

And now I'm fighting off an urge to dress up as this person's cat and stand outside their house. But it's early yet, and it's a weeknight. Maybe after a few more gin rickeys.

AW

From the comments:

I'm not entirely convinced you've seen your characters come alive, but as someone who suffers from writer's block all the time, it's amazing to me that you can joke about your situation as much as you do on this site, especially when your actual job is on the line. If I were you, I would be wetting my pants right about now.

Oh, trust me. I am. I so very *am.* My local Pavilions is entirely out of Depends right about now. I shop for them at night, so my neighbors won't see me. And when I'm done with them I put them in my next door neighbor's trash can so they can't be traced back to me. I'm not proud. Or dry.

I'm going to let you in on a little secret, Internet: Part of the reason I'm writing this blog right now is in fact to keep from shitting myself in abject fear. The last time I went a week without writing something creative was when I was in college and I spent six days in the hospital for a truly epic case of food poisoning. (Dorm food. Not always the freshest. I wasn't the only one. For the rest of the year my dorm was known as the Puke Palace. I digress.) And even then, when I thought I was going to retch my lower intestine right out past my tongue, I was plotting stories and trying out dialogue in my head. Right now, I try plotting a story or thinking about dialogue for a script and a big wall comes down in my brain. I. Just. Cannot. Write.

This has never happened to me before. I am absolutely terrified that *this is it,* that the creative tank is all out of gas and that from here on out there's nothing for me but residuals and occasional teaching gigs at the Learning Annex. I mean, fuck, kill me now. It terrifies me so much that there's only two things I can think to do at the moment:

1. Make a special cocktail of antifreeze and OxyContin and then take a long, luxurious bath with my toaster.

2. Write on this blog like it's a methadone treatment.

One of these options doesn't have me found as a bloated corpse a week later. Guess which one.

As for the joking, well, look. When I was twelve, my appendix burst, and as they were wheeling my ass into the operating room, I asked the doctor, "How will this affect my piano playing?" and he said, "Don't worry, you'll still be able to play the piano," and I said, "Wow! I wasn't able to before!"

And then they gassed me.

My point is that even when I was about to die of imminent peritonitis I was still going for the joke. Failing, but going for it. (Actually, as my father said in the recovery room, "All the jokes in the world you could have made at that moment, and that's the one you go for. You are no son of mine." Dad took his jokes seriously.)

Shorter version of all of the above: If I actually wrote in a way that indicated how bowel-voidingly scared I am at the moment, you would have all fled by now. And I probably would have gone to play in traffic. It's better to joke, I think.

Don't you?

AW

Hey, now we're getting somewhere. The following e-mail from the next person on my list:

Dear Anon-a-Writer:
Your e-mail intrigues me on several levels. In fact, there is some crossover between what happens in my books and what happens in my real life. Your canny ambiguity in asking the question suggests to me you might have some of that same crossover.

As it happens, I'll be coming to LA tomorrow to meet with my film agent about a project we're pitching at XXXXXXXXX Studios. After I'm done with the industry glad-handing, I'd be happy to meet and chat. I'm staying at XXX XXXX XXXXXXX; let's meet in the bar there about 5, if you have the time.

Yours,
XXXXXX XXXXXX

So *that* sounds wildly promising. Now all I have to do is keep myself from *exploding with anxiety* for the next 24 hours or so. Fortunately I have meetings all day tomorrow. And yes, I said *fortunately* — the more meetings I have to sit in at work, the less anyone asks about the scripts I'm supposed to be working on. This is getting harder to keep up. I did suggest to one of the other staff writers that he and I collaborate on a script, and that he bang out the story outline and maybe the first draft. I can make him do the first draft because I'm senior. I can do it without guilt because he owes me money. I question my moral grounding. But at the moment, not as much as I would otherwise.

Hopefully the writer I'm meeting tomorrow will have something useful for me. Meetings and taking advantage of underlings only goes so far.

AW

Okay. I've met with the other writer. She's Denise Hogan. And in order to describe our "conversation," I'm going to use a format I'm used to.

INT. COFFEE SHOP — CORNER TABLE — DAY

Two people are sitting at the table, coffees in hand, the remains of muffins on the table. They are ANON-A-WRITER and DENISE HOGAN. They have been talking for an hour as ANON-A-WRITER has described his crisis to DENISE in detail.

DENISE
That's really a very interesting situation
you've gotten yourself into.

ANON-A-WRITER
"Interesting" isn't the word I would use for
it. "Magnificently screwed" is the phrase I
would use.

DENISE
Yes, that would work, too.

AW
But this has happened to you too, right?
When you write the characters in your
novels, they are always arguing with you
and ignoring how you want the plot to go
and running off and doing their own thing.
It's your trademark. You write it like it
actually happens.

DENISE
(gently)
Well, I think we need to have some
definition of terms on this.

AW
(draws back)
Definition of terms? That sounds like code
for "No, it doesn't actually happen to me
that way, you crazy crazy person."

DENISE
(beat)
AW, may I be honest with you?

AW
Considering what I just splashed out to
you over the last hour? Yes, would you,
please.

DENISE
I'm here because I read your blog.

AW
I don't have a blog.

DENISE
You don't have one under your actual
name. You have one as Anon-a-Writer.

AW
(beat)
Oh. Oh, *shit.*

DENISE
(holds up hands)
Relax, I'm not here to out you.

AW
Fuck!
(gets up, thinks about leaving, shuffles
back and forth for a moment, sits back
down)
How did you find it?

DENISE
How anyone with an ego finds anything
on the Internet. I have a Google alert tied
to my name.

AW
(runs hands through hair)
Fucking *Google,* man.

DENISE
I clicked through to see if it was some
sort of feature piece on writers who break
the fourth wall and then I saw what your
blog was really about, and I put it into my
RSS feed. I knew you were going to

contact me before you sent your e-mail.

AW
You're not actually in town to see your
film agent.

DENISE
Well, no. I had lunch with him today, and
we *did* talk about that Paramount thing.
But I called him after I got your e-mail
and told him I was going to be in town.
Don't worry, I didn't tell him why else I
was here.

AW
So your characters aren't actually alive
and talking to you.

DENISE
Other than the usual thing writers mean
about making their characters come alive,
no.

AW
Swell.
(stands up again)
Thank you for wasting a large portion of
my day.
Nice to meet you.

355

DENISE
But you and I have something in
common.

AW
Besides the wasted afternoon?

DENISE
(crossly)
Look, I didn't come here to get a close-up
look at a freak show. I already have my
first husband for that. I came here
because I think I understand your
situation better than you think. I had
writer's block too. A bad one.

AW
How bad?

DENISE
More than a year. Bad enough for you?

AW
Maybe.

DENISE
I think I can help you with yours. Because
whether I believe you or not about your
characters being actually real, I think my

own writer's block situation is close to
what yours is now.

AW
If you don't believe what I'm saying, I
don't see how your situation could be like
mine.

DENISE
Because we both had characters we're
scared to do anything with.

AW
(sits back down, warily)
Go on.

DENISE
For whatever reason, you have
characters you're scared of killing or
hurting, and it's blocking you. For me, I
had characters who I couldn't make do
anything critical. I would push them to a
crisis point in my stories, but when it
came time for them to pull the trigger —
to do something significant — I could
never get them to do it. I'd devise all
these ways to get them out of the holes I
spent chapters putting them into. The way
I was doing wasn't good. Finally I froze
up completely. I just couldn't write.

AW
But that's about *you* —

DENISE
(holds up hand)
Wait, I'm not done. Finally, one day as I
was sitting in front of my laptop, doing
nothing with my characters, I typed one of
them turning to me as the writer and
saying, "Would you just fucking make up
your mind already? No? Fine. I'll do it,
then." And then he did something I didn't
expect — that I wasn't even wanting him
to do — and when he did it, it was like a
huge flood of possibilities broke through
the dam of my writer's block. My
character did what I was afraid of him
doing.

AW
Which is what?

DENISE
Having agency. Doing things that even if
they were disastrous in the long run for
the character, was still doing something.

AW
Trust me, agency is not a problem with
my characters.

358

DENISE

I didn't say it was. But my characters
were also doing something else. They
were rebelling against something.

AW
What?

DENISE

My own bad writing. I wouldn't do for my
characters what they needed for me to do
— be courageous enough in my writing to
make them interesting. So they did it
themselves. And by they, I mean me, or
some part of my writing brain that I wasn't
willing to connect with before. Maybe
that's something you need to do too.

AW
Wait. Did you just call me a bad writer?

DENISE
I didn't call you a bad writer.

AW
Good.

DENISE
But I've watched your show. Most of the
scripts are pretty terrible.

AW
(throws up hands)
Oh, come *on.*

DENISE
(continuing)
And they're terrible for no good reason!

AW
(leaning forward)
Do you write scripts? Do you know how
hard it is to work on a weekly deadline for
a television show?

DENISE
No, but you do. Let me ask you: Do you
really think you're making a good effort?
Remember, I'm reading your blog. I've
read you make excuses for the quality of
your output, even when you pat yourself
on the back for the speed you crank it
out.

AW
This doesn't have anything to do with why
I'm blocked.

DENISE
Doesn't it? I was blocked because I knew
I was writing badly, and I didn't have the

courage to fix it. You know you're writing badly, but you give yourself an excuse for it. Maybe that block is telling you the excuse isn't working anymore.

AW
I'm not blocked because I'm writing badly, goddamn it! I'm blocked because I don't want anyone else to die!

DENISE
(nods)
I believe that's your new excuse, yes.

AW
(standing up again)
I thought I was wasting my time before. Now I know. Thanks ever so much. I'll be sure not to use your name when I write this up on the blog.

DENISE
If you actually do put it on your blog, use my name. And then ask your readers if what I've said makes sense. You said you wanted their help. I want to see if you're really interested in that help.

ANON-A-WRITER WALKS OUT.

And that's how I completely wasted my evening tonight, listening to a woman who I thought might actually be helpful to me explain how I'm a bad writer — oh, wait, not a bad *writer,* just doing bad *writing.* Because *there's* a distinction with a difference.

And no, I've never said my writing for the show was bad. I said it's not Shakespeare. I said it's not Emmy-winning good. That's not the same as *bad.* I think I'm honest enough about myself that I would admit to bad writing. But you don't stay on a writing staff for years if you can't write, or if all you write is bad shit. Believe it or not, there is a minimum level of competence you have to have. I have an M.F.A. in film from USC, people. They don't just *give* those away. I wish they did. I wouldn't have had student loans for six years until I caught my first break. But they don't.

My point is, fuck you, Denise Hogan. I'm not your cheap entertainment in L.A. I came to you with a real problem and your solution is to crap all over me and my work. Thanks so much for that. One day I look forward to returning the favor.

In the meantime, enjoy the Internet knowing how you "helped" me today. I'm sure they're going to love it.

AW

So, that was a reporter from Gawker on my cell phone. She told me that they figured out I was Anon-a-Writer based on what I've been writing here, like how my show was on basic cable, it was an hour-long show, it's been on for several seasons, it's a show where a lot of people get killed, and that I'm a USC alum who got his first regular gig in the business six years after graduating.

And also because once I named Denise Hogan, they went on Facebook and did an image search on her name and found a picture of her dated today, at a coffee shop in Burbank, sitting with a guy who looks like me. The picture was taken by a fan of hers with her iPhone. She didn't come up to talk to Denise because she was too nervous. But not too nervous, apparently, that she couldn't upload the damn picture to a social network with half the population of the entire wired world on it.

So that's the story and Gawker's going to be posting it in, like, twenty minutes. The chipper little Gawker reporter wanted to know if I had anything I wanted to say about it. Sure, here's what I want to say:

Fuck.

That is all.

And now I'm going to spend the remaining few hours as a writer on *The Chronicles of the Intrepid* doing what I probably should have been doing the moment all this shit started: sitting on my couch with a big fat bottle of Jim Beam and getting really fucking drunk.

Thanks, Internet. This little adventure has certainly been an eye-opener.

Love,
Apparently Not-So-Anon-a-Writer, After All

Dear Internet:

First, I'm hung over and you're too damn bright. Tone it down.

Oh, wait, that's something I can fix on my end. Hold on.

There. Much better.

Second, something important's happened. I need to share it with you.

And to share it with you I need to go into script mode again. Bear with me.

EXT — FEATURELESS EXPANSE WITH ENDLESS GROUND REACHING TO THE HORIZON — POSSIBLY DAY

ANON-A-WRITE — aw, fuck it, half the Internet already knows anyway: NICK WEINSTEIN comes to in the expanse, clutching his head and wincing. ANOTHER MAN is by him, kneeling casually. Some distance behind him is a crowd of people. They, like the MAN near NICK, are all wearing red shirts.

                    MAN
                  Finally.

                    NICK
              (looks around)
        Okay, I give up. Where am I?

                    MAN
        A flat, gray, featureless expanse
        stretching out to nowhere. A perfect
      metaphor for the inside of your own brain,
                    Nick.

                    NICK
              (looks at MAN)
         You look vaguely familiar.

                    MAN
                 (smiles)
        I should. You killed me. Not too many
              episodes ago, either.

NICK
(gapes for a second, then)
Finn, right?

FINN
Correct. And do you remember how you
killed me?

NICK
Exploding head.

FINN
Right again.

NICK
Not *your* head exploding, though.

FINN
No, someone else's. I just happened to
be in the way.
(stands, points over to the crowd, at one
guy in particular)
He's the guy whose head you blew off.
Wave, Jer!

JER waves. NICK waves back, cautiously.

NICK
(stands, also, unsteadily, peering)
His head looks pretty good for having
been blown off.

FINN
We figured it would be easier for you if
you didn't see us all in the state you killed
us in. Jer would be headless, I would be
severely burned, others would be
dismembered, partially eaten, have their
flesh melted off their bones from horrible
disfiguring diseases. You know. Messy.
We thought you'd find that distracting.

NICK
Thanks.

FINN
Don't mention it.

NICK
I'm assuming this can't be real and that
I'm having a dream.

FINN
This is a dream. It doesn't mean it's not
also real.

NICK
(rubbing his head)
That's a little deep for my current state of
sobriety, Finn.

FINN
Then try this: It's real and taking place in
a dream, because how else can your
dead talk to you?

NICK
Why do you want to talk to me?

FINN
Because we have something we want to
ask of you.

NICK
I'm already not killing any more of you.
I've got writer's block, because of you.
And I'm about to lose my job, because of
the writer's block.

FINN
You've got writer's block, yes. It's not
because of us. Not directly, anyway.

NICK
It's my writer's block. I think I know why I
have it.

FINN

I didn't say you didn't know why you had
it. But you're not admitting the reason
why to yourself.

NICK

Don't take this the wrong way, Finn, but
your Yoda act is getting old quick.

FINN

Fine. Then I'll put it this way: Denise
Hogan? She was right.

NICK

(Throws up his hands)
Even in my own brain, I get this.

FINN

You're a decent enough writer, Nick. But
you're lazy.
(motions toward the crowd)
And most of us are dead because of it.

NICK

Come on, that's not fair. You're dead
because it's an action show. People die in
action shows. It's one of the reasons it's
called an action show.

FINN
(looks at NICK, then points to a face in
the crowd)
You! How did you die?

REDSHIRT #1
Ice shark!

FINN
(turning to NICK)
Seriously, an ice shark? What's even the
biology on that?
(turns back to the crowd)
Anyone else randomly eaten by space
animals?

REDSHIRT #2
Pornathic crabs!

REDSHIRT #3
A Great Badger of Tau Ceti!

REDSHIRT #4
Borgovian Land Worms!

NICK
(to REDSHIRT #4)
I didn't write the land worms!
(to FINN)
Seriously, those aren't mine. I keep

getting blamed for those.

FINN

That's because you're the senior writer on
the show, Nick. You could have raised a
flag or two about the random animal
attacks, whether you wrote them or not.

NICK

It's a weekly science fiction show —

FINN

It's a weekly science fiction show, but lots
of weekly shows aren't *crap,* Nick.
Including science fiction shows. A lot of
weekly science fiction shows at least *try*
for something other than mere sufficiency.
You're using schedule and genre as an
excuse.
(back to the crowd)
How many of you were killed on decks
six through twelve?

Dozens of hands shoot up. FINN turns
back to NICK, looking for an answer.

NICK

The ship needs to take damage. The
show has to have drama.

FINN

The ship needs to take damage. Fine. It
doesn't mean you have to have some
bastard crewman sucked into space
every time it happens. Maybe after the
first dozen times it happened, the
Universal Union should have started
engineering for space defenestration.

NICK

Look, I get it, Finn. You're unhappy with
being dead. So am I. That's why I'm
blocked!

FINN

You don't get it. None of us are pissed off
at being dead.

REDSHIRT #4
I am!

FINN
(to REDSHIRT #4)
Not now, Davis!
(back to NICK)
None of us except for Davis are pissed
off at being dead. Death happens. It
happens to everyone. It's going to
happen to you. What we're pissed off
about is that our deaths are so

completely *pointless.* When you killed us off, Nick, it doesn't do anything for the story. It's just a little jolt you give the viewers before the commercial break, and they've forgotten it before the first Doritos ad fades off the screen. Our lives had meaning, Nick, if only to us. And you gave us really shitty deaths. Pointless, shitty deaths.

NICK

Shitty deaths happen all the time, Finn. People accidentally step in front of buses, or slip and crack their head on the toilet, or go jogging and get attacked by mountain lions. That's life.

FINN

That's *your* life, Nick. But you don't have anyone writing you, as far as you know. *We* do. It's you. And when we die on the show, it's because *you've killed us off.* Everyone dies. But we died how you decided we were going to die. And so far, you've decided we'd die because it's easier than writing a dramatic moment whose response is earned in the writing. And you *know* it, Nick.

NICK
I don't —

FINN
You do. We're dead, Nick. We don't have
time for bullshit anymore. So admit it.
Admit what's actually going on in your
head.

NICK
(sits down, dazed)
All right. Fine. All right. I wrote my last
script, the one we used to send everyone
back, and I remember thinking to myself,
'Wow, we didn't actually kill anyone off
this time.' And then I started thinking
about all the ways we've killed off crew
on the show. Then I started thinking about
the fact that for them, they were real
deaths. Real deaths of real people. And
then I started thinking of all the stupid
ways I've killed people off. Not just them
being stupid by themselves, but
everything around them too. Stupid
reasons to get people in a position where
I could kill them off. Ridiculous
coincidences. Out-of-nowhere plot twists.
All the little shitty tricks I and the other
writers use because we can and no one

calls us on it. Then I went and got
drunk —

FINN
(nodding)
And when you woke up you went to do
some writing and nothing came out.

NICK
I thought it was about not wanting to kill
people. About being responsible for their
deaths.

FINN
(kneeling again)
It's the fact you weren't acting responsibly
when you killed them that's eating at you.
Even if you hadn't written our deaths, all
of us would have died one day. That's a
fact. I think you know it.

NICK
And I gave you bad deaths when I could
have given you better ones.

FINN
Yes. You're not a grim reaper, Nick.
You're a general.
Sometimes generals send soldiers to their
deaths.

Hopefully they don't do it stupidly.

NICK
(looking back at the crowd)
You want me to write better deaths.

FINN
Yeah. Fewer deaths wouldn't hurt, either.
But better deaths. We're all already dead.
It's too late for us. But each of us have
people we care about who are still alive,
who might pass under your pen, if you
want to put it that way. We think they
deserve better. And now you know you do
too.

NICK
You're assuming I'll still have a job after
all this.

FINN
(standing again)
You'll be fine. Just tell everyone you were
exploring the boundaries between fiction
and interactive performance in the online
media. It's a perfectly meta excuse, and
anyway, no one's going to believe your
characters actually came to life. At most
people will think you were kind of an
asshole with this thing. But then some

people think you're kind of an asshole anyway.

NICK
Thanks.

FINN
Hey, I told you, I'm dead. No time for bullshit. Now pass out again and wake up for real this time. Then get over to your computer. Try writing. Try writing better. And stop drinking so much. It does weird things to your head.

NICK nods, then passes out. FINN and his crew of redshirts disappear (I assume).
And then I woke up.
And then I went and powered up my laptop.
And then I wrote thirty pages of the *best goddamned script* I've ever written for the show.
And then I collapsed because I was still sort of drunk.
And now I'm awake again, and hung over, and writing this crying because I can write again.

And this is where I end the blog. It did what it was supposed to — it got me over my writer's block. Now I have scripts to write and writers to supervise and a show to be part of. It's time for me to get back to that.

Some of you have asked — is it really a hoax? Did I ever really have writer's block, or was this an exercise in alternate creativity schemes, a weird little side project from someone who writes too many pages about lasers and explosions and aliens? And did my characters ever actually come to life?

Well, think about it. I trade in fiction. I trade in science fiction. I make up weird shit all the time. What's the most logical explanation in a case like this: more fiction, or everything in the blog being really real, and really happening?

You know what the most logical answer is.

Now you have to ask yourself if you believe it.

Think about it and let me know.

Until then:

Bye, Internet.

Nick Weinstein, Senior Writer,
The Chronicles of the Intrepid

■ ■ ■ ■

CODA II:
SECOND PERSON

■ ■ ■ ■

Coda II: Second Person

You've heard it said that people who have been in horrific accidents usually don't remember the accident — the accident knocks their short-term memory right out of them — but you remember your accident well enough. You remember the rain making the roads slick, and you reining yourself in because of it. You remember the BMW running the red and seeing the driver on his cell phone, yelling, and you knew he wasn't yelling because of you because he never looked in your direction and didn't see your motorcycle until it crushed itself into his front fender.

You remember taking to the air and for the briefest of seconds enjoying it — the surprising sensation of flight! — until your brain had just enough time to process what had happened and douse you in an ice-cold bath of fear before you hit the pavement helmet first. You felt your body

twist in ways human bodies weren't supposed to twist and heard things inside your
body pop and snap in ways you did not
imagine they were meant to pop and snap.
You felt the visor of your helmet fly off and
the pavement skip and scrape off the
fiberglass or carbon fiber or whatever it
was that your helmet was made of, an inch
from your face.

Twist pop snap scrape and then stop,
and then your whole world was the little
you could see out of the ruined helmet,
mostly facing down into the pavement. You
had two thoughts at that moment: one, the
observation that you must be in shock,
because you couldn't feel any pain; two,
that given the crick of your neck, you had
a sneaking suspicion that your body had
landed in such a way that your legs were
bunched up underneath you and your ass
was pointing straight up into the sky. The
fact that your brain was more concerned
about the position of your ass than the
overall ability to feel anything only served
to confirm your shock theory.

Then you heard a voice screaming at
you; it was the driver of the BMW, outraged
at the condition of his fender. You tried to
glance over at him, but without being able
to move your head, you were only able to

get a look at his shoes. They were of the sort of striving, status-conscious black leather that told you that the guy had to work in the entertainment industry. Although truth be told it wasn't just the shoes that told you that; there was also the thing about the asshole blowing through a red light in his BMW because he was bellowing into his phone and being gasket-blowing mad at you because you had the gall to hurt his car.

You wondered briefly if the jerk might know your dad before your injuries finally got the best of you and everything went out of focus, the screaming agent or entertainment lawyer or whoever he was softening out to a buzzy murmur that became more relaxing and gentle as you went along.

So that was your accident, which you remember in what you now consider absolutely terrifying detail. It's as clear in your head as a back episode of one of your father's television shows, preserved in high definition on a Blu-ray Disc. At this point you've even added a commentary track to it, making asides to yourself as you review it in your head, about your motorcycle, the BMW, the driver (who as it turns out was an entertainment lawyer, and who was sentenced to two weeks in county jail and three hundred hours of community service for his third violation of California law banning driving while holding a cell phone) and your brief, arcing flight from bike to pavement. You couldn't remember it more clearly.

What you can't remember is what came after, and how you woke up, lying on your bed, fully clothed, without a scratch on you, a few weeks later.

It's beginning to bother you.

"You have amnesia," your father said, when you first spoke to him about it. "It's not that unusual after an accident. When I was seven I was in a car accident. I don't remember anything about it. One minute I was in the car going to see your great-grandmother and the next I was in a hospital bed with a cast and my mother standing over me with a gallon of ice cream."

"You woke up the next day," you said to your father. "I had the accident weeks ago. But I only woke up a few days ago."

"That's not true," your father said. "You were awake before that. Awake and talking and having conversations. You just don't remember that you did it."

"That's my point," you said. "This isn't like blacking out after an accident. This is losing memory several weeks after the fact."

"You *did* land on your head," your father said. "You landed on your head after sailing through the air at forty-five miles an hour. Even in the best-case scenario, like yours was, that's going to leave some lingering trauma, Matthew. It doesn't surprise me that you've lost some memories."

"Not *some,* Dad," you said. "All of them. Everything from the accident until when I woke up with you and Mom and Candace and Rennie standing over me."

"I told you, you fainted," your dad said. "We were concerned."

"So I faint and then wake up without a single memory of the last few weeks," you said. "You understand why I might be concerned about this."

"Do you want me to schedule you for an MRI?" your dad asked. "I can do that. Have the doctors look around for any additional signs of brain trauma."

"I think that might be a smart thing to do, don't you?" you said. "Look, Dad, I don't want to come across as overly paranoid about this, but losing weeks of my life

385

bothers me. I want to be sure I'm not going to lose any more of it. It's not a comfortable feeling to wake up and have a big hole in your memory."

"No, Matt, I get it," your dad said. "I'll get Brenda to schedule it as quickly as she can. Fair enough?"

"Okay," you said.

"But in the meantime I don't want you to worry about it too much," your father said. "The doctors told us you would probably have at least a couple of episodes like this. So this is normal."

" 'Normal' isn't what I would call it," you said.

"Normal in the context of a motorcycle accident," your dad said. "Normal such as it is."

"I don't like this new 'normal,' " you said.

"I can think of worse ones," your father said, and did that thing he's been doing the last couple of days, where he looks like he's about to lose it and start weeping all over you.

While you're waiting for your MRI, you go over the script you've been given for an episode of *The Chronicles of the Intrepid*. The good news for you is that your character plays a central role in the events. The bad news is that you don't have any lines, and you spend the entire episode lying on a gurney pretending to be unconscious.

"That's not true," Nick Weinstein said, after you pointed out these facts to him. He had stopped by the house with revisions, which was a service you suspected other extras did not get from the head writer of the series. "Look" — he flipped to the final pages of the script — "you're conscious here."

" 'Crewman Hester opens his eyes, looks around,' " you said, reading the script direction.

"That's consciousness," Weinstein said.

"If you say so," you said.

"I know it's not a lot," Weinstein said. "But I didn't want to overtax you on your first episode back."

You achieved that, you said to yourself, flipping through the script in the MRI waiting room and rereading the scenes where you don't do much but lie there. The episode is action-packed — Lieutenant Kerensky in particular gets a lot of screen time piloting shuttles and running through exploding corridors while redshirts get impaled by falling scenery all around him — but it's even less coherent than usual for *Intrepid,* which is really saying something. Weinstein isn't bad with dialogue and keeping things moving, but neither him nor anyone on his writing staff seems overly invested in plotting. You strongly suspected that if you knew more about the science fiction television genre, you could probably call out all the scenes Weinstein and pals lifted from other shows.

Hey, it paid for college, some part of your brain said. *Not to mention this MRI.*

Fair enough, you thought. But it's not unreasonable to want the family business to be making something other than brainlessly extruded entertainment product, indistinguishable from any other sort of brainlessly extruded entertainment product. If that's all you're doing, then your family might as well be making plastic coat hangers.

"Matthew Paulson?" the MRI technician said. You looked up. "We're ready for you."

You enter the room the MRI machine is in, and the technician shows you where you can slip into a hospital gown and store your clothes and personal belongings. Nothing metal's supposed to be in the room with the machine. You get undressed, get into your gown and then step into the room, while the technician looks at your information.

"All right, you've been here before, so you know the drill, right?" the technician asked.

"Actually, I don't remember being here before," you said. "It's kind of why I'm here now."

The technician scanned the information again and got slightly red. "Sorry," he said. "I'm not usually this much of an idiot."

"When was the last time I was here?" you asked.

"A little over a week ago," the technician said, and then frowned, reading the information again. "Well, maybe," he said after a minute. "I think your information may have gotten mixed up with someone else's."

"Why do you think that?" you asked.

The technician looked up at you. "Let me hold off on answering that for a bit," he said. "If it *is* a mix-up, which I'm pretty sure it is, then I don't want to be on the hook for sharing another patient's information."

"Okay," you said. "But if it is my information, you'll let me know."

"Of course," the technician said. "It's your information. Let's concentrate on this session for now, though." And with that he motioned for you to get on the table and slide your head and body into a claustrophobic tube.

"So what do you think that technician was looking at?" Sandra asked you, as the two of you ate lunch at P.F. Chang's. It wasn't your favorite place, but she always had a weakness for it, for reasons passing understanding, and you still have a weakness for her. You met her outside the restaurant, the first time you had seen her since the accident, and she cried on your shoulder, hugging you, before she pulled back and jokingly slapped you across the face for not calling her before this. Then you went inside for upscale chain fusion food.

"I don't know," you said. "I wanted to get a look at it, but after the scan, he told me to get dressed and they'd call with the results. He was gone before I put my pants on."

"But whatever it was, it wasn't good," Sandra said.

"Whatever it was, I don't think it matched up with me walking and talking," you said. "Especially not a week ago."

"Medical record errors happen," Sandra said. "My firm makes a pretty good living with them." She was a first year at UCLA School of Law and interning at the moment at one of those firms that specialized in medical class-action suits.

"Maybe," you said.

"What is it?" Sandra said, after a minute of watching your face. "You don't think your parents are lying to you, do you?"

"Can you remember anything about it?" you asked. "About me after the accident."

"Your parents wouldn't let any of us see you," Sandra said, and her face got tight, the way it did when she was keeping herself from saying something she would regret later. "They didn't even call us," she said after a second. "I found out about it because Khamal forwarded me the *L.A. Times* story on Facebook."

"There was a story about it?" you said, surprised.

"Yeah," Sandra said. "It wasn't really about you. It was about the asshole who ran that light. He's a partner at Wickcomb Lassen Jenkins and Bing. Outside counsel for half the studios."

"I need to find that article," you said.

"I'll send it to you," Sandra said.

"Thanks," you said.

"I resent having to find out you were in a life-threatening accident through the *Los Angeles Times*," Sandra said. "I think I rate better than that."

"My mom never liked you as much after you broke my heart," you said.

"We were sophomores in high school," Sandra said. "And *you* got over it. Pretty quickly, too, since you were all over Jenna a week later."

"Maybe," you said. The Jenna Situation, as you recalled it now, had been fraught with fraughtiness.

"Anyway," Sandra said. "Even if she or your dad didn't tell me, they could have told Naren. He's one of your best friends. Or Kel. Or Gwen. And once we did find out, they wouldn't let any of us see you. They said they didn't want us to see you like that."

"They actually said that to you?" you asked.

Sandra was quiet for a moment. "They didn't say it out loud, but there was sub-text there," she said. "They didn't want us to see you in that condition. They didn't want us to have a memory of you like that. Naren was the one who pushed them the most about it, you know. He was ready to come back from Princeton and camp out on your doorstep until they let him see you. And then you got better."

You smiled, remembering the blubbery conversation the two of you had when you called him to let you know you were okay. And then you stopped smiling. "It doesn't make any sense," you said.

"What specifically?" asked Sandra.

"My dad told me that I'd been recovered and awake for days before I got my memory back," you said. "That I was acting like myself during that time."

"Okay," Sandra said.

"So why didn't I call you?" you said. "We talk or see each other pretty much every week when I'm in town. Why didn't I call Naren? I talk to him every other day. Why didn't I update Facebook or send any texts? Why didn't I tell anyone I was okay? It's just about the first thing I did when I *did* regain my memory."

Sandra opened her mouth to respond, but then closed it, considering. "You're right, it doesn't make sense," she said. "You would have called or texted, if for no other reason than that any one of us would have killed you if you didn't."

"Exactly," you said.

"So you *do* think your parents are lying to you," Sandra said.

"Maybe," you said.

"And you think that somehow this is related to your medical information, which shows something weird," Sandra said.

"Maybe," you said again.

"What do you think the connection is?" Sandra asked.

"I have no idea," you admitted.

"You know that by law you're allowed to look at your own medical records," Sandra said. "If you think this is something medical, that's the obvious place to start."

"How long will that take?" you asked.

"If you go to the hospital and request them? They'll make you file a request form and then send it to a back room where it's pecked at by chickens for several days before giving you a précis of your record," Sandra said. "Which may or may not be helpful in any meaningful sense."

"You're smiling, so I assume there's an Option B," you said to Sandra.

Sandra, who was indeed smiling, picked up her phone and made a call, and talked in a bright and enthusiastic voice to whoever was on the other end of the line, passing along your name and pausing only to get the name of the hospital from you. After another minute she hung up.

"Who was that?" you asked.

"Sometimes the firm I'm interning for needs to get information more quickly than the legal process will allow," Sandra said. "That's the guy we use to get it. He's got moles in every hospital from Escondido to Santa Cruz. You'll have your report by dinnertime."

"How do you know about this guy?" you asked.

"What, you think a *partner* is going to get caught with this guy's number in his contact list?" Sandra said. "It's always the intern's job to take care of this sort of thing. That way, if the firm gets caught, it's plausible deniability. Blame it on the stupid, superambitious law student. It's brilliant."

"Except for you, if your guy gets caught," you noted.

Sandra shrugged. "I'd survive," she said. You're reminded that her father sold his software company to Microsoft in the late 1990s for $3.6 billion and cashed out before the Internet bubble burst. In a sense, law school was an affectation for her.

Sandra noted the strange look on your face. "What?" she asked, smiling.

"Nothing," you said. "Just thinking about the lifestyles of the undeservingly rich and pampered."

"You'd better be including yourself in that thought, Mr. I-changed-my-major-eight-times-in-college-and-still-don't-know-what-

I-want-to-do-with-my-life-sad-bastard,"
Sandra said. "I'm not so happy to see you
alive that I won't kill you."

"I do," you promised.

"You've been the worst of us," Sandra
pointed out. "I only changed my major four
times."

"And then took a couple of years off fart-
ing around before starting law school," you
said.

"I founded a start-up," Sandra said. "Dad
was very proud of me."

You said nothing, smiling.

"All right, fine, I founded a start-up with
angel investing from my dad and his
friends, and then proclaimed myself
'spokesperson' while others did all the real
work," Sandra said. "I hope you're happy
now."

"I am," you said.

"But it was still *something*," Sandra said.
"And I'm doing something now. Drifting
through grad school hasn't done you any
favors. Just because you'll never have to
do anything with your life doesn't mean
you *shouldn't* do anything with your life.
We both know people like that. It's not
pretty."

"True," you agreed.

"Do you know what you want to do with

your life now?" Sandra asked.

"The first thing I want to do is figure out what's happening to me right now," you said. "Until I do, it doesn't feel like I have my life back. It doesn't even feel like it's really my life."

You stood in front of your mirror, naked, not because you are a narcissist but because you are freaking out. On your iPad are the medical records Sandra's guy acquired for you, including the records from your car crash. The records include pictures of you, in the hospital, as you were being prepped for the surgery, and the pictures they took of your brain after they stabilized you.

The list of things that were broken, punctured or torn in your body reads like a high school anatomy test. The pictures of your body look like the mannequins your father's effects crews would strew across the ground in the cheapo horror films he used to produce when you were a kid. There is no way, given the way in which you almost died and what they had to do to keep you alive, that your body should, *right now,* be anything less than a patch-work of scars and bruises and scabs parked in a bed with tubes and/or catheters in every possible orifice.

You stood in front of your mirror, naked, and there was not a scratch on you.

Oh, there are a few things. There's the scar on the back of your left hand, commemorating the moment when you were thirteen that you went over your handlebars. There's the small, almost unnoticeable burn mark below your lower lip from when you were sixteen and you leaned over to kiss Jenna Fischmann at the exact moment she was raising a cigarette to her mouth. There's the tiny incision mark from the laparoscopic appendectomy you had eighteen months ago; you have to bend over and part your pubic hair to see it. Every small record of the relatively minimal damage you've inflicted on your body prior to the accident is there for you to note and mark.

There's nothing relating to the accident at all.

The abrasions that scraped the skin off much of your right arm: gone. The scar that would mark where your tibia tore through to the surface of your left leg: missing. The bruises up and down your abdomen where your ribs popped and snapped and shredded muscle and blood vessels inside of you: not a hint they ever existed.

You spent most of an hour in front of the mirror, glancing at your medical records for specific incidents of trauma and then looking back into the glass for the evidence of what's written there. There isn't any. You are in the sort of unblemished health that only someone in their early twenties can be. It's like the accident never happened, or at the very least, never happened to you.

You picked up your iPad and turned it off, making a special effort not to pull up the images of your latest MRI, complete with the MRI technician's handwritten notation of, "Seriously, WTF?" because the disconnect between what the previous set of MRIs said about your brain and what the new ones said is like the disconnect between the shores of Spain and the eastern seaboard of the United States. The previous MRI indicated that your future would be best spent as an organ donor. The current MRI showed a perfectly healthy brain in a perfectly healthy body.

There's a word for such a thing.

"Impossible." You said it to yourself, looking at yourself in the mirror, because you doubted that at this point anyone else would say it to you. "Just fucking impossible."

You looked around your room, trying to see it like a stranger. It's larger than most people's first apartments and is strewn with the memorabilia of the last few years of your life and the various course corrections you've made, trying to figure out what it was you were supposed to be doing with yourself. On the desk, your laptop, bought to write screenplays but used primarily to read Facebook updates from your far-flung friends. On the bookshelves, a stack of anthropology texts that stand testament to a degree that you knew you would never use even as you were getting it; a delaying tactic to avoid facing the fact you didn't know what the hell you were doing.

On the bedside table is the Nikon DSLR your mother gave you as a gift when you said you were giving some thought to photography; you used it for about a week and then put it on the shelf and didn't use it again. Next to it, the script from *The Chronicles of the Intrepid,* evidence of your latest thing, dipping your toe into the world of acting to see if it might be for you.

Like the screenwriting and anthropology and photography, it's not; you already know it. As with everything else, though, there'd be the period between when you discovered the fact and when you could exit gracefully from the field. With anthropology, it was when you received the degree. With the screenwriting, it was a desultory meeting with an agent who was giving you twenty minutes as a favor to your father. With acting, it will be doing this episode of the show and then bowing out, and then returning to this room to figure out what the next thing will be.

You turned back to the mirror and looked at yourself one more time, naked, unblemished, and wondered if you would have been more useful to the world as an organ donor than you are right now: perfectly healthy, perfectly comfortable and perfectly useless.

You lay on your stretcher on the set of *The Chronicles of the Intrepid,* waiting for the crew to move around to get another shot and becoming increasingly uncomfortable. Part of that was your makeup, which was designed to make you look pallid and sweaty and bruised, requiring constant application of a glycerin substance that made you feel as if you were being periodically coated in personal lubricant. Part of it was that two of the other actors were spending all their time staring at you.

One of them was an extra like you, a guy named Brian Abnett, and you mostly ignored him because you knew it was common knowledge on the set that you're the son of the show's producer, and you knew that there was a certain type of low-achieving actor who would love to become chummy with you on the idea that it would advance their own status, a sort of work-through-entourage thing. You knew what he's about and it's not anything you wanted to deal with.

The other, though, was Marc Corey, who was one of the stars of the show. He was already in perfectly well with your father, so he didn't need you to advance his career, and what you knew of him from Gawker, TMZ and the occasional comment from your father suggested that he's not the sort of person who would be wasting any of his precious, precious time with you. So the fact he couldn't really keep his eyes off of you is disconcerting.

You spent several hours acting like a coma patient while Corey and a cast of extras hovered over your stretcher during a simulated shuttle attack, ran with it down various hallway sets, and swung it into the medical bay set, where another set of extras, in medical staff costumes, pretend to jab you with space needles and waved fake gizmos over you like they were trying to diagnose your condition. Every now and again you cracked open an eye to see if Abnett or Corey was still gawking at you. One or the other usually was. Your one scene of actual acting had you opening your eyes as if you were coming out of a bout of unconsciousness. This time they were both staring at you. They were supposed to be doing that in the script. You still wondered if either or both of them were thinking of hitting on you after the show wraps for the day.

Eventually the day was done, and you scraped off the KY and bruise makeup, formally ending your acting career forever. On your way out, you saw Abnett and Corey talking to each other. For a reason you couldn't entirely explain to yourself, you changed your course and walked right up to the both of them.

"Matt," Marc said to you as you walked up.

"What's going on?" you asked, in a tone that made it clear that the phrase was not a casual greeting but an actual interrogative.

"What do you mean?" Marc said.

"The two of you have been staring at me all day," you said.

"Well, yes," Brian Abnett said. "You've been playing a character in a coma. We've been carting you around on a stretcher all day. That requires us to look at you."

"Spare me," you said to Abnett. "Tell me what's going on."

Marc opened his mouth to say something, then closed it and turned to Abnett. "I still have to work here after today," he said.

Abnett smiled wryly. "So I get to be the redshirt on this one," he said to Marc.

"It's not like that," Marc said. "But he needs to know."

"No, I agree," Abnett said. He slapped Marc on the shoulder. "I'll take care of this, Marc."

"Thanks," Marc said, and then turned to you. "It's good to see you, Matt. It really is." He walked off quickly.

"I have no idea what that was about," you said to Abnett, after Marc walked off. "Before today I'm pretty sure he never gave me a thought whatsoever."

"How are you feeling, Matt?" Abnett said, not directly answering you.

"What do you mean?" you asked.

"I think you know what I mean," Abnett

said. "You feeling good? Healthy? Like a new man?"

You felt a little cold at that last comment. "You know," you said.

"I do," Abnett said. "And now I know that you know, too. Or at least, that you know something."

"I don't think I know as much as you do," you said.

Abnett looked at you. "No, you probably don't. In which case, I think you and I need to get out of here and go somewhere we can get a drink. Maybe several."

You returned to your room late in the evening and stood in the middle of it, searching for something. Searching for the message that had been left for you.

"Hester left you a message," Abnett had told you, after he explained everything else that had happened, every other absolutely impossible thing. "I don't know where it is because he didn't tell me. He told Kerensky, who told Marc, who told me. Marc says it's somewhere in your room, somewhere you might find it but no one else would look — and someplace you wouldn't look, unless you went looking for it."

"Why would he do it that way?" you had

asked Abnett.

"I don't know," Abnett had said. "Maybe he figured there was a chance you wouldn't actually figure it out. And if you didn't figure it out, what would be the point in telling you? You probably wouldn't believe it anyway. I barely believe it, and I met my guy. *That* was some weirdness, I'll tell you. You never met yours. You could very easily doubt it."

You didn't doubt it. You had the physical evidence of it. You had you.

You went first to your computer and looked through the folders, looking for documents that had titles you didn't remember giving any. When you didn't find any, you rearranged the folders so you could look for files that were created since you had your accident. There were none. You checked your e-mail queue to see if there were any e-mails from yourself. None. Your Facebook page was jammed with messages from friends from high school, college and grad school, who heard you were back from your accident. Nothing from yourself, no new pictures posted into your albums. No trace of you leaving a message for you.

You stood up from your desk and turned around, scanning the room. You went to your bookshelves. There you took down the blank journals that you had bought around the time you decided to be a screenwriter, so you could write down your thoughts and use them later for your masterworks. You thumbed through them. They were as blank as they had been before. You placed them back on the shelf and then ran your eyes over to your high school yearbooks. You pulled them down, disturbing the dust on the bookshelf, and opened them, looking for a new inscription among the ones that were already there. There were none. You returned them to the shelf, and as you did so you noticed another place on the bookshelf where the dust had been disturbed, but not in the shape of a book.

You looked at the shape of the disturbance for a minute, and then you turned around, walked to your bed table and picked up your camera. You slid open the slot for the memory card, popped it out, took it to your computer and opened up the pictures folder, arranging it so you could see the picture files by date.

There were three new files made since your accident. One photo and two video files.

The picture file was of someone's legs

and shoes. You smiled at this. The first video file consisted of someone panning across the room with the camera, swinging it back and forth as if they were trying to figure out how the thing worked.

The third video was of you. In it, your face appeared, followed by some wild thrashing as you set down the camera and propped it up so you would stay in the frame. You were sitting. The autofocus buzzed back and forth for a second and then settled, framing you sharply.

"Hi, Matthew," you said. "I'm Jasper Hester. I'm you. Sort of. I've spent a couple of days with your family now, talking to them about you, and they tell me you haven't touched this camera in a year, which I figure means it's the perfect place to leave you a message. If you wake up and just go on with your life, then you'll never find it and there's no harm done. But if you do find this, I figure it's because you're looking for it.

"If you are looking for it, then I figure either one of two things have happened. Either you've figured out something's weird and no one will tell you anything about it, or you've been told about it and you don't believe it. If it's the first of these, then no, you're not crazy or had some sort of weird psychotic break with your life. You haven't had a stroke. You did have a massive brain injury, but not with the body you're in now. So don't worry about that. Also, you don't have amnesia. You don't have any memory of this because it's not you doing it. I guess that's pretty simple.

"If you've been told what happened and you don't believe it, hopefully this will convince you. And if it doesn't, well, I don't know what to tell you, then. Believe what you want. But in the meantime indulge me for a minute."

In the video Hester who is not you but also is ran his fingers through his hair and looked away, trying to figure what to say next.

"Okay, here's what I want to say. I think I exist because you exist. Somehow, in a way I really couldn't ever try to explain in any way that makes any sense, I believe that the day you asked your dad if you could try acting in his show, on that day something happened. Something happened that meant that in the universe I live in, events twisted and turned and did whatever they do so that I was born and I lived a life that you could be part of, as me, as a fictional character, in your world. I don't know how it works or why, but it does. It just does.

"Our lives are twisted together, because we're sort of the same person, just one universe and a few centuries apart. And because of that, I think I can ask you this next question.

"Honestly, Matthew, what the *fuck* are we doing with our lives?

"I've been talking to your family about you, you know. They love you. They all do. They love you and when you had your accident it was like someone came along and stabbed them in the heart. It's amazing how much love they have for you. But, and again, I can tell you this because you're me, I can tell they think you need to get your ass in gear. They talk about how you have so many interests, and how you're waiting for that one thing that will help you achieve your potential, and what I hear is what they won't say: You need to grow up.

"I know it because I'm the same way. Of course I'm the same way, I'm *you*. I've been drifting along for years, Matthew. I joined the Universal Union navy not because I was driven but because I didn't know what to do with myself. And I figured as long as I didn't know what I wanted to do with myself I might as well see the

410

universe, right? But even then I've always just done the bare minimum of what I had to do. There wasn't much point to doing more.

"It wasn't bad. To be honest I thought I was pretty clever. I was getting away with something in my own way. But then I get here and saw you, brain-dead and with tubes coming out of every part of your body. And I realized I wasn't getting away with anything. Just like you didn't get away with anything. You were just born, fucked around for a while, got hit by a car and died, and that's your whole life story right there. You don't win by getting through all your life not having done anything.

"Matthew, if you're looking at this now it's because one of us finally did something useful with his life. It's me. I decided to save your life. I swapped bodies with you because I think the way it works means that I'll survive in my world in your messed-up body, and you'll survive in mine. If I'm wrong and we both die, or you survive and I die, then I'll have died trying to save you. And yes, that sucks for me, but my life expectancy because of your dad's show wasn't all that great to begin with. And all things considered, it was one of the best ways I could have died.

411

"But I'm going to let you in on a secret. I think this is going to work. Don't ask me why — hell, don't ask me why about *any* of this situation — I just think it will. If it does, I have only one thing I want from you. That you do something. Stop drifting. Stop trying things until you get bored with them. Stop waiting for that one thing. It's stupid. You're wasting time. You almost wasted all of your time. You were lucky I was around, but I get a feeling this isn't something we'll get to do twice.

"I'm going to do the same thing. I'm done drifting, Matthew. Our lives are arbitrary and weird, but if I pull this off — if me and all my friends from the *Intrepid* pull this off — then we get something that everyone else in our universe doesn't get: a chance to make our own fate. I'm going to take it. I don't know how yet. But I'm not going to blow it.

"Don't you blow it either, Matthew. I don't expect you to know what to do with yourself yet. But I expect you to figure it out. I think that's a fair request from me, all things considered.

"Welcome to your new life, Matthew. Don't fuck this one up."

Hester reached over and turned off the camera.

412

You clicked out of the video window, closed the laptop and turned around to see your father, standing in the doorway.

"It's not amnesia," he said. There were tears on his face.

"I know," you said.

■ ■ ■ ■

CODA III:
THIRD PERSON

■ ■ ■ ■

CODA III: THIRD PERSON

Samantha Martinez sits at her computer and watches a short video of a woman who could be her reading a book on a beach. It's the woman's honeymoon and the videographer is her newlywed husband, using a camera the two of them received as a wedding gift. The content of the video is utterly unremarkable — a minute of the camera approaching the woman, who looks up from her book, smiles, tries to ignore the camera for several seconds and then puts her book down and stares up at the camera. What could be the Santa Monica Pier, or some iteration of it, hovers not too distantly in the frame.

"Put that stupid thing down and come into the water with me," the woman says, to the cameraman.

"Someone will take the camera," says her husband, offscreen.

"Then they take the camera," she says. "And all they'll have is a video of me reading a book. You get to have me."

"Fair point," says the husband.

The woman stands up, drops her book, adjusts her bikini, looks at her husband again. "Are you coming?"

"In a minute," the husband says. "Run to the water. If someone does steal the camera, I want them to know what they're missing."

"Goof," the woman says, and then for a minute the camera wheels away as she comes toward the husband to get a kiss. Then the picture steadies again and the camera watches her as she jogs to the water. When she gets there, she turns around and makes a beckoning motion. The camera switches off.

Samantha Martinez watches the video three more times before she gets up, grabs her car keys and walks out of the front door of her house.

"Samantha," Eleanor, her sister, says, waving her hand to get Samantha's attention. "You're doing that thing again."

"Sorry," Samantha says. "What thing again?"

"That thing," Eleanor says. "That thing

when no matter what someone else is saying you phase out and stare out the window."

"I wasn't staring out of a window," Samantha says.

"You were phased out," Eleanor says. "The staring out the window part isn't really the important part of that."

The two of them are sitting in the Burbank P.F. Chang's, which is empty in the early afternoon except for a young couple in a booth, across the entire length of the restaurant from them. Eleanor and Samantha are sitting at a table near the large bank of windows pointing out toward a mall parking structure.

Samantha is in fact not looking out the window; she's looking at the couple and their discussion. Even from a distance she can see the two aren't really a couple, although they might have been once, and Samantha can see that the young man, at the very least, wouldn't mind if they were again. He is bending toward her almost imperceptibly while they sit, telling her that he'd be willing. The young woman doesn't notice, yet; Samantha wonders if she will, and whether the young man will ever bring it to her attention.

"Samantha," Eleanor says forcefully.

"Sorry," Samantha says, and snaps her attention to her sister. "Really, E, sorry. I don't know where my head is these last few days."

Eleanor turns to look behind her and sees the couple in the booth. "Someone you know?" she asks.

"No," Samantha says. "I'm just watching their body language. He likes her more than she likes him."

"Huh," Eleanor says, and turns back to Samantha. "Maybe you should go over there and tell him not to waste his time."

"He's not wasting his time," Samantha says. "He just hasn't let her know how important she is to him yet. If I was going to tell him anything, that's what I would tell him. Not to stay quiet about it. Life is too short for that."

Eleanor stares at her sister, strangely. "Are you okay, Sam?" she asks.

"I'm fine, E," Samantha says.

"Because what you just said is the sort of line that comes out of a Lifetime movie character after she discovers she has breast cancer," Eleanor says.

Samantha laughs at this. "I don't have breast cancer, E," she says. "I swear."

Eleanor smiles. "Then what is going on, sis?"

"It's hard to explain," Samantha says.

"Our waiter is taking his time," Eleanor says. "Try me."

"Someone sent me a package," Samantha says. "It's pictures and videos and love letters from a husband and wife. I've been looking through them."

"Is that legal?" Eleanor asks.

"I don't think that's something I need to worry about," Samantha says.

"Why would someone send those to you?" Eleanor asks.

"They thought they might mean something to me," Samantha says.

"Some random couple's love letters?" Eleanor asks.

"They're not random," Samantha says, carefully. "It made sense to send them to me. It's just been a lot to sort through."

"I get the sense you're skipping a whole bunch of details here," Eleanor says.

"I did say it was hard to explain," Samantha says.

"So what's it been like, going through another couple's mail?" Eleanor asks.

"Sad," Samatha says. "They were happy, and then it was taken away."

"It's good they were happy first, then," Eleanor says.

"E, don't you ever wonder about how

421

your life could have been different?" Samantha asks, changing the subject slightly. "Don't you ever wonder, if things just happened a little differently, you might have a different job, or different husband, or different children? Do you think you would have been happier? And if you could see that other life, how would it make you feel?"

"That's a lot of philosophy at one time," Eleanor says, as the waiter finally rolls up and deposits the sisters' salads. "I don't actually wonder how my life could be different, Sam. I like my life. I have a good job, Braden's a good kid and most days I don't feel like strangling Lou. I worry about my little sister from time to time, but that's as bad as it gets."

"You met Lou at Pomona," Samantha says, mentioning her sister's alma mater. "But I remember you flipping a quarter for your college choice. If the coin had landed on heads instead of tails, you would have gone to Wesleyan. You never would have met Lou. You wouldn't have married him and had Braden. One coin toss and everything in your life would have gone another way completely."

"I suppose so," Eleanor says, spearing leaves.

"Maybe there's another you out there," Samantha says. "And for her the coin landed another way. She's out there leading your other life. What if you got to see that other life? How would that make you feel?"

Eleanor swallows her mouthful of greens and points her fork at her sister. "About that coin toss," she says. "I faked it. Mom's the one who wanted me to go to Wesleyan, not me. She was excited about the idea of two generations of our family going there. I always wanted to go to Pomona, but Mom kept begging me to consider Wesleyan. Finally I told her I would flip a coin over it. It didn't matter which way the coin would have landed, I was still going to choose Pomona. It was all show to keep her happy."

"There are other places your life could have changed," Samantha says. "Other lives you could have led."

"But it didn't," Eleanor says. "And I don't. I live the life I live, and it's the only life I have. No one else is out there in the universe living my alternate lives, and even if they were, I wouldn't be worrying about them because I have my life to live here, now. In my life, I have Lou and Braden and I'm happy. I don't worry about what else could have been. Maybe that's lack of imagination on my part. On the other hand, it keeps me from being mopey."

Samantha smiles again. "I'm not mopey," she says.

"Yes you are," Eleanor says. "Or maudlin, which is the slightly more socially respectable version. It sounds like watching these couple's home videos is making you wonder if they're happier than you are."

"They're not," Samantha says. "She's dead."

A letter from Margaret Jenkins to her husband Adam:

Sweetheart:

I love you. I'm sorry that you're upset. I know the *Viking* was supposed to be back to Earth in time for our anniversary but I don't have any control of our missions, including the emergency ones, like this one is. This was part of the deal when you married a crewman on a Dub U ship. You knew that. We discussed it. I don't like being away from you any more than you like it, but I also love what I do. You told me when you proposed to me that you knew this would be some-

424

thing you would have to live with. I'm asking you to remember you said that you would live with it.

You also said that you would consider joining the navy yourself. I asked Captain Feist about the Special Skills intake process and she tells me that the navy really needs people who have experience with large-scale computer systems like you do. She also tells me that if you make it through the expedited training and get on a ship, the Dub U will pick up the tab for your college loans. That would be one less thing hanging over us.

Captain also tells me that she suspects there'll be an opening on the *Viking* for a systems specialist in the next year. No guarantees but it's worth a shot and the Dub U does make an effort to place married couples on the same ship. It believes it's good for morale. I know it would be good for *my* morale. Monogamy sucks when you can't exercise the privilege. I know you feel the same way.

I love you. Think about it. I love you. I'm sorry I can't be there with you. I love you. I wish I was. I love you. I wish you were here with me. I love you. Maybe you could be. I love you. Think

about it. I love you.
  Also: I love you.

(I) love (you),
M

To placate Eleanor, who became more worried about her sister the more she thought about their conversation at P.F. Chang's, Samantha sets off on a series of blind dates, selected by Eleanor apparently at random.

The dates do not go well.

The first date is with an investment banker who spends the date rationalizing the behavior of investment bankers in the 2008 economic meltdown, interrupting himself only to answer "urgent" e-mails sent to him, or so he claims, from associates in Sydney and Tokyo. At one point he goes to the bathroom without his phone; Samantha pops open the back and flips the battery in the compartment. Her date, enraged that his phone has inexplicably stopped working, leaves, barely stopping to ask Samantha if she minds splitting the bill before stalking off in search of a Verizon store.

The second date is with a junior high English teacher from Glendale who is an aspiring screenwriter and who agreed to the date because Eleanor hinted that Samantha might still have connections at *The Chronicles of the Intrepid,* one of the shows she had been an extra on. When Samantha explains that she had only been an extra, and that was years ago, and she had gotten the gig through a casting director and not through personal connections, the teacher is silent for several minutes and then begs Samantha to read the script anyway and give him feedback. She does, silently, as dinner is served. It is terrible. Out of pity, Samantha lies.

The third date is with a man so boring that Samantha literally cannot remember a thing about him by the time she gets back to her car.

The fourth date is with a bisexual woman co-worker of Eleanor's, whose gender Eleanor obfuscated by referring to her as "Chris." Chris is cheerful enough when Samantha explains the situation, and the two have a perfectly nice dinner. After the dinner Samantha calls her sister and asks her what she was thinking. "Honey, it's been so long since you had a relationship, I thought maybe you just weren't telling me something," Eleanor says.

The fifth date is a creep. Samantha leaves before the entrée.

The sixth date is with a man named Bryan who is polite and attentive and charming and decent looking and Samantha can tell he has absolutely no interest in her whatsoever. When Samantha says this to him, he laughs.

"I'm sorry," he says. "I was hoping it wasn't obvious."

"It's all right," Samantha says. "But why did you agree to the date?"

"You've met your sister, right?" Bryan says. "After five minutes it was easier just to say yes than to find excuses to say no. And she said you were really nice. She was right about that, by the way."

"Thank you," Samantha says, and looks at him again silently for a few seconds. "You're a widower," she says, finally.

"Ah," Bryan says. "Eleanor told you." He takes a sip of his wine.

"No," Samantha says. "I just guessed."

"Eleanor should have told you, then," Bryan says. "I apologize that she didn't."

"It's not your fault," Samantha says. "Eleanor didn't mention to me that she had set me up on a date with a woman two weeks ago, so it's easy to see how she might skip over you being widower."

They both laugh at this. "I think maybe you ought to fire your sister from matchmaking," Bryan says.

"How long has it been?" Samantha asks. "That you've been widowed, I mean."

Bryan nods to signal that he knows what she means. "Eighteen months," he says. "It was a stroke. She was running a half-marathon and she stumbled and died at the hospital. The doctors told me the blood vessels in her brain had probably been thin her whole life and just took that moment to go. She was thirty-four."

"I'm sorry," Samantha says.

"So am I," Bryan says, and takes another small drink from his wine. "A year after Jen died, friends started asking me if I was ready to date again. I can't think of a reason to say no. Then I go on them and I realize I don't want anything to do with them. No offense," he says quickly. "It's not you. It's me."

"No offense taken," Samantha says. "It must have been love."

"That's the funny thing," Bryan says, and suddenly he's more animated than he's been the entire evening and, Samantha suspects, more than he's been for a long time. "It wasn't love, not at first. Or it wasn't for me. Jen always said that she knew I was going to be hers from the first time she saw me, but I didn't know that. I didn't even much like her when I met her."

"Why not?" Samantha asks.

"She was *pushy*," Bryan says, smiling. "She didn't mind telling you what she thought, whether you had asked for an opinion or not. I also didn't think she was that attractive, to be entirely honest. She definitely wasn't the sort of woman I thought was my type."

"But you came around," Samantha says.

"I can't explain it," Bryan admits. "Well, that's not true. I can. Jen decided I was a long-term project and invested the time. And then the next thing I knew I was under a chuppah, wondering how the hell I had gotten myself there. But by then, it was love. And that's all I can say. Like I said, I can't explain it."

"It sounds wonderful," Samantha says.

"It was," Bryan says. He finishes his wine.

"Do you think that's how it works?" Samantha asks. "That you have just that one person you love?"

"I don't know," Bryan says. "For everyone in world? I don't think so. People look at love all sorts of ways. I think there are some people who can love someone, and then if they die, can love someone else. I was best man to a college friend whose wife died, and then five years later watched him marry someone else. He was crying his eyes out in joy both times. So, no, I don't think that's how it works for everyone. But I think maybe that's how it's going to work for *me.*"

"I'm glad that you had it," Samantha says.

"So am I," Bryan says. "It would have been nice to have it a little longer, is all." He sets down his wineglass, which he had been fiddling with this entire time. "Samantha, I'm sorry," he says. "I've just done that thing where I tell my date how much I love my wife. I don't mean to be a widower in front of you."

"I don't mind," Samantha says. "I get that a lot."

"I can't believe you still have that camera," Margaret says to her husband, once again behind the lens. They are walking through the corridors of the *Intrepid.* They have just been assigned together to the ship.

"It was a wedding present," her husband says. "From Uncle Will. He'd kill me if I threw it out."

"You don't have to throw it out," Margaret says. "I could arrange an accident."

"I'm appalled at such a suggestion," her

husband says.

Margaret stops. "Here we are," she says. "Our married quarters. Where we will spend our blissfully happy married life together on this ship."

"Try saying that without so much sarcasm next time," her husband says.

"Try learning not to snore," Margaret says, and opens the door, then sweeps her hand in a welcoming motion. "After you, Mr. Documentary."

Her husband walks through the door and pans around the room, which takes a very short amount of time. "It's larger than our berth on the *Viking*," he says.

"There are broom closets larger than our berth on the *Viking*," Margaret points out.

"Yes, but this is almost as large as *two* broom closets," her husband says.

Margaret closes the door and faces her husband. "When do you need to report to Xenobiology?" she asks.

"I should report immediately," her husband says.

"That's not what I asked," Margaret says.

"What do you have in mind?" her husband asks.

"Something you're not going to be able to document," Margaret says.

■ ■ ■ ■

"Did you want to make a confession?"
Father Neil asks.

Samantha giggles despite herself. "I
don't think I could confess to you with a
straight face," she says.

"This is the problem of coming to a priest
you used to date in high school," Father
Neil says.

"You weren't a priest then," Samantha
notes.

The two of them are sitting in one of the
back pews of Saint Finbar's Church.

"Well, if you decide you need confession,
you let me know," Neil says. "I promise
not to tell. That's actually one of the
requirements, in fact."

"I remember," Samantha says.

"So why did you want to see me?" Neil
asks. "Not that it isn't nice to see you."

"Is it possible that we have other lives?"
Samantha asks.

"What, like reincarnation?" Neil asks.
"And are you asking about Catholic doctrine, or something else?"

"I'm not exactly sure how to describe it,"
Samantha says. "I don't think it's reincarnation exactly." She frowns. "I'm not sure

433

there's any way to describe it that doesn't sound completely ridiculous."

"It's popularly believed theologians had great debates about how many angels could dance on a head of a pin," Neil says. "I don't think your question could be any more ridiculous."

"Did they ever find out how many angels could dance on the head of a pin?" Samantha asks.

"It was never actually seriously considered," Neil says. "It's kind of a myth. And even if it weren't, the answer would be: As many as God needed to. What's your question, Sam?"

"Imagine there's a woman who is like a fictional character, but she's real," Samantha says, and holds up her hand when she sees Neil about to ask a question. "Don't ask how, I don't know. Just accept that she's the way I've described her. Now suppose that woman is based on someone in our real world — looks the same, sounds the same, from all outward appearances they could be the same person. The first woman wouldn't exist without having the second woman as a model. Are they the same person? Are they the same soul?"

Neil furrows his brow and Samantha is reminded of him at age sixteen and has to suppress a giggle. "The first woman is based on the second woman, but she's not a clone?" he asks. "I mean, they don't take genetic material from one to make the other."

"I don't think so, no," Samantha says.

"But the first woman is definitely made from the second woman in some ineffable way?" Neil asks.

"Yes," Samantha says.

"I'm not going to ask for details of how that gets managed," Neil says. "I'm just going to take it on faith."

"Thank you," Samantha says.

"I can't speak for the entire Catholic Church on this, but my own take on it would be no, they're not," Neil says. "This is a gross oversimplification, but the Church teaches us that those things that have in themselves the potential to become a human being have their own souls. If you were to make a clone of yourself, that clone wouldn't be you, any more than identical twins are one person. Each has its own thoughts and personal experiences and are more than the sum of their genes. They're their own person, and have their own individual souls."

"You think it would be the same for her?" Samantha asks.

Neil looks at Samantha oddly but answers her question. "I'd think so. This other person has her own memories and experiences, yes?" Samantha nods. "If she has her own life, she has her own soul. The relationship you describe is somewhere between a child and an identical sibling — based on someone else but *only* based, not repeating them exactly."

"What if they're separated in time?" Samantha asks. "Would it be reincarnation then?"

"Not if you're a Catholic," Neil says. "Our doctrine doesn't allow for it. I can't speak to how other faiths would make the ruling. But the way you're describing it, it doesn't seem like reincarnation is strictly necessary anyway. The woman is her own person however you want to define it."

"Okay, good," Samantha says.

"Remember, this is just me talking," Neil says. "If you want an official ruling, I'd have to run it past the pope. That might take a while."

Samantha smiles. "That's all right," she says. "What you're saying makes sense to me. Thank you, Neil."

"You're welcome," Neil says. "Do you mind me asking what's this about?"

"It's complicated," Samantha says.

"Apparently," Neil says. "It sounds like you're researching a science fiction story."

"Something like that, yes," Samantha says.

Sweetheart,

Welcome to Cirqueria! I know Collins has you cranking away on a project so I won't see you before we go to the surface for the negotiations. I'm part of the Captain's security detail; he expects things to proceed in boring and uneventful ways. Don't wait up any longer than Collins makes you. I'll see you tomorrow.

Kiss kiss love love,
M

P.S.: Kiss.

P.S.S.: Love.

Samantha buys herself a printer and a couple hundred dollars' worth of ink and prints out letters and photographs from the collection that she was given a month previously. The original projector had disappeared mysteriously as promised, collapsing into a crumbling pile that evaporated over the space of an hour. Before that happened, Samantha took her little digital camera and took a picture of every document, and video capture of every movie, that she had been given. The digital files remained on the camera card and on her hard drive; she's printing documents for a different purpose entirely.

When she's done, she's printed out a ream of paper, each with a letter from or a picture of Margaret Jenkins. It's not Margaret's whole life, but it's a representation of the life that she lived with her husband; a representation of a life lived in love and with love.

Samantha picks up the ream of paper, walks over to the small portable shredder she's purchased and runs each sheet of paper through it, one piece at a time. She takes the shredded papers into her small backyard and places them into a small metal garbage can she has also purchased. She packs the paper down so that is loosely compacted, lights a kitchen match and places it into the trash can, making sure the paper catches. When it does, Samantha places the lid on top of the garbage can, set slightly askew to allow oxygen in while keeping wisps of burning paper from floating away.

The paper burns down to ashes. Samantha opens the lid and pours a bucket of beach sand into the trash can, smothering any remaining embers. Samantha goes back into her house to retrieve a wooden spoon from her kitchen and uses it to stir the sand, mixing it with the ashes. After a few minutes of this, Samantha upends the trash can and carefully pours the mixture of sand and ashes into the bucket. She covers the bucket, places it into her car and drives toward Santa Monica.

Hello.

I don't know what to call you. I don't know if you will ever read this or if you will believe it even if you do. But I'm going to write like you will read it and believe it. There's no point in doing it otherwise.

You are the reason that my life has had joy. You didn't know it, and you couldn't have known it. It doesn't mean it's not true. It's true because without you, the woman who was my wife would not have been who she was, and who she was to me. In your world, you played her, as an actress, for what I believe was only a brief amount of time — so brief that it's possible you don't even remember that you played her.

But in that brief time, you gave her life. And where I am, she shared that life with me, and gave me something to live for. When she stopped living, I stopped living too. I stopped living for years.

I want to start living again. I know she would want me to start living again. To do that I need to give her back to you. Here she is.

I wish you could have known her. I wish you could have talked to her, laughed with her and loved her as I did. It's impossible now. But at the very least I can show you what she meant to me, and how she lived with me and shared her life with me.

I don't know you; I will never know you. But I have to believe that a great part of who my wife was comes from you — lives in you even now. My wife is gone, but knowing that you are out there gives me some comfort. I hope that what was good in her, those things I loved in her, live in you too. I hope that in your life you have the love that she had in hers. I have to believe you do, or at the very least that you can.

I could say more, but I believe the best way to explain everything is simply to show you everything. So here it is. Here she is.

My wife's name was Margaret Elizabeth Jenkins. Thank you for giving her to me, for the time I had her. She's yours again.

With love,
Adam Jenkins

Samantha Martinez stands ankle deep in the ocean, not too far from the Santa Monica Pier, and sprinkles the remains of Margaret Jenkins' life in the place where she will have one day been on her honeymoon. She does not hurry in the task, taking time between each handful of ash and sand to remember Margaret's words, and her life, and her love, bringing them inside of her and letting them become part of her, whether for the first time or once again.

When she's done, she turns around to walk up the beach and notices a man standing there, watching her. She smiles and walks up to him.

"You were spreading ashes," he says, more of a statement than a question.

"I was," Samantha says.

"Whose were they?" he asks.

"They were my sister's," Samantha says. "In a way."

"In a way?" he asks.

"It's complicated," Samantha explains.

"I'm sorry for your loss," the man says.

"Thank you," Samantha says. "She lived a good life. I'm glad I got to be a part of it."

"This is probably the worst possible thing I could say to you right this moment," the man says, "but I *swear* you look familiar to me."

"You look familiar to me too," Samantha says.

"I swear to you this isn't a line, but are you an actress?" the man asks.

"I used to be," Samantha says.

"Were you ever on *The Chronicles of the Intrepid*?" the man asks.

"Once," Samantha says.

"You're not going to believe this," the man says. "I think I played your character's husband."

"I know," Samantha says.

"You remember?" the man asks.

"No," Samantha said. "But I know what her husband looks like."

The man holds out his hand. "I'm Nick Weinstein," he says.

"Hello, Nick," Samantha says, shaking it. "I'm Samantha."

"It's nice to meet you," Nick says. "Again,

I mean."

"Yes," Samantha says. "Nick, I'm think-ing of getting something to eat. Would you like to join me?"

Now it's Nick's turn to smile. "I would like that. Yes," he says.

The two of them head up the beach.

"It's kind of a coincidence," Nick says, after a few seconds. "The two of us being here like this."

Samantha smiles again and puts her arm around Nick as they walk.

ACKNOWLEDGMENTS

I wrote this novel in the wake of having worked on a science fiction television show, so before I do anything else, let me make the following disclaimer: *Redshirts* is not even remotely based on the television show *Stargate: Universe.* Anyone hoping this is a thinly veiled satire of that particular experience of mine is going to have to be disappointed. Indeed, I would argue that *Stargate: Universe* was all the things that *The Chronicles of the Intrepid* wasn't — namely, smart, well-written and interested in having its science nod in the direction of plausibility.

I was really pleased to have worked on *SG:U* as its creative consultant; I also had a lot of fun with it. And of course I genuinely enjoyed *watching* it, both as a fan of the genre and as someone who worked on it and could see where my contributions showed up on the screen. *That* was cool.

I've co-dedicated this book to Brad Wright and Joe Mallozzi, the *SG:U* producers who brought me into the show, but I'd also like to take a moment here to bow deeply to the cast, crew, writers and staff of *SG:U* as well. It's a shame it couldn't have lasted longer, but no good thing lasts forever.

I also wrote this novel while serving as president of the Science Fiction and Fantasy Writers of America, the largest organization of SF/F writers in the world (and possibly in the entire universe, although of course there's no way to confirm this, yet). Over the years, there's been a bit of received wisdom that if one serves as SFWA's president, one has to essentially lose a year of creative productivity to the gig, and possibly one's sanity as well. I'm happy to say I have not found this to be true — and the reason it was not true in my case was that I was fortunate to have an SFWA board of directors filled with very smart, dedicated people, who worked together for its members as well as or better than any board in recent memory.

So to Amy Sterling Casil, Jim Fiscus, Bob Howe, Lee Martindale, Bud Sparhawk, Sean Williams and in particular Mary Robinette Kowal, my sincere thanks, admiration and appreciation. It was an honor to serve

446

with each of you. Thanks also to all those who volunteer for SFWA and make it a writers' organization I am proud to be a part of.

Every time I write a novel, I am amazed at how much *better* it is when it finally comes out in book form. It's because so many excellent people improve it along the way. This book was helped along by Patrick Nielsen Hayden, my editor; Irene Gallo, Tor's art director; cover artist Peter Lutjen; copy-editor Sona Vogel; text designer Heather Saunders and also production editor Rafal Gibek. Thanks are also due to Cassie Ammerman, my publicist at Tor, and of course to Tom Doherty, who continues to publish my work, for which I continue to be ridiculously pleased. Thanks are also due to my agent, Ethan Ellenberg, and to Evan Gregory, who keeps track of my foreign sales.

Redshirts was read by a small core of first-line readers who offered invaluable feedback and assured me that the thing was something more than just a piss-take on televised science fiction (although obviously it is that too). My appreciation, then, to Regan Avery (as always), Karen Meisner, Wil Wheaton, Doselle Young, Paul Sabourin, Greg DiCostanzo and my wife, Kristine Scalzi, who also

447

deserves thanks for putting up with me in a general sense. I'm really glad she does.

And finally, thank you, dear reader. I'm glad you keep coming back for more. If you keep coming back, I'll keep writing them. That's a promise.

John Scalzi,
July 22, 2011

ABOUT THE AUTHOR

John Scalzi is the author of several SF novels including the bestselling Old Mans War sequence, comprising *Old Mans War, The Ghost Brigades,* and the *New York Times* bestselling *The Last Colony.* He is a winner of science fictions John W. Campbell Award for Best New Writer, and he won the Hugo Award for "Your Hate Mail Will Be Graded," a collection of essays from his popular blog *Whatever.* His latest novel, *Fuzzy Nation,* hit the *New York Times* bestseller list in its first week on sale. He lives in Ohio with his wife and daughter.